Enderby Outside

novels

The Long Day Wanes:
  Time for a Tiger
  The Enemy in the Blanket
  Beds in the East
The Right to an Answer
The Doctor is Sick
The Worm and the Ring
Devil of a State
One Hand Clapping
A Clockwork Orange
The Wanting Seed
Honey for the Bears
Inside Mr Enderby
Nothing like the Sun: A Story
  of Shakespeare's Love-Life
The Eve of Saint Venus
A Vision of Battlements
Tremor of Intent
Enderby Outside
MF
Napoleon Symphony
The Clockwork Testament;
  or, Enderby's End
Beard's Roman Women
Abba Abba
Man of Nazareth
1985
Earthly Powers
The End of the World News

for children

A Long Trip to Teatime
The Land Where the
  Ice Cream Grows

verse

Moses

non-fiction

English Literature: A Survey
  for Students
They Wrote in English
Language Made Plain
Here Comes Everybody: An
  Introduction to James Joyce for
  the Ordinary Reader
The Novel Now: A Student's Guide
  to Contemporary Fiction
Urgent Copy: Literary Studies
Shakespeare
Joysprick: An Introduction to
  the Language of James Joyce
New York
Hemingway and His World
On Going to Bed
This Man and Music

translator

The New Aristocrats (with Llewela
  Burgess)
The Olive Trees of Justice (with
  Llewela Burgess)
The Man Who Robbed Poor Boxes
Cyrano de Bergerac
Oedipus the King

editor

The Grand Tour
Coaching Days of England
A Shorter Finnegans Wake

Enderby Outside

Anthony Burgess

McGraw-Hill Book Company
New York   St. Louis   San Francisco   Bogotá   Guatemala
Hamburg   Lisbon   Madrid   Mexico   Montreal   Panama   Paris
San Juan   São Paulo   Tokyo   Toronto

First McGraw-Hill edition, 1984

1 2 3 4 5 6 7 8 9   FGRFGR   8 7 6 5 4

ISBN 0-07-008974-4 {H.C.}
ISBN 0-07-008971-X {PBK.}

Library of Congress Cataloging in Publication Data

Burgess, Anthony, 1917–
     Enderby outside.

     Reprint. Originally published as book 2 of: Enderby.
New York : Norton, [1968]
     I. Title.
PR6052.U638E55   1984   823'.914   83-26816
ISBN 0-07-008974-4
ISBN 0-07-008971-X (pbk.)

TO *Deborah*

Esperad todavía.
El bestial elemento se solaza
En el odio a la sacra poesía
Y se arroja baldón de raza a raza.

—Rubén Darío

I

1

One

I T's,' said this customer at the bar, 'what I personally would
want to call—and anyone else can call it what the hell
they like for all I care—' Hogg listened respectfully, half-bowed,
wiping dry a glass from which a very noisy woman, an actress or
something, had drunk and eaten a Pimm's Number One. 'But it's
what I, speaking for myself, would call—' Hogg burnished an
indelible veronica of lipstick, waiting for some highly idiosyncratic pay-off, not just the just word but the word just with just
this customer's personal brand of justness. 'A barefaced liberty.'
Hogg bowed deeper in tiny dissatisfaction. He had been a word-
man himself once (nay, still—but best to lock all that up: they
had said those days were past, trundled off by time's rollicking
draymen, empties, and they knew best, or said they did. Still—)
'A man's name's his name, all said and done.' You couldn't say
what this man had just said. A liberty was diabolical; it was lies
that were barefaced. Hogg had learned so much during his season with the salt of the earth, barmen and suchlike. But he said,
blandly:

'It's very kind of you, sir, to feel that way about it.'

'That's all right,' said this customer, brushing the locution towards Hogg as though it were a tip.

'But they didn't call it after me, sir, in a manner of speaking.' That was good, that was: genuine barman. 'They brought me in here, as you might say, because the place was already called what it is.'

'There's been plenty named Hogg,' said the customer sternly. 'There was this man that was a saint and started these schools where all these kids were in rags. They had to be in rags or they wouldn't have them in. It was like what they call a school uniform. And there's this Hogg that was a lord and gave it up to be prime minister but he didn't get it so he goes round ringing bells and telling them all off.'

'There was also James Hogg, the poet,' said Hogg, unwisely.

'You leave poets out of it.'

'The Ettrick shepherd he was known as, in a manner of speaking. Pope in worsted stockings.'

'And religion as well.' This customer, who had had no lunch except whisky, grew louder. 'I might be an Arsee, for all you know. Respect a man's colour and creed and you won't go far wrong. I take a man as I find him.' He spread his jacket like wings to show green braces. Hogg looked uneasily across the near-empty bar. The clock said five to three. John, the tall sardonic Spaniard who waited on, the Head Steward's nark, he was taking it all in all right. Hogg sweated gently.

'What I mean is,' said flustered Hogg, 'this bar was called Piggy's Sty because of the man that was here before me.' John the Spaniard sneered across. 'Sir,' added Hogg.

'And you won't go far wrong is what I say.'

'It was to do with the people that started these hotels,' said Hogg urgently. 'They had a Hogg over there when they started. He brought them luck and he died. Americans they were.'

'I can take them or leave them. We fought side by side in both lots. They did as much good as harm, and I hope they'll say as much about you.' He slid his empty glass towards Hogg, impelling it as though it were a child's match-box ten-ton truck.

'Similar, sir?' asked Hogg, barman's pride pushing through the fluster.

'No, I'll try one of theirs. If the Yanks run this place then they'll likely know what's what.' Hogg didn't get that. 'What they call bourbon. That bottle there with the nigger on.' Hogg measured out a double slug of Old Rastus. 'With branch-water,' said this customer. Hogg filled a little pig-shaped jug from a tap. He rang up the money and said:

'They wouldn't have false pretences, that being their policy, as you might say. They said that customers like things genuine in the States and it's got to be the same here too. So it had to be a Hogg.'

The customer, as though testing his neck for fracture, swivelled his head slowly, taking in Piggy's Sty. It was one of many whimsically-named bars in this tall but thin hotel, London's new pride. This bar and the Wessex Saddleback, where at this moment there were a lot of thick-necked Rotarians sweating on to charred gristle, made up nearly the whole of the tenth floor. You could see much of autumn London from the windows of the bar (on which artificial trotter-prints were like a warning). You could see an ape-architecture of office-blocks, the pewter river, trees that had scattered order-paper leaves all about Westminster, Wren and his God like babes in the wood, the dust of shattered Whig residences thrown by the wind. But this customer looked only on the frieze of laughing tumbling porkers, the piggy-banks with broken saddles to make ashtrays, little plastic troughs with plastic chrysanthemums in them. He turned back to Hogg to nod at him in grudging admiration as though he, Hogg, had made all this.

'Closing now, sir,' said Hogg. 'One for the road, sir?'

'You wouldn't catch them daring to take the mike out of *my* name,' said the customer. He now winked pleasantly at Hogg. 'Not that I'd give them the chance. A man's name is his own.' He laid his finger to his nose, as though to cool the inflammation which Hogg's stepmother had used to call Harry Syphilis, winking still. 'Catch *me*.' He smirked, as though his name was something he had won and was going to hug greedily to his chest till he got home. 'I'll have some of our own now after that nigger stuff. A wee drappie. Och aye. There's a wee wifey waiting.' Hogg daringly poured Scotch into the glass that had held bourbon. John had his eyes on his two leaving customers.

'Electric shepherds,' said one of these, a man who might well be a pig-farmer and yet had not seemed really at home in Piggy's Sty. 'It'll come to that, I daresay.' He was with a man in clerical grey, etiolated as by a life of insurance. They both nodded at Spanish John and then went out. John showed them a baroque shrine of golden teeth and said: 'Zhentilmen.' Then he picked up their glasses and brought them to the counter for Hogg to wash. Hogg looked on him with hate.

'But what I say is,' said the one customer left, 'it's an insult to the name of your old dad. That's the way to look at it.' He descended his stool with care. John bowed and bowed, his gob all bits of fractured doubloon. The customer grunted, dove into his trouser-pocket and brought up a half-crown. This he gave to John; to Hogg he gave nothing. John bowed and bowed, baring deeper and deeper gold deposits. Hogg said:

'Actually, it was my mother's.'

'Eh?' The customer squinted at him.

'What I mean is, Hogg was my mum's name, not my dad's.'

'I don't come in here,' said the customer, 'to have the piss took.' A certain lowness was coming out now. 'You watch it.'

Hogg sulked. He had gone too far again. And this horrible John had, as before, been a witness. But Hogg had spoken truth. Hogg had been the maiden name of that barely imaginable sweet woman, singing 'Passing By' to her own accompaniment, Banksia and Macartney and Wichuraiana vainly opposing their scents to hers through the open french window. His father, O-ing out the smoke of a Passing Cloud while he listened, his father had been called—

'I like a laugh same as the next one, but watch it, that's all.' And the customer left, going aaarkbrokhhh on his stomach of whisky. Hogg and Spanish John faced each other.

'Puerco,' said John, for so he translated Hogg's mother's name. 'You speak other time of poetry, not good. Get on with bloody job is right way.'

'Nark,' growled Hogg. 'Tell Holden if you want to. A fat lot I care.' Holden was the Head Steward, a big man hidden behind secretaries and banks of flowers, an American who sometimes pretended he was Canadian. He would talk of cricket. It was something to do with American trade policy.

'I say bugrall this time,' promised John generously. 'This time not big. Last time very big.'

Well, it hadn't really been Hogg's fault. A group of young fattish television producers had been there for dinner, cramming down peanuts with the martinis, going 'Ja' when they meant 'yes.' They had talked loudly of the sexual *mores* of certain prominent actresses and, by a natural transition, had been led on to a discussion of poetry. They had misquoted something by T. S. Eliot and Hogg, off his guard, had put them right. This had interested them, and they had tried him on other poets, of all of whom—Wunn, Gain, Lamis, Harkin, some such names—Hogg had never heard. The television men had seemed to sneer at him, a common barman, for knowing; now they sneered at him for not knowing. The leader of the *ja*-sayers fed himself, in the manner of a Malaysian rice-eater, with a shovel-hand loaded with salty peanuts, sneering at the same time. He said, indistinctly, 'Wenggerggy.'

'Who?' said Hogg. He had begun to tremble. There was a phantom girl hovering near the pig-pink (chopped-ham-and-pork-pink, to be accurate) ceiling, a scroll in her hand, queenly shoulders nacreous above a Regency ballgown. Hogg knew her all too well. Had she not deserted him a long time ago? Now she smiled encouragingly, unrolling her scroll coquettishly though, an *allumeuse*. 'Did you say *Enderby?*' asked Hogg, shaking beneath his barman's white bum-freezer and frowning. The girl swooped down to just behind him, flat-handed him on the nape, and then shoved the wide-open scroll in front of his eyes. He found himself reciting confidentially, as in threat:

'Bells broke in the long Sunday, a dressing-gown day.
The childless couple basked in the central heat.
The papers came on time, the enormous meat
Sang in the oven. On thick carpets lay
Thin panther kittens locked in clawless play—'

'Ah, Jesus—'
'A *sonnet* yet—'
Hogg glowered at this one, a small gesturing man, and prepared to say 'For cough.' But instead he went stoutly on:

'Bodies were firm, their tongues clean and their feet
Uncalloused. All their wine was new and sweet.
Recorders, unaccompanied, crooned away—'

At this moment another television man came in, one they had
apparently all been waiting for. He was much like the others,
very pasty. They clawed at him passionately, shouting.

'The Minetta Tavern—'

'Goody's on Sixth Avenue—'

There was a solitary man at the counter, one who had ordered
by pointing; he wore dark glasses; his mouth had opened at
Hogg and let cigarette smoke wander out at him. The tabled
customers, aware of the intrusion of verse-rhythm into the form-
lessness of chat, had all been looking at Hogg. Spanish John
stood shaking his head, nastily pleased.

'No more verse-fest,' said the chief peanut-eater to Hogg.
'More martinis.'

'Wait,' said Hogg, 'for the bloody sestet.'

'Oh, let's go in,' the newcomer said, 'I'm *starving*.' And so
they all shouted off to the Wessex Saddleback, clawing and going *ja*. Hogg turned gloomily to the man in dark glasses and
said:

'They could have waited for the bloody sestet. No manners
nowadays. It's a miracle, that's what they don't seem to realise. I
tried for years to get that thing right, and only then it just came
to me.' He suddenly felt guilty and began to excuse himself.
'Another man, though. Not really me. It's a long story. Rehabilitation they call it.' The man had said:

'*Nye ponimaiu.*' That was why he had started pointing again.
Hogg, sighing, had measured out a large globule of an Iron Curtain glycerine-smelling apéritif. Must watch himself. He was
happy now, wasn't he? Useful citizen.

It was after that occasion that he had been summoned to see
Mr Holden, a man desperately balding as though to get into
Time magazine. Mr Holden had said:

'You were on a sticky wicket there, *ja*. A straight bat and keep
your eye on the pitcher. This is a respectable hotel and you are a
sort of gliding presence in white, that's your image, *ja*. You've
done well to get here after so short an innings in the profession.

Self-employed before, that's what it says in your dossier. Well,
whatever it was is no concern of the management. Though it's
beginning to sound as though it wasn't quite com eel foe. Still,
the pairst is pairst. The cream of global citizenry pairsses
through these portals. They don't want bar-tenders telling them
to keep their tongues clean. And you said something about our
cellar that was libellous, but he may have balled that up, so we'll
let it pairss. It's your name that's your asset, remember that.
Carry your bat, brother, or you'll find yourself no-balled PDQ.'
Past, was it? The past, that is. He did something there was no
law against doing shortly after. If anybody found out they
would have him on television, sandwiched between a dustman
who collected Meissen and a bank-clerk who had taught his dog
to smoke a pipe. A curiosity at best. At worst a traitor. To what,
though? To what a traitor would he be regarded as? And now, a
month after, he was frowning while he compared his takings
with the roll in the till that recorded each several amount rung.
He would have to take the money in a little box to the huge
clacking hotel treasury full of comptometers that—so Larry in
the Harlequin Bar upstairs had asserted—if programmed proper
could be made to see right through to your very soul. And then
he had an appointment. In (his breast swelled minimally) Harley Street. To your very soul, eh? He felt uneasy. But, damn it,
he had done no real wrong, surely? When John Milton clocked
in to do his daily stint of translation of Cromwell into Latin, had
they not perhaps used to say: 'All right that was, that thing you
pinned up on the wall about Fairfax and the siege of Colchester.
You carry on'? He, Hogg, had not pinned anything up, though,
by God, one of these days—He had merely—
    'My brother,' John was saying, 'now he work in Tangier. At
Big Fat White Doggy Wog, bloody daft name for bar. Billy
Gomez, everybody know him. Good on knife if trouble, ah yes,
man.' He made a bloodthirsty queeeeeking noise and drove a
ghost-stiletto at Hogg's hidden puddings. 'He say poetry, but
now not. *Good* poetry. *Spanish* poetry. Gonzalo de Berceo, Juan
Ruiz, Ferrant Sánchez Calavera, Jorge Manrique, Góngora—
good poetry. England too fackin cold for good poetry. English
man no *fuego*. Like bloody fish, *hombre*.'
    'I'll give you no *fuego*,' said Hogg, incensed. 'We gave you

mucho bloody *fuego* in 1588, bastards, and we'll do it again. Garlicky sods. I'll give you no good poetry.' A ruff went round his neck. He stroked a spade-beard, enditing. The sky was red with fireships. Then he saw himself in the gross reredos mirror, his cross reflection framed in foreign bottles, a decently shaven barman in glasses, going, like Mr. Holden, rapidly bald.

'We go eat now,' said John. In the hotel's intestines steamed an employees' cafeteria, full of the noise of shovelled chips and heady with Daddies Sauce. A social organiser walked regularly between the tables, trying to get up table-tennis tournaments. John's empty stomach castanetted dully.

'I don't want to eat,' sulked Hogg. 'I'm full up already. Chocker, that's what I am.'

Two

Hogg walked to Harley Street, much set upon by leaves and blowing bits of paper. He knew his way about these defiled streets, London Hogg as he was. His stepmother in Purgatory or wherever she was would have a fit to see how well he knew London. Bruton Street, New Bond Street, across Oxford Street, then through Cavendish Street and across Cavendish Square, then into Harley Street, knowing also that Wimpole Street was the next one, where Robert Browning had read bits of *Sordello*, a very obscure and long poem, to that woman who had looked like and, indeed, possessed a spaniel, and under the bed there had been big spiders. Her father had made her drink very black stout. Hogg tried to pretend that he did not know these things, since they were outside his barman's province, but he knew that he knew them. He frowned and set his shoulders in defiance. A man who sold newspapers and dirty magazines said, 'Cheer ap, gav.'

Hogg, in working trousers and decent dogtooth—patterned sports-jacket, was soon seated in Dr Wapenshaw's waiting-room. He had received, some three days before, a curt summons from Dr Wapenshaw, chief agent of his rehabilitation from failed suicide to useful citizen. He could think of only one possible reason for the curtness, but it was a reason so unlikely that he was fain to reject it. Still, when you thought about these cybernetic triumphs and what they were capable of, and how a psychiatrist as cunning as Dr Wapenshaw would be quite likely to have banks of electronic brains working for him (and all at National Health expense), then it was just about possible that the summons might be about this particular hole-in-the-corner thing that Hogg had done, an act of recidivism, to use the fashionable jargon. Otherwise, he, Hogg, and Dr Wapenshaw had achieved a condition of mutual love and trust that, however official and Government-sponsored, had been looked on as a wonder in that green place of convalescence. Had not Dr Wapenshaw shown him, Hogg, off as an exemplary cure, inviting colleagues of all nations to prod and finger and smile and nod and ask cunning questions about Hogg's relationship with his Muse and his stepmother and his lavatory and his pseudo-wife, cooling all that turbulent past to the wan and abstract dignity of a purely clinically interesting case to be handled by fingers smelling of antiseptics? Yes, that was so. Perhaps that curtness was, after all, the official wrapping that enclosed warmth and love and protected them from the eyes of strangers. Still and nevertheless.

The waiting-room had a gas-fire, and the only other waiting patient was crouched over it, as though it were a wicket and he its keeper. The chill of autumn was reflected in the covers of copies of *Vogue* and *Vanity Fair* that lay on the polished table that turned the vase of real, not plastic, chrysanthemums into a kind of antipodeal ghost. These covers showed thin young women in mink against the falling of the leaves. Something like winter cold struck Hogg as he noticed a deck of copies of *Fem.* Those days, not so long ago, when he had actually written ghastly verses for *Fem*, set as harmless prose ('I lift my baby to the air. He gurgles because God is there') and pseudonymously signed Faith Fortitude; those incredible days when he had actually been married to its features editress, Vesta Bainbridge; those days should, officially, be striking him with little more than mild and condescending curiosity. That had been another man, one from a story read yawning. But the past was fastening its suckers on him once more, had been doing ever since that night of the goddess and the television *ja*-sayers and the unpremeditated

chrysostomatic utterance. Hogg nodded, sighing heavily. Dr
Wapenshaw knew; he knew everything. That was what this
interview was going to be about.

'For a load of blasphemous balderdash,' said the man by the
gas-fire, 'you ought to read this lot.' He turned to Hogg, waving
a thin little book. He had, then, been holding it to the gas-fire, as
if, as with bread in some study feed in some school story of pre-
electric days, deliberately toasting it. He was a man with wild
grey hair who spoke with a cultivated accent which made his
demotic vocabulary seem affected, which, if he was, as he evidently was, one of Dr Wapenshaw's patients, being rehabilitated
in the same modes as Hogg himself had been, if he really had
been, it probably was. 'And they say it's *us* that are crackers,' he
said. 'You and me,' he clarified, 'are supposed to be the barmy
ones.' Hogg prepared to dissociate himself from that predica-
tion, but he let it pass. The man launched wild fluttering wings
of paper at Hogg and Hogg deftly caught them. The man did
not say 'Fielded'; that was rather for Mr Holden or for Dr
Wapenshaw himself, at least the Dr Wapenshaw of the chummy
green days with his 'Good show' and 'That's the ticket.' Hogg
leafed through the little book, frowning. He caught the title and
further frowned: *The Kvadrat's Kloochy.* He said, with care:
'What does it mean, then?'

'Oh,' said the man, irritably, 'what does *anything* mean? It's
all a *merde universelle*, as that French Irishman says. You read
it, that's all.' Hogg read, at random:

The miracle of this uncomplicated monody with its minimal
chordal accompaniment is not diminished by our hindsight
knowledge that it had been there waiting, throughout recorded
history, yet unnoticed by the bearded creaking practitioners of
the complex. They built up their multivocal counterpoint, their
massive orchestras, their fugal and sonata forms, seeking a per-
fection that, if they could have cleansed the rheum from their
old-man's eyes, they would have known had to lie in the simple
and direct rather than the periphrastic and complicated. And
yet it is in the error of the traditional equating of age with
wisdom that one may find the cause of their blindness or, to be
kind, presbyopia. The answer to all problems, aesthetic as much
as social, religious, and economic, resides, in a word, in Youth.

'I don't see what all this is about,' said Hogg. He frowned still, turning over the page to find a photograph of four common louts who leered up at him, one bearing a guitar from which electrical flex sprouted, the others poising sticks over gaudy side-drums.

'Ah,' growled the man, 'don't bother *me* with it. You stick to your world and I'll stick to mine.' And then he cried, very loud: 'Mother, you've forsaken your son.' Hogg nodded without fear. Had he not spent an entire summer among men given to sudden despairing ejaculations or, worse, quiet confident assertions about the nature of ultimate reality, often delivered, Hogg and other patients shaken awake for the intimation, in the middle of the night? He read on:

Jack Cade and the Revolters established the fruitful device of a heavy ictus on the fourth beat in their disc *Like He Done That Time*, pressed in April, 1964. In May of the same year this was further developed by Nap and the Bonies, who, in their *Knee Trembler*, transferred it to the quaver between the third beat and the fourth. Needless to say, this was achieved instinctually, these youthful performers being unburdened by traditional technical knowledge. In June both groups were superseded by the Tumers who, intuitively aware of a new shift in the *Zeitgeist*, perhaps wisely reverted to a greater simplicity of rhythmical texture and . . .

'Ah, Hogg!' cried a voice both fierce and plummy. Hogg looked up to see a different Dr Wapenshaw from the one he remembered—an urban Dr Wapenshaw in a natty suit of char-coal grey with discreet stripes, more formidable than the one who, in that country retreat, had dressed for his consultations as if for outdoor games. The chubby face was stern. Meekly Hogg went into the consulting-room. 'Sit you down,' said Dr Wapen-shaw. Hogg sat on the seat nearest the door, a sort of creepy-stool. 'Here,' said Dr Wapenshaw, throwing a fierce fistful of air at a seat drawn up to the desk, a desk massive enough to contain any number of small secret electronic monitors. He himself went round the desk to its window-side and stood behind his swivel-chair, grey Harley Street framed behind him, while he watched Hogg, who still had *The Kvadrat's Kloochy* in his hand, shamble over. 'Very well, then,' said Dr Wapenshaw, in the manner of a sour grace. Consultant and patient sat simultaneously.

'Soon be winter now,' said Hogg in a conversational manner. 'The nights are drawing in very fast. Could do with a fire, really, in a manner of speaking.' Suddenly noticing that Dr Wapenshaw's consulting-room had a grate conspicuously empty, he added, 'Not that I meant that in any spirit of criticism, as you might say. All I meant was that it gets a bit chilly at nights.' Dr Wapenshaw held him with a disgusted look; Hogg grew flustered. 'What I mean is, some feel the cold more than others, so to speak. But'—and he struck hard at Dr Wapenshaw's flint, desperately seeking some of that old warmth—'nobody can deny that it's late autumn now, and after autumn, if you'll pardon the observation—'

'Shut up!' cried Dr Wapenshaw. ('No, no, don't,' whimpered the patient in the waiting-room.) 'I'll do all the talking.' But all he did was to hurl a thick book bound in green paper across at Hogg. Hogg was already growing tired of having books hurled at him; still, he caught it deftly, just like the other one, which was now on his knee. 'Look at that,' ordered Dr Wapenshaw. 'Page 179. Read it, man.'

Hogg fingered the book rather tenderly. It was, he saw, a proof copy. He had, in the remote past when he was another man altogether, handled proof copies of his own work, very slim proof copies, poems. He flicked through the massive prose-work with a certain envy, then admired the title. '*Rehabilitations*,' he read out. 'There used to be a lot like that in the old days. F. R. Leavis and such people. The New School of Criticism, they called it. But it's all changed now. They have different ideas now and more flowery titles. *The Romantic Orgasm* was one I saw in a shop. And *The Candle in the Thigh* was another. They get a lot of the titles from poor Dylan, you know, who died. It's nice to see a good old-fashioned title like this again. That,' he said diffidently, though with a wisp of ancient authority, when he had lighted at last on Page 179, 'isn't the right symbol for a deletion and close up, if you'll pardon the correction. It should be like a little balloon on the tip of a stick—'

'Read it, man, read it!' And Dr Wapenshaw thumped his desk thrice. Hogg read where he was ordered, wonderingly. Dr Wapenshaw tattooed the desk-top softly, as though his fingers at least were appeased—three beats in the left hand against two beats in the right, as though playing in some children's nonsense by Benjamin Britten, with tuned teacups and tin-whistles but also Peter Pears as an old man. 'Well?' he said at length.

'You know,' said Hogg, 'this case seems pretty close to what my own was. This chap here, K you call him, was a poet, and that made him into a protracted adolescent. He spent a lot of his time writing verse in the lavatory—a kind of womb you say it is here, but that's a lot of nonsense, of course—and this woman made him marry her and it was a mess and he ran away and then he tried to go back to the old life, writing poetry in the lavatory and so on, and it didn't work so he attempted suicide and then you cured him by reorientating his personality, as it's called here, and then he became a useful citizen and forgot all about poetry and—Well,' Hogg said, 'that, if I may say so, is an astonishing coincidence, you might call it.' He tried to beam, but Dr Wapenshaw's black look was not irradiable. Dr Wapenshaw leaned across the desk and said, with terrible quietness and control:

'You bloody fool. That *is* you.'

Hogg frowned slightly. 'But,' he said, 'it can't be. It says here that this K had delusions about other people stealing his work and making horror films out of his poetry. That's not quite the same, is it? I mean, this bloody man Rawcliffe did pinch the plot of my *Pet Beast* and make a bloody awful Italian picture out of it. I even remember the name. *L'Animal Binato* it was called in Italy—that's from Dante, you see: *The Double-Natured Animal* or something like it—and in England it was called *Son of the Beast from Outer Space*.' He read more intently, frowning further. 'What's all this,' he said, 'about a sexual fixation on this bloke K's stepmother? That can't be me, this bloke can't. I hated her, you know how much for I told you. And,' he said blushing, 'about masturbating in the lavatory. And about this woman being very refined and trying to make a real married man out of him.' He looked up, his sternness a remote (fourth or fifth or something) carbon copy of Dr Wapenshaw's own. 'That woman,' he said clearly, 'was *not* refined. She was a bitch. She wanted my bit of money, which she got, and she wanted a bit of my honour and glory. When I was dead, that is,' he said, less as-

sertively. 'In my biography, if such should come to be written.'
The great expensive consulting-room tasted that, shrugged,
grimaced, swallowed it.

'Can you see it?' said Dr Wapenshaw, his upper lip lifted.
'Can you honestly say that you see it, man? The most elegant
woman in Europe, controller of the best pop-groups in the business?' Hogg stared at this wink of evidence of knowledge of a
very vulgar world (he knew it all; he read the *Daily Mirror* dog-
gedly every morning before opening his bar) in an eminent consultant. He said:

'I've not seen her name in the papers—'

'She's married again. A *real* marriage. A man with *real* money
and *real* talent, also younger than you and, moreover, *handsome.*'

'—But that confirms what I always thought, what you said
then, I mean. I mean *not* refined. A bitch.' *The Kvadrat's
Kloochy* fell off his knees, as in conscious failure to convert. Dr
Wapenshaw said harshly:

'Right. Now look at this.' And Hogg had hurled at him his
third fluttering paper bird of the afternoon. He caught it without
much skill; he was already weary; it was a journal he at once
recognised; it was called *Confrontation,* a cisatlantic quarterly
transatlantically financed and of, he understood, little general
appeal. He nodded, unsurprised. Dr Wapenshaw knew everything, then. Hogg understood all. He knew now what it was all
about. This was it. He turned to the page where the sestet of
that sonnet, which the *ja*-sayers had not wished to hear, spoke to
no frequenters of expensive bars, though the octave certainly
had:

> Coiled on the rooftree, bored, inspired, their snake
> Crowed Monday in. A collar kissed the throat,
> Clothes braced the body, a benignant ache
> Lit up a tooth. The papers had a note:
> 'His death may mean an empire is at stake.'
> Sunday and this were equally remote.

And it was signed with that former, forbidden, name. Hogg said,
stuttering:

'I can explain everything. I started that before, you see, before you got hold of me. Cured me, I mean. Of antisocial activities, that is. But I couldn't finish it. And then one night when I was working in the bar it just came. It had sort of tidied itself up behind my back. It was perfect, if you'll pardon the expression. So I sent it off and they published it. A kind of last fling, as you might term it. Or posthumous, perhaps you could even say. And then no more poetry, not never no more.' That last phrase was perhaps too ingratiating, too consciously the old-time barman. Dr Wapenshaw did not fall for it. Instead, he rose in wrath and cried:

'That's right, that's right, indulge yourself at my expense.' He strode across to a little table near the empty grate, picked up a human skull from it, and then waved it threateningly at Hogg. 'What you won't or can't realise, *you traitor*, is that that treacherous effusion of yours has been seen, yes, seen. Shorthouse saw it, Dr Shorthouse to you. You wouldn't know who Dr Shorthouse is, in your wilful treachery, but Dr Shorthouse is the author of *The Poetic Syndrome* and *Art and the Spirochaete* and other standard clinical works. Shorthouse saw it and Shorthouse showed it to me.' He crept towards Hogg, his eyes blowlamping in shame and anger, holding the skull in both hands like a pudding. 'And,' he cried, 'I felt a fool, because I'd already discussed your case with Shorthouse.'

'Dr Shorthouse,' kindly emended Hogg.

'Now do you see? *Do you see?* I boast about you as a cure, and here you are again with your bloody poetry.' Thumbs in skull's eye-sockets, he tore outwards in his anger, though the skull stayed firm.

'If it's the page-proofs of that thing of yours you're worried about,' said Hogg, still kindly, 'I'd be only too pleased to help you to correct them. What I mean is, to say that I wasn't cured after all and that my case was a failure. If that would be of any use,' he added humbly. 'You see,' he explained, 'I know all about altering things when they're in proof. I was a writer by profession, you see, as you know (I mean, that's what you tried to cure me of, isn't it?), and to you, who are really a doctor, it's only a sort of hobby when all's said and done.' He tried to smile at Dr Wapenshaw and then at the skull, but only the latter responded. 'Or if you like,' suggested Hogg, 'I'll tell everybody that I'm really cured and that that sonnet was only a kind of leftover from the old days. Or that that bloke K isn't really me but somebody else. In any case, that Shorthouse man won't say anything to anybody, will he? I mean, you doctors stick together, you have to, don't you? In one of those papers of yours I could do it,' expanded Hogg. 'The Lancet and The Scalpel and all those things.'

Dr Wapenshaw tore at the skull with his tense strong-nailed hairy fingers, but the skull, as though, it shot into Hogg's mind, remembering Housman's line about the man of bone remaining, grinned in armoured complacency. Dr Wapenshaw seemed about to weep then, as though this skull were Yorick's. After that, he made as to hurl the skull at Hogg, but Hogg got down to the floor to pick up the copy of The Kvadrat's Kloochy. Dr Wapenshaw put the skull back on its table, took a great breath and cried:

'Get out! Get out of my bloody consulting-room!'

'I,' said Hogg, still on his knees, mildly, 'only came here because you told me to.'

'Go on, get out! I expended skill and time and patience and, yes, bloody love on your case, and this is the thanks I get! You want to ruin my bloody career, that's what it is!'

Hogg, who had forgotten that he was still kneeling, said with continued mildness: 'You could always put what they call an erratum slip in the book, you know. I had one once. The printers had printed "immortal" instead of "immoral." It'll be a great pleasure to help you, really and truly. In any case, if the worst comes to the worst, they can always take that whole section out of the book and you can put something else in. Although,' he added seriously, 'you'll have to make sure it's exactly the same length. You could sit down tonight and make something up.'

Dr Wapenshaw now stomped over to kneeling Hogg and began to lift him by his collar. 'Out!' he cried again. 'Get out of here, you immoral bastard!' He thumped to the door, opened it and held it open. The patient by the gas-fire was weeping quietly. 'As for you, you scrimshanker,' Dr Wapenshaw cried at him, 'I'll deal with you in a minute. I know you, leadswinger as you are.' Hogg, in sorrowful dignity that would, he foreknew, become a brew of rage when he could get to somewhere nice and quiet, walked to the door and said:

'You take too much on yourselves, if you don't mind me saying so.' He waved *The Kvadrat's Kloochy* in a kind of admonition. 'I'd say it was the job of people like you to set the rest of us a good example. It's you who want a good going over, not this poor chap here.'

'Out!'

'Just going,' said Hogg, just going. He went, shaking his head slowly. 'And,' he said, turning back to Dr Wapenshaw, though from a safe distance, 'I'll write what poetry I want to, thanks very much, and not you nor anybody else will stop me.' He thought of adding 'So there,' but, before he could decide, Dr Wapenshaw slammed his consulting-room door; the patient by the gas-fire went 'Oh!' as though clouted by his mother. Not a very good man after all, thought Hogg, leaving. He ought to have suspected that heartiness right at the beginning. There had always, he felt, been something a bit insincere about it.

Three

Some short time later, Hogg sat trembling in a public lavatory. He could actually see the flesh of his inner thighs jellying with rage. Up above him diesel trains kept setting off to the west, for this was Paddington Station, whither he had walked by way of Madam Tussaud's, the Planetarium, Edgware Road and so on. He had put a penny in the slot and was having more than his pennyworth of anger out. The whole poetry-loathing world had the face of Dr Wapenshaw but, he felt, having soundly and legitimately bemerded that face in imagination and micturated on it also, the world was content merely to loathe, while Dr Wapenshaw had had to go further, deliberately liquidating the poet. Or trying to. He, Hogg, was maligning the world. The world was very bad, but not as bad as Dr Wapenshaw. But then again, was not the bloody Muse bad too, withholding her gifts as she had done and then coming forward with a most ill-timed bestowal? The point was, what was the position? What precisely and the hell did she want him to do? He caught a most agonising and fragrant whiff of himself as he had once been, seated like this in the workroom of his seaside flat, scratching bared legs that were mottled by the electric fire, working away steadily at his verse, the Muse and he set in a calm and utterly professional relationship. Would she, coaxed (which meant, among other things, not calling her bad or bloody as he had done just then), be willing to return on a sort of chronic basis? An acute spasm like that one which there had just been the row about really did nobody anything but harm.

But, of course, in those days, before that bloody woman had married him and made him squander his capital, it had been possible for him to be a professional (*i.e.* non-earning, or earning very little) poet. Now he had to have a wage. Even if the gift returned properly it would have to be expended in the form of what was called a nice hobby. Of course, he had been able to save a little. He had a little bedroom in the hotel, his food, a few tips. His trousers being down, he was able to find out at once how much he had saved. He still kept his cash in a sponge-bag whose string was wound about a fly-button. He trusted neither banks nor his colleagues at the hotel. Keys there were a mockery, because of pass-keys. Once he had entered his little bedroom to find Spanish John in it, with a shirt of Hogg's in one hand and one of Hogg's razor-blades in the other, and Hogg had been quite sure he had locked his door. John had smiled falsely and said that he had found the door unlocked and had entered to borrow a razor-blade, he being out of them, and at the same time had been filled with a desire to admire Hogg's shirts, which he considered to be very good ones. Hogg did not believe that. Anyway, he kept his money in a bag in his trousers. It was also a kind of testicle-protector, for there were some dirty fighters among the Maltese and Cypriot commis waiters. He now took his roll of five-pound notes out of the bag and counted them earnestly. A crude drawing of a man, a sort of naked god of fertility, looked down without envy.

Twenty-five drawings of a clavigerous lion guarding a rather imbecilic teenage Britannia. That was not bad. That was one hundred and twenty-five pounds. And, in his trouser pocket, there was about thirty shillings in silver, made up of mostly very mean gratuities. The value of certain other gratuities, dispensed

in foreign notes, he had not yet troubled to ascertain. These—
dirhams, lire, newfrancs, deutschmarks and so on—he kept
folded in his passport, which was in the inside pocket of his
sports-jacket, now hanging from the door-hook. It was necessary,
he had learned, for every employee of the hotel to keep close
guard on his passport, because of the thievery and shady trade
in passports that went on among the dark scullions, outcasts of
the islands, creatures of obscure ethnic origin, cunning, vicious,
and unscrupulous. Despite Britain's new despised status in the
world, a British passport was still prized. So there it was, then.
Enough to buy time to write, say, a really careful sestina or a
rambling Pound-type canto, if the Muse would be willing to co-
operate. He blew very faint wind. That was not, he told her, in
case she were around, acting silly, meant in any spirit of acri-
mony or impatience: it was a legitimate efflation, paid for in advance.

He was calmer now. He looked with sympathy at the graffiti
on the walls and door. Some of these must, he thought, be considered a kind of art, since they were evidently attempts to
purge powerful emotion into stylised forms. There were also
wild messages, pleas for assignations at known places, though
the dates were long gone; there were boasts too extravagant to
be capable of fulfilment, also succinct desiderations of sexual
partners too complaisant to be of this world. Sex. Well, he,
Hogg, had tried, following the rehabilitatory pattern imposed by
Dr, now bloody, Wapenshaw, to go in for sex like everybody
else, but it had not been very successful. In any case, you really
had to be young nowadays to go in properly for sex: that had
been made fairly clear to him by such of the young—Italian
chambermaids and so on—as he had met, as also by some of the
popular art he had, again in fulfilment of the Wapenshaw
bloody pattern, tried glumly to appreciate. So there it was, then.
He must stop himself saying that to himself all the time.

On the walls there were also little verses, most of them set—
like those works of Faith Fortitude—as prose. They were all
traditional verses, mostly on cloacal subjects, but it was somehow warming to find that verse was still in regard for its gnomic
or mnemonic properties. Among the common people, that was.
He could not imagine bloody Wapenshaw writing or drawing

anything in a lavatory. There was, Hogg noticed, a nice little patch of naked wall by his right arm. He did not need his Muse for what he now took out his ballpoint pen to write. He wrote:

> Think, when you ease your inner gripe
> Or stand with penis in your paw,
> A face is lodged within the pipe
> And it belongs to Wapenshaw.

That, perhaps, would be learned by heart and reproduced else-where underground, imperfect memory blurring the sharp elegance but perhaps not wholly losing that name, in some allomorph or other. Enderby, folk poet. Enderby, not Hogg. And Wapenshaw given a proper immortality.

Hoggerby now felt hungry. He girded himself, pulled the chain, donned his jacket and went out. He nodded kindly at the wash-and-brush-up man, who was reading the *Evening Standard* by his glazed partition, then mounted to the light. He walked out of the station and found a sufficiently dirty-looking little eating-hell in a sidestreet, nearly filled with slurping men. He knew the sort of meal he wanted: a rebellious meal. From the tooth-sucking man with glasses behind the counter he ordered a mug of very strong tea, eggs and fat bacon, marged doorsteps. He was going to give himself indigestion. That would show bloody Wapenshaw.

2

One

A GREAT honour, *ja*,' said Mr Holden from behind massed flowers of the season. In the adjoining office typewriters clacked.
Standing before Mr Holden were Hogg and John the Spaniard,
respectively flashing gold and caries and looking dour about the
great honour. 'Smallish and very select, and the Saddleback is
just about the right-sized pitch, *ja*. So it'll be cocktails in the Sty,
and this is where you, brother Hogg, show your batting strength.
We'll be having some waiters from the Sweet Thames Run Softly
bar, sort of extra cover. You'd better start boning up on your
cocktails, fella, read up your sort of bar-tender's Wisden. Horse's
necks, sidecars, manhattans, snowballs, the lot. You reckon you
can carry your bat?'

'I know them all,' said Hogg, 'including some that haven't
been thought of yet.'

'I show him,' said John, 'if he not know.'

'A pop-group, you say?' said Hogg.

'You ought to know these things,' said Mr Holden. 'You get
plenty of time for reading the papers. A sort of belated celebra-

tion, a kind of late cut to the off. They've been making this movie in the Bahamas, as you should know, and only now have they been able to get this fixture organised. There's a lot to celebrate. A new golden disc, the birthday honours, and now Yod Crewsy gets this F.L.R.S. thing. *Ja,* plenty to celebrate. *Mucho,*' he added for John's benefit.

'*Usted habla bien español.*'

'F.R.S.L.?' Hogg queried. 'Fellow of the Royal Society of Literature?'

'Not bad, not bad, fella. Keep on like that, eye on the ball and all that palooka. *Ja,* he got the Hangman award for some book of poems he wrote and then this F.S. thing sort of automatically followed.'

'Heinemann award?' frowned Hogg. 'And what do you say this lot are called?'

'Ah, Jesus, you'll never get off the reserve list,' said Mr Holden. 'The Crewsy Fixers. You mean to say you never heard of the Crewsy Fixers? England's best ambassadors they've been termed, a little Test team all on their own, *ja,* doing all in their power to protect the wicket of your shattered economy. Foreign earnings, that is, an export drive to the boundary, and Her Majesty the Queen' (Mr Holden bowed his head) 'is no doubt dooly grateful. Hence, fella, those medals. So now you know, but I guess you should have known already.'

'*Sí sí sí,*' agreed John. 'Already he should know.'

'I would call that a very blasphemous name,' said Hogg coldly. 'Not,' he added hastily, 'that I'm at all a religious man, you understand. What I mean is, it seems to me in very bad taste.'

'To the pure,' said Mr Holden, 'all things are pure. There's Yod Crewsy and his Fixers, so they become the Crewsy Fixers. Right? If you're thinking it sounds like something else, then you're on a very shaky wicket yourself, fella, so far as taste goes. And they're very very religious boys, which again you should have known. *Molto religioso,*' he added to John.

'*Lei parla bene italiano.*'

'I bet,' divined Hogg, 'that he called himself Crewsy just so he could make up that blasphemous name. And that Yod bit doesn't sound Christian to me. Yod,' he told Mr Holden, 'is a letter of the Hebrew alphabet.'

'Now you'd better watch that,' said Mr Holden very sternly. 'Because that sounds to me very much like racial prejudice. And if there's one thing the policy of this hotel group says out out out to, it's racial prejudice. So watch it.'

'He say too,' intimated John, 'about Spanish people not good.'

'Right, then,' said Mr Holden. 'We'll have harmony, efficiency, and team spirit. A very special luncheon for very special people. The confectionary chefs are working out a very special ice pudding for the occasion. And there's going to be a very exotic dish not before served here. It's called—' he consulted a draft menu on his desk, '—*lobscowse*. Something Arabic, I guess. Those boys sure scored big in Saudi-Arabia.'

Hogg stood transfixed. 'Ice pudding,' he said. 'In Saudi-Arabia. It melts as it is made. Like time, you know.'

'You feeling all right, Hogg?' While Mr Holden frowned, John the Spaniard poked his right temple with a brown finger, shaking his head in sad glee. 'You sure you feel up to this, fella? If not, we can always get Juanito here to take over. I reckon he can face the bowling if you can't.'

'It has to be a Hogg,' said Hogg, distracted. 'He may be a pig but he's not a Hogg. It's coming,' he added. 'There's something there all right. The gift's coming back. Something special. I'll have to go and put it down on paper.'

'Ah, a cocktail,' nodded Mr Holden, relieved. 'That's okay, then. Something special, eh? You go right off and get it down, fella. And don't forget that we own the copyright. One more thing. Wigs. There's got to be wigs. They needn't fit too good, but there's got to be wigs. Okay. Back to the pavilion.'

Hogg left in a small daze. 'Useless to hope to hold off,' he muttered, 'the unavoidable happening.' What the hell was it all about? She was there all right; she was playing silly hide-and-seek, finger in mouth, up and down the corridors. She was wearing a very short dress. John the Spaniard said:

'What you mean, *hombre*? You call me pig.'

'Big, I said big,' said Hogg, distracted. 'Look, the bar doesn't open for another hour. I've got to go to my room.'

'Big pig, you say? I hear. Not bloody daft, man.'

Hogg made a dash for the staff lift which, he saw, was just about to land. It opened, and a very natty though puffy young man came out, bearing what looked like the disgorgements of one of the hotel computers. He seemed to look direly at Hogg, as though it was his character that had been programmed. Hogg got in frowning, his brain full of words that were trying to marshal themselves into an ordered, though cryptic, statement. John the Spaniard tried to follow, but the puffy young man was in the way. Hogg pressed the right button and saw the door slice fist-shaking John laterally until there was nothing left of him save the after-image of the glow of his fillings. The lift-car seemed to remain where it was, and only the flash of the floor-numbers spoke of rising to 34A, a floor not accessible to the hotel guests. A high-powered car rushing on to it, whether you will or not. Hogg nearly fainted.

He got out blindly when the door automatically opened, fumbled for his key, almost tumbled into his cheerless cell. Paper. He had a lined writing-pad, in keeping with his new image. He sat panting heavily on his cot and began to scribble. She breathed hard into his left ear; her voice had become, for some reason, a lisping child's one. He wrote:

> Useless to hope to hold off
> The unavoidable happening
> With that frail barricade
> Of week, day or hour
> Which melts as it is made,
> For time himself will bring
> You in his high-powered car,
> Rushing on to it,
> Whether you will or not.

And then sudden silence. What was it all about? What did it mean? Too much meaning in your poetry, Enderby. Somebody had said that once. You worry, my dear Enderby, far too much about meaning. Rawcliffe, one of the special trinity of enemies. And there was Wapenshaw, trying to crush his skull. He saw the strong hairy fingers, but the skull only grinned. The consolation of bone, the bone's resignation. But what thing was going to happen that he had to resign himself to? A handshake of finality, the welcome of whole fields of empty time. No, no, it was not quite that. With a rush like blood it came:

> So, shaking hands with the grim
> Satisfactory argument,
> The consolation of bone
> Resigned to the event,
> Making a friend of him,
> He, in an access of love,
> Renders his bare acres
> Golden and wide enough.

The prophetic tingling, as of something thrilling to welcome and then to lose and not to mind losing. He could have wept. The Muse stood by his wash-basin. What, then? What was the covenant to be? He might have to wait for a dream for the full disclosure. There was a hammering on the door. She hid, sliding through its door, into his tiny clothes-cupboard.

'*Puerco, puerco!*' called John the Spaniard. 'You get tonic water for bloody bar, man!'

'For cough!' cried Hogg. 'Go away, you garlicky bastard!'

And then, radiating from the clothes-cupboard, it announced itself as the last stanza:

> And this last margin of leaving
> Is sheltered from the rude
> Indiscreet tugging of winds.

'*You* bastard! You pull pudding in there! I bloody *know!*' Hogg wrote, like a dying message:

> For parting, a point in time,
> Cannot have magnitude
> And cannot cast shadows about
> The final

John's thudding drowned the final whatever it was. The Muse, hidden in the cupboard, shook her sad child's head. Hogg-Enderby, enraged, got up and unlocked his door. Then he pulled it open. John almost fell in.

'Right,' Hogg-Enderby clenched. 'You've had this coming a long time, bloody *hombre*. You and bloody Franco and wanting bloody Gibraltar. Right.' Well, Wapenshaw and the rest wished him to be involved in the world, didn't they—low, vulgar, an ordinary citizen ungiven to civilised restraints? John grinned dirty gold and put out mean claws. Hogg, as low barman, at once kicked him on the shin. While John was hopping mad, Hogg pushed him on to the bed. John sat there nursing his pain and trying to kick at the same time, mouthing the foulest bodega provincial Spanish with no refined lisp in it. Hogg looked for something to hit him with and picked up the cheap bedroom chair from near the clothes-cupboard. By the time he had raised it John was on his feet again. He leered very terribly and said:

'*Momento de verdad.*' Hogg thought he saw peasant's muscles underneath the cheap bar-waiter's clothes; his heart failed; he was too old; he shouldn't have started this. He put the chair gently down on the floor again. He said:

'All right. Here's my bloody throat.' And he proffered it. John did not expect this. He said:

'You give kick on flaming leg, *hombre*. Not good.'

'Listen,' said Hogg, 'listen.' He, who had done Latin at school, who had spoken soldier's Italian in Catania but also read Dante with a crib, for some reason was now impelled to draw on this Romance equipment and create, nearly from scratch, not merely a language for Spain but a literature as well. '*La consolación del osso,*' he suggested. John cocked an ear and said:

'*Hueso.*'

'That's right,' Hogg agreed. '*La consolación del hueso resignado al evento.*' He didn't know whether that was right or not, but he felt it ought to have a place somewhere along the line of colonial deformation of Latin. In any case, John went pale. It was Orpheus with his lute, by God, who (so Hogg as schoolboy Enderby had believed, taking the first line of the song as a semantic entity) made trees. 'And,' said Hogg, very recklessly now, 'To say *adiós, no è que un punto temporál.*'

'*Sí sí.*'

'*Y un punto* can't have a bloody *ombra.*'

'*No puede tener sombra, sí, claro.*'

'And so there can't be any *sombras* around the something *finál.*' (There was a rhyme there, wasn't there? He was actually rhyming in Spanish.)

'Ah,' and as though they were both merely trying to remember a Spanish poem that actually existed, *'el beso.'*
Beso, baiser, bacio. Kiss.

> And cannot cast shadows about
> The final kiss

Tears came into Hogg's eyes. He felt unutterably wretched. He said to John, tearfully, 'You can have the job any time you like. I don't want it. I want to be a poet again, that's all.' John nodded. Garlicky sod as he was, he understood. 'Poetry no money,' he said. 'Go on National Assistance, man.' Like most immigrants, he knew everything about the resources of the British Welfare State. And then he said: 'No, no good. Wait is best. Wait.' He knew all about destiny too, being a foreigner. 'Wait for,' he said, *'el acaso inevitable.'*
Hogg looked at him in wonder. The unavoidable happening.

Two

They got on a good deal better after that, though John exaggerated the limp from Hogg's shin-kick. When the day for the luncheon arrived, they were working in accord, and Mr Holden was pleased. *'Ja,'* he said. 'All we want here is harmony. Like a real good opening pair. Hobbs and P. G. Grace, or two guys like that.' But Mr Holden fussed in nervousness at midday on the day. Everything had to be just right. Out of stereophonic speakers there excreted (Hogg could think of no other word) pseudo-music composed and performed by the guests of honour, and Mr Holden tried to adjust the volume so as to secure the correct balance between the subliminally insinuating and the overtly assertive. Furniture-music, like Erik Satie, but set cunningly for the barking of ears: that was the aim. Hogg considered that he had never in his whole life heard anything so, at the same time, obscene, noisy, and insipid. He was mixing cocktails in big crocks, selecting the ingredients aleatorically. After all, poetry was compounded of chance elements, and cocktail-making was by far the inferior art. He set out now to blend his special, intended for people he already disliked, like this blasphemous gang that was a collective guest of honour, and those he would dislike when he saw them. He threw together Scotch whisky and British port-type wine, adding flat draught bitter beer, grenadine, angostura, and some very sour canned orange juice which the management had bought up cheap some months before. As the resultant colour seemed rather subfusc for a festive drink, he broke in three eggs and electrically whisked all up to a yellowy pinkish froth. He tasted a little gingerly from a dram-measure and found it tasted of nothing. It left, however, a sickish residual gust that would do very well. Nodding, he put it in the refrigerator to keep cold with the other crocks.

'You better get your wig on, fella,' said Mr Holden. Hogg looked around, seeing John the Spaniard and the three Albanian waiters from the Sweet Thames Run Softly bar downstairs all looking terrible in coarse golliwog toupees that were meant to be a kind of homage, so Hogg understood, to an enviable aspect of youth typified by these blasphemous obscenities—namely, a riotous and sickening excess of head-hair. Hogg picked up his own wig and crammed it on. He did not like what he saw in the mirrored reredos. He seemed to resemble very much his stepmother surfacing from blurred after-stout sleep, taken with her glasses on and teeth in, her head a very unsavoury Medusa-tangle.

The first man to arrive seemed to be the man who had been deputed to organise this luncheon by the various interests concerned. Hogg frowned: the face seemed familiar. It was a stormy Irish face that appeared to fight against its London sleeking. The lapelless jacket and tapering trousers were of a kind of healthy stirabout colour.

'You'll find everything in order,' said Mr Parkin, a very much more important man than Mr Holden. He was British, not American, and he wore striped trousers and a short black jacket, like a member of parliament meeting his constituents in the lobby. He had obviously, considered Hogg, been cast rather than appointed. He was distinguished greying butler-talking British, which meant, thought Hogg, that he was probably a con-man reformed out of fear of another stretch. He was in charge of banquets and luncheons for the distinguished and the like. He was above knowing Hogg's name. 'Barman,' he said, 'a drink for Mr Macnamara.'

So that was who it was. Shem Macnamara, once a poet himself but now, analogously to Mr Parkin, reformed. 'Scatch on the racks,' said Shem Macnamara, like an American. He did not recognise Hogg. He breathed a kind of mouthwash as he opened meaty lips for his drink. Hogg remembered that luncheon long ago that had been given for him, himself, Enderby as he had been, when he had won the Goodby Gold Medal for poetry. Then Shem Macnamara had been very poor, only too ready for a free meal and a quiet sneer at the success of a fellow-poet. Then, instead of expensive mouthwash, he had breathed on Hogg-Enderby bafflingly (for no banquet would serve, because of the known redolence of onions, onions) onions.

'Onions,' said Hogg. He was frowned on in puzzlement. 'Cocktail onions,' he offered. Well, just imagine, Shem Macnamara. Shem Macnamara deepened his frown. Something in that voice saying 'Onions'? He did not take any onions.

The guests began to arrive. There were ugly tall girls, very thin, showing bony knees, whom Hogg took to be photographer's models, or some such thing. He filled out tray-loads of his special cocktail for them, and told the waiters to say it was called a Crucifier. It seemed to do none of these girls any harm, blasphemous bitches as they were. There were young men who seemed to be literary men, and some of these ordered drinks that had to be freshly made up and were very complicated. Hogg cursed under his wig when one young man stood over him at the bar while some exotic nonsense called a Papa Doc was painfully put together—rum, lemon juice, vermouth, tabasco (two drops), stir with a cock's feather. 'This,' groused Hogg, 'is a hen's feather. Does it make much difference?' Mr Holden hovered, looking black. Some very important New York Jews came in, all stroking some of the model-girls as if thereby to conjure humps of voluptuousness. A most insolent Negro in native robes was made much of; Hogg had a large helping of the Crucifier ready for him, but he asked for plain milk, and this had to be sent downstairs for, and then, when it had been handed to him, he merely carried it round unsipped, as if to demonstrate that he was not totally anti-white. Photographers struck with flashes from opposed corners, like a little war, and there were, though not practising their art today, some, so Hogg heard from John, very great photographers among the guests.

The Crucifier was, to Hogg's annoyance, rather popular. Atrophy of the gustatory sense or anaesthesia of the stomach lining, or something. He prepared a sicklier version—whiskey and port-style British wine diluted with warm water from the washing-up tap—and this too was well appreciated. It was the name, that was what it was: it was a small and unbargained-for poetic victory. Suddenly, while Hogg was sucking on the sour lozenge of an image of himself, sweating under a dyed-wool wig into the American-type martinis he was pouring from the gin bottle, there was a reverent hush. The Prime Minister had arrived. He was a little bumptious man in a baggy suit to show he had just come from work, and he was at his ease with everyone and full of little pleasantries. Hogg begged John the Spaniard to make sure he got a Crucifier, but the Prime Minister asked for orange juice. Hogg was happy to serve some of the cheap acid variety. Then he got down to a batch of champagne cocktails for a bunch of exquisite young men who grinned at his wig, himself longing for a mug of very strong, or stepmother's, tea. There was a lot of loud chatter and some giggles (as though the session were proceeding at once, without the interim of a meal, towards seduction); under it the ghastly pseudo-music swelled up, reached its sonic level, then rose above to drown it. It was a fanfare. There were cheers. The guests of honour had come at last, embraced and worshipped from their very entrance. Hogg stopped mixing to have a good look at them.

They were, he thought, about as horrible in appearance as it was possible to imagine any four young men to be. The one Hogg knew to be their leader, Yod Crewsy, received, because of his multiple success, the most homage, and he accepted this as his due, simpering out of a lopsided mouth that was too large to be properly controlled and, indeed, seemed to possess a kind of surrealist autonomy. The other three were vulgarly at home, punching each other in glee and then doing a kind of ring-a-roses round the Prime Minister. The working photographers flashed and flashed like an epidemic of sharp sneezes. With the four, Hogg now noticed, there was a clergyman. He was small, old, and vigorous, and he champed and champed, nodding at everyone and even, before he came up to Hogg at the bar, sketching a general blessing. He said, nodding:

'If there's such a thing as a Power's among that heathen army you have up there on your shelves, then I'll have a double Power's. And I'll trouble you for a glass of fresh water.'

Hogg surveyed his small stock of Irish. 'Will a Mick Sullivan do?'

'Ah, well then, I'll try it. Such a big place as you are and divil a drop of Power's to bless yourself with.'

'If you'd like something for a change,' said Hogg, 'there's this special cocktail here I've mixed in honour. A Crucifier, it's called.' He at once realised that that must sound like deliberate insult to this man's cloth. 'Blasphemous, I know,' he said. 'I apologise. But I consider that the name itself. Of these four, I mean. The guests of honour, that is. Father,' he added.

'Well now, shouldn't we all be sticking to our own vocations and not stepping outside the lines to deliver judgments on what isn't our proper province at all? Perhaps you'd be willing to allow that it's myself as would be the proper and qualified judge of what's blasphemous and what isn't, me being the chaplain to those boys?' While he spoke his eyes roamed everywhere in Irish neurosis. In the corner there was the sound of someone being sick, a woman from the pitch of the retchings. Hogg showed minimal satisfaction, then swiftly shut it off. The chaplain saw. 'Taking pleasure itself, is it, in the misfortune of some poor body's weak and delicate stomach and it fasting from dawn maybe?' The Prime Minister was heard to say:

'Well, as long as nobody blames it on the Government.' There was dutiful laughter, though one young man, standing alone by the bar, nodded seriously. He had, like the Crewsy Fixers, very long hair, but it seemed as seedy as Hogg's own wig. His suit was not new; the side-pockets bulged. The chaplain poured himself another measure from the whisky bottle. Yod Crewsy and one of his group, a guffawing youth with very white dentures, came over to the bar, bearing glasses, Hogg was glad to see, of the later version of the Crucifier. Yod Crewsy said to Hogg:

'What you on then, dad?' Before Hogg could make an evasive reply, Yod Crewsy feigned to be surprised and overjoyed by the sudden sight of the seedy-maned young man with the bulging

pockets. He put on a large record-sleeve smile and then embraced him with arms whose thinness the cut of his serge jerkin
did nothing to disguise, saying: 'Jed Foot. Me old Jed, as
ever was. Glad like you could make it, boy.' Jed Foot,
mouth closed, smiled with his cheek-muscles. Hogg could not
remember whether Jed belonged to the same alphabet as Yod.
Yod Crewsy said to his chaplain: 'Look who's here, Father.
We're back to the old days. Happy times them was,' he said to
Jed Foot. 'Pity you got out when you did. What they call a
miscalculation. Right?' he said to Hogg cheekily.

'A memento mori,' said Hogg, with poet's acuity. The chaplain chewed darkly over that before taking more whisky, as
though Hogg had revealed himself as an anti-vernacularist.

'You got your mementos,' said Jed Foot to Yod Crewsy. 'Them
songs. Pity I never learned how to write down music.'

'Every man to his own like opinion,' said Yod Crewsy. 'You
said the groups was finished. What you been on—the Western
Australia run? Dead horrible, I know. Collie and Merredin and
Bullfinch. They've been working you hard, boy. I can see that.'

'I've been doing the clubs. The clubs is all right.'

'Have another of these,' said Hogg to Yod Crewsy. 'A *big*
one. A Crucifier, it's called.'

'What I want,' said Yod Crewsy, 'is me dinner. Her ladyship
here yet?'

'Herself will be the last to come,' said the chaplain. ' 'Tis a
lady's privilege. You,' he said to Hogg, 'have the face of a man
who's been a long time away from the altar. A Catholic face I
said to meself as soon as I clapped eyes on it, and very guilty
and shifty too with your self-knowledge of being in the presence
of a priest of your Church and you with the boldness to be
speaking of blasphemy and many a long year between yourself
and the blessed sacrament.'

'Look here,' said Hogg. Swirls of toothed worshippers were
about Yod Crewsy and his accomplices, but this Jed Foot drank
bitter gin alone. 'You,' said Hogg, 'and your bloody ecumenical
nonsense.'

'Is it yourself as would be daring to flaunt the shame of your
apostasy in the face of a priest of your Church and spitting
venom on the blessed enactments of the Holy Father himself?'

He took more whisky. 'I'll be troubling you,' he said, 'for another glass of fresh water.'

It had been part of Hogg's cure to attend the services of the Church of England, a means of liquidating for ever his obsession with his dead stepmother who, Dr Wapenshaw had said, was really the Catholic Church. He was about to tell this chaplain that the liturgy of traditional Anglicanism was superior to that of reformed Papistry when the chaplain turned his face towards the entrance with mouth open in joy. Everybody else turned too. A lady was entering and, with her, a handsome and knowing Jewish man in his thirties. Hogg's heart turned over several times, as on a spit. Of course, of course, blast it: he should have known. Had not bloody Wapenshaw said something about her running the best pop-groups in the business? This was too much. He said to Mr Holden, who was standing by the bar, though not drinking:

'I've got to get out of here, I've *got to.*'

'You stay where you are, fella, on the crease.'

'But I've got to get to a lavatory.'

'Now listen,' said Mr Holden, his tea-coloured eyes very hard. 'I've had about enough from you, fella, that I have. Obstruction for its own sake and going against the rules. You stay in till you're given out, right? And another thing, there's too many been made sick, and hard drinkers too from the look of them. See, they're taking that poor girl off now. I reckon those drinks you've been mixing will have to be looked into. Now what in hell's name—' for Hogg had pulled his wig down over his eyes like a busby. Even so he could see her clearly enough through the coarse fringe.

'Vesta, me dear,' the chaplain was saying. 'Five Our Fathers and five Hail Marys for being late.' She smiled from her clever green eyes. She, never behind in the fashions, was in a new long-length skirt of palest pink and a brown biki-jacket. On the shining penny-coloured hair was a halo hat of thrushes' feathers. Her purse and shoes were quilled. All the other women at once began to look dated in their bright reds and greens. Hogg moaned to himself, desperately washing a champagne-glass below the level of the counter-top.

'You know my husband, I think,' Vesta said.

'And isn't it meself he's been coming to for his preliminary in-
struction? Well, praise be to God, as one goes out another comes
in.' He swivelled his long Irish neck to frown at Hogg.

'What a strange little man,' Vesta said. 'Is he serving only
from the top of his head, or something?' And then she turned to
greet the Prime Minister with every sign of ease and affection.
Her chief pop-group came over whooping to kiss her cheeks
extravagantly, calling her, though in evident facetiousness,
'mum.' The photographers opposed fresh lightnings at each
other.

'Oh God God God.' groaned Hogg.

'Repentance, is it?' the sharp-eared chaplain said. 'Well, you
have a long penance in front of you for scoffing at the True
Church itself.'

A man with glasses, dressed in hunting pink, came to the door
to bawl that luncheon was served. There was a ragged shouting
exodus towards the Wessex Saddleback. Some, though, as Hogg
saw, with very little satisfaction now, on the clearing of the bar,
would not be wanting any lunch. Himself included. Shem Macnamara was one of the last to leave. He turned frowning to look
at Hogg, mouthing the word 'onions.' He had, he was sure,
heard that voice somewhere before.

Three

Hogg and John the Spaniard washed glasses companionably together, Hogg in a daze though, though he responded to John's
excited comments on the event still proceeding with his usual
courtesy. John had been swigging from half-empty glasses and
was more garrulous than usual.

'You see that bloody thing, *hombre*? All ice cream and done
like big *monumento*.' It appealed to John's baroque taste and
prompted memories of the victorious group-effigies erected by
the Caudillo: the Crewsy Fixers, with drums and guitar, in
highly compressed frozen confectioner's custard—whether really
to be eaten or not was not clear, though the sound of laughing
chiselling was coming through at that moment.

'Oh?' said Hogg.

'See this bloody *vaso*? One *párpado* dropped in. Daft, *hombre*.' It was not so much a false eyelid as a set of false eyelashes for one eye.

'Ah,' said Hogg. Some of the glasses were very filthy.

'One thing,' said John. 'We not serve no *coñac* from in here. Bottles on the *mesa* already. *Vasos* too. Not bar job, *hombre*.'

'No.'

John sang. It was a kind of flamenco without words. Soon he desisted. The rhythms, if not the sense, of an after-lunch speech were coming through. It was the Prime Minister. 'He speak bloody good, man. But always same thing. I hear on telly.' Hogg could tell exactly what the Prime Minister was saying: selling country short; legacy of misrule; determination to win through to solvency despite treacherous and frivolous opposition of opposition; teamwork of these four boys here, not unfortunately his constituents but he would be proud to have them, example to all; people's art; art of the people; the people in good art, heart; struggles to come; win through to solvency; legacy of misrule. After long clapping there was the sound of a kind of standing ovation. Suddenly the door of Piggy's Sty was burst open. It was Jed Foot lurching in, very white. He said:

'Give us something strong. Can't stand it, I tell you. The bastard's on his feet.' Sympathetic, Hogg poured him a large brandy. Jed Foot downed it in one. 'Taught him all he knows,' he whined. 'Bloody treachery. Give us another one of them.' Hogg poured an even larger brandy. Jed Foot gave it, in one swig, to his gullet. John tut-tutted. He said:

'We finish now here, *hombre*. I go see.'

'I'm getting out,' said Hogg. 'Out. Bloody fed-up, that's what I am.'

'Bloody fed-up, mate?' said Jed Foot, his mouth quivering. 'You don't know what bloody fed-upness is. I'll have another one of them.'

'I'm off duty now,' Hogg said. He had already discarded that shameful wig. Now he took off his barman's coat. His own mufti jacket was in the little storeroom at the back of the bar. He went to get it. John was just opening the door that led to the exit-corridor; the door of the Wessex Saddleback was opposite. When Hogg, decently jacketed, was making his way out, he found that

that door had been thrown wide open so that hotel employees could listen and look. The whole of Europe was represented there among the chambermaids and small cooks who, with open mouths, worshipped this global myth. Jed Foot was at the back of them; John had pushed to the front. Hogg, shambling in wretchedness towards the staff lift, suddenly heard familiar noises:

> 'And so the car plunged in the singing green
> Of sycamore and riot-running chestnut and oak
> That squandered flame, cut a thousand arteries
>   and bled
> Flood after summer flood, spawned an obscene
> Unquenched unstanchable green world sea, to choke
> The fainting air, drown sun in its skywise tread.'

It was being read wretchedly, as though the reader was decoding it from ill-learnt Cyrillic. Yod Crewsy now said: 'Me teeth is slipping a bit.' Laughter. 'I can write em but I can't say em. Anyway, here's how it finishes:

> But the thin tuning-fork of one of the needs of
>   men,
> The squat village letter-box, approached, awoke,
> Called all to order with its stump of red;
> In a giant shudder, the monstrous organ then
> Took shape and spoke.'

There was applause. Yod Crewsy said: 'Don't ask me what it means; I only wrote it.' Laughter. 'No, serious like, I feel very humble. But I put them poems together in this book just like to show. You know, show that we do like think a bit and the kvadrats, or squares which is what some of you squares here would like call yourselves, can't have it all their own way.' Cheers.

Hogg stood frozen like an ice cream *monumento*. He had left, when he had run away from that bitch in there, several manuscript poems in her Gloucester Road flat. They had been written; later they had been written off. The holograph of *The Pet Beast* had been among them. Unable to reconstitute them from memory, he could not now be absolutely sure—But wait. A painter

friend of that bitch, his name Gideon Dalgleish, had said something on some social occasion or other about driving with a
friend through green summer England and being overwhelmed
with its somehow, my dear, *obscene* greenness, a great prolif-
erating green carcinoma, terrifying because shapeless and *huge*.
And then the sudden patch of red from a letter-box concentrated
and tamed the green and gave it a comprehensible form. Nature
needs man, my dear. The words CURTAL SONNET had flashed
before his, Hogg's, Enderby's, eyes, and the rhymes had lined up
for inspection. And then—He stood gaping at nothing, unable to
move. He heard Yod Crewsy's voice again, calling microphon-
ically over loud cheers:

'Right. So much for the F.S.L.S. lot, or whatever it is. And I'd
like to say a very 'artfelt *ta* to our mum here, who like encouraged me. Now we're going to do our new disc, and not mime
neither. I see the lads is all ready up there. All they want is me.'
Ecstasy.

Hogg painfully turned himself about. Then, as against a G
science-fictionally intensified twentyfold, he forced his legs to
slide forward towards the open door of the Wessex Saddleback.
Jed Foot was trembling. Across the smoky luncheon-room, now
darkened by drawn curtains, he saw, glorious in floodlighting,
the Crewsy Fixers ranged grinning on a little dais. Yod Crewsy
held a flat guitar with flex sprouting from it. In front of each of
the others was a high-mounted sidedrum. They poised white
sticks, grinning. Then they jumped into a hell of noise belched
out fourfold by speakers set at the ceiling's corners.

> 'You can do that, *ja,* and do this. *Ja.*
> You can say that you won't go beyond a kiss. *Ja.*
> But where's it goin to get ya, where's
> It goin to get
> Ya (*ja*), babaaah?'

Where was she, that was the point? Where was she, so that he
could go in there and expose her, the whole blasphemous crew
of them, before high heaven, which did not exist? Hogg squinted
through the dark and thought he saw that cruel feathered halo
hat. Then, in that little group by the open door, there seemed to
be violent action, noise, the smell of a sudden pungent fried

breakfast. A couple of chambermaids screamed and clutched each other. The sidedrums on the dais rimshotted like mad. Yod Crewsy did a crazy drunken dance, feet uplifted as if walking through a shitten byre. His autonomous mouth did a high scream, while his eyes crossed in low comedy. The crowd clapped.

'Here yare,' panted Jed Foot, and he handed something to Hogg. Hogg automatically took it, a barman used to taking things. Too heavy for a brandy glass. Jed Foot hared off down the corridor.

'Lights! Lights!' called somebody, the king in *Hamlet*. 'He's shot, he's hurt!' Yod Crewsy was down, kicking. The dullest of the Crewsy Fixers still leered, singing inaudibly. But drums started to go over. Hogg was being started back from, John incredulous, the chambermaids pointing and screaming, a minor cook, like a harvest-caught rabbit, wondering whither to run, whimpering. Hogg looked down at his hand and saw a smoking gun in it. Shem Macnamara was yelling: 'Him! Stop him! I knew that voice! Sworn enemy of pop! Murderer!' John the Spaniard was quick, perhaps no stranger to such southern public violence. He yapped like a dog, most unspanishly, at Hogg: 'Out out out out out out!' It was like a Mr Holdenish nightmare of umpires. Hogg, with an instinct learnt from the few films he had seen, pointed the gun at Shem Macnamara, marvelling. Some of the guests still thought this part of the show. Others called for a doctor. Hogg, gun in hand, ran. He ran down the corridor to the service lift. The indicator said it was on another floor, resting. He called it and it lazily said it was coming. He kept the gun pointing. John was in everybody's way, but some were thinking of coming for him. Vesta now would be weeping over her favourite client, the impersonal and opportunist camera-lights cracking. The lift arrived and Hogg entered, still marvelling. Armed. Dangerous. The lift-door snapped off the sound of running and falling feet. Drunk, that was the trouble with them: all drunk. Hogg stood dazed in a fancied suspension of all movement, while the lighted floor-pointer counted down. He had pressed, for some reason, the button marked B for basement. As low as you could get. He landed on a stone corridor, full of men trundling garbage bins. Useless to hope to hold off. It was a matter of running, if he could, up a short dirty flight to a ground-level back entrance. He remembered, near-dead with breathlessness, to drop the gun at the top of the stairs. It clanked down and, the safety-catch still off, somehow managed to fire itself at nothing. *El acaso inevitable.* With that frail barricade. Would the frozen monument be melting now up there, Yod Crewsy dissolving first? Men were coming to the noise of firing. He was out. It was a staff car-park, very unglamorous. For time himself will bring. You in that high-powered car. A taxi. London lay in autumn after-lunch gloom, car-horns bellowing and yapping. Rushing on to it. Air, air. Hogg gasped for it. 'Taxi,' he breathed, waving like mad, though feebly. Amazingly, one stopped. 'Air,' he said. 'Air.'

'Airport?' the driver wore sinister dark glasses. 'Air terminal? Cromwell Road?' Hogg's head sank to his chest; the driver took it for a nod. 'Right, gav. Hop in.' Hogg hopped in. Fell in, rather.

Four

So they were trying to go west, Gloucester Road way, despite the opposition (frivolous and treacherous) of contrary traffic and stultified red signals. There, he supposed, his days of misery had really begun, in the flat of that woman. And now the unavoidable happening was rushing him (well, hardly rushing) to the same long street to make his escape from not merely Vesta's world but Wapenshaw's as well. Well, they were the same world, they had to be the same. They were not the poet's world. Did such a world really exist? Where, anyway, did he think he was going to? He had better make up his mind. He could not say, 'What planes do you have, please?' Quite calm now, iced by his wrongs, he got his five-pound notes out of their hiding-place. His passport rode in hard protectiveness over his right pap. It was decidedly an ill wind. About passports, he meant. He had nothing in the way of luggage, which was a pity. Airlines, he thought, must be like hotels so far as luggage was concerned. But you had to pay in advance, didn't you? Still, there must be nothing to arouse suspicion. The newspapers would be cried around the streets shortly. Man answering to this description.

May be using an alias. Was he being followed? He looked out of the rear window. There were plenty of vehicles behind, but from none of them were hands and heads broadcasting agitation. He would be all right, he was sure he would be all right. He was innocent, wasn't he? But he hadn't behaved innocent. Who would speak up for him? Nobody could. He had pointed a loaded gun at Shem Macnamara. Besides, if that ghastly yob was dead he was glad he was dead. He had desire and motive and opportunity.

The taxi was now going up the ramp that led into the air terminal, a stripped-looking and gaudy place like something from a very big trade exhibition. He paid off the driver, giving a very unmemorable tip. The driver looked at it with only moderate sourness. Would he remember when he saw the evening papers? Yus yus, I picked him ap ahtside the otel. Fought vere was summink a bit fishy. Flyin orf somewhere he was. Hogg entered the terminal. Where the hell was he going to go to? He suddenly caught the voice of John the Spaniard, talking of his brother Billy Gomez. In some bar or other, very exotic, knifing people. Where was that now? Hogg had a confused image of the Moorish Empire: dirty men in robes, kasbahs without modern sanitation, heartening smells of things the sun had got at, muezzins, cockfights, shady men in unshaven hiding, the waves slapping naughty naughty at boats full of contraband goods. Hogg noticed a raincoated man pretending to read an evening paper near an insurance-policy machine. The news would not be in yet, but it wouldn't be long. There was a crowd of people having its luggage weighed. Hogg got in there. One married man was unpacking a suitcase on the floor, almost crying. His wife was angry.

'You should have read it proper. I leave them sort of things to you. Well, it's your stuff that'll have to stay behind, not mine.'

'How was I to know you couldn't take as much on a charter flight as on one of them ordinary uns?' He laid a polythene-wrapped suit, like a corpse, on the dirty floor. Hogg saw a yawning official at a desk. Above him stretched a title in neon Egyptian italic: PANMED AIRWAYS. Panmed. That would mean all over the Med or Mediterranean. He went up and said politely:

'A single to Morocco, please.' Morocco was, surely, round the

Mediterranean or somewhere like that. Hogg saw the raincoated paper-reader looking at him. Lack of luggage, no coat over arm, a man obviously on the run.

'Eh?' The official stopped yawning. He was young and ginger with eyes, like a dog's, set very wide apart. 'Single? Oh, one person you mean.'

'That's right. Just me. Rather urgent, actually.' He shouldn't have said that. The young man said:

'You mean this air cruise? Is that what you mean? A last-minute decision, is that it? Couldn't stand it any longer? Had to get away?' It was as though he were rehearsing a report on the matter; he was also putting words into Hogg's mouth. Hogg said:

'That's right.' And then: 'I don't *have* to get away, of course. I just thought it would be a good idea, that's all.'

'Charlie!' called the young official. To Hogg he said: 'It looks as though you're going to be in luck. Somebody died at the last minute.'

Hogg showed shock at the notion of someone dying suddenly. The man called Charlie came over. He was thin and harassed, wore a worn suit, had PANMED in metal on his left lapel. 'They won't ever learn,' said Charlie. 'There's one couple there brought what looks like a cabin-trunk. They just don't seem able to *read*, some of them.'

'The point is,' said the young ginger man, 'that you've had this cancellation, and there's this gentleman here anxious to fill it. Longing to get to the warmth, he is. Can't wait till the BEA flight this evening. That's about it, isn't it?' he said to Hogg. Hogg nodded very eagerly. Too eagerly, he then reflected.

Charlie surveyed Hogg all over. He didn't seem to care much for the barman's trousers. 'Well,' he said, 'I don't know really. It's a question of him being able to pay in cash.'

'I can pay in nothing else,' said Hogg with some pride. He pulled out a fistful in earnest. 'I just want to be taken to Morocco, that's all. I have,' he said, improvising rapidly, 'to get to my mother out there. She's ill, you see. Something she ate. I received a telegram just after lunch. Very urgent.' *Very* urgent: the typesetters would be setting up the type now; the C.I.D. would be watching the airports.

Charlie had a fair-sized wart on his left cheek. He fiddled with it as though it activated a telegraphic device. He waited. Hogg put his money back in his trouser-pocket. A message seemed to come through. Charlie said: 'Well, it all depends where in Morocco, doesn't it? And how fast you want to get there. We'll be in Seville late tonight, see, and not in Marrakesh till tomorrow dinner-time. This is an air cruise, this is. If it's Tangier you want to get to, we shan't be there for another fortnight. We go round the Canaries a bit, you see.'

'Marrakesh would do very nicely,' said Hogg. 'What I mean is, that's where my mother is.'

'You won't get anybody else, Charlie,' said the young ginger official. 'That seat's going begging, all paid for by the bloke who snuffed it. He's got cash.' He spoke too openly; he seemed to know that Hogg was making a shady exit. 'The bus,' he looked at the big clock, 'leaves in ten minutes.'

'Shall we say fifty?' Charlie licked his lips; the young official picked up the gesture. 'In cash, like I said.'

'Done,' said Hogg. He lick-counted the money out. A good slice of his savings. Savings. The word struck, like a thin tuning-fork (he was glad Yod Crewsy was dead, if he *was* dead), a pertinent connotation. He put the money on the counter.

'Passport in order, sir?' said the ginger official. Hogg showed him. 'Luggage, sir?'

'Wait,' said Hogg. 'I've got it over there.' He pierced the waiting crowd. That unpacking man had finished unpacking. In the big suitcase lay only a pair of Bermuda shorts, some shaving gear, and two or three paperbacks of a low sort. The unpacked garments were on his arm. 'They said I could leave them in their office here,' he puffed. 'Collect them on the way back. Still, it's a bloody nuisance. I've practically only got what I stand up in.' Hogg said:

'Saw you were in a bit of trouble over weight.' He smiled at the couple as if they were going to do him a favour, which they were. 'That suitcase could go with mine, if you like. I'm taking practically nothing, you see.'

The couple looked at him with proper suspicion. They were decent fattish short people in late middle age, unused to kindness without a catch in it. The man groused: 'It means I'll have to shove it all in again.'

'That's right,' said Hogg. 'Shove it all in again.' The man, shaking his head, once more got down heavily on his knees.

'It's very kind, Mr er,' said the wife, grudgingly.

They never took their eyes off Hogg as he swung the reconstituted bag to the weighing. Charlie and the ginger official had seen nothing: they were busy doing a split on Hogg's money. The raincoated paper-reader, Hogg noticed, had gone. Perhaps to buy a later edition. Hogg was glad to be herded to the bus.

Five

This Charlie seemed to be what they called a dragoman. He counted his charges on and then, when they were on, counted them again. He frowned, as if the numbers did not tally. Hogg was seated next to a rather dowdy woman in early middle age, younger than himself, that was. She smiled at him as to a companion in adventure. She wore churchgoing clothes of sensible district-nurse-type hat and costume in a kind of underdone piecrust colour. Her stockings, of which the knees just about showed, were of some kind of lisle material, opaque gunmetal. Hogg smiled back very tentatively, and then warily surveyed the other members of the party. They were mostly unremarkable people subduedly thrilled at going off to exotic places. The men were already casting themselves for parts, as if the trip were really going to be full of enforced privations and they had somehow to make their own entertainment. One beef-necked publican-type was pointing out the sights on the way to the airport and inventing bogus historical associations, like 'Queen Lizzy had a milk stout there.' There was cautious fencing for the rôle of low comedian, and one man who, his teeth out, could contort his face in a rubbery manner seemed likely to win. There was a loud and serious man, a frequenter presumably of public libraries, who was giving a preliminary account of the more hurtful fauna of North Africa. Another man could reel off exchange rates. Hogg's seat-companion smiled again at him, as if with pleasure that everything was going to be so nice and cosy. Hogg closed his eyes in feigned (but was it feigned?) weariness.

When they got to the airport the news was still unbroken. Perhaps the management, on the instructions of the police, had sealed everything off, and it was no good the Prime Minister saying he had to get back to the House. Twenty minutes before take-off. Hogg spent most of that time in one of the lavatories, sitting gloomily on the seat. Could he do anything about disguising himself? With teeth out he would be expected to compete for the part of cruise comedian perhaps. Spectacles off? He tried that; he could just about see. Rearrange hair-style? Too little hair really, but he combed what he had down in a Roman emperor arrangement. Walk with a limp? Easy enough, if he could remember to keep on doing it. He heard ladylike intonations from a loudspeaker, so he pulled the chain and went to join his party. The man with the overweight luggage had suddenly woken up to the fact of Hogg's kindness; he did not seem to notice any change in Hogg's appearance. With bleary unfocused eyes, top denture out (a compromise that a sudden feeling of nausea had forced upon him on leaving the lavatory), and scant imperial coiffure, Hogg nodded and nodded that that was really quite all right, only too glad to oblige.

They all walked to the aircraft. Wind blew grit across the tarmac. Farewell, English autumn. It did not seem to Hogg to be a very elegant aircraft. There was a button missing from the stewardess's uniform jacket, and she herself, though insipidly and blondly pretty, had a look of vacancy that did not inspire confidence. Things done on the cheap, that was about it. Hogg sat down next to a starboard window, taking his last look at England. Somebody sat next to him, a woman. She said, in a semi-cultured Lancashire accent:

'We seem destined, don't we?' It was the one who had sat next to him on the bus. Hogg grunted. The unavoidable happening. In the elastic-topped pocket on the back of the seat in front of him, Hogg sadly found reading-matter, very cheerful and highly coloured stuff. No need to worry if we go down into the sea. We have a fine record for air safety. Keep calm, the stewardess will tell you what to do. But who, wondered Hogg, would tell her? There were brochures about the ports of call on the air cruise.

'This is my first time,' said the woman next to Hogg. 'Is it yours?' Her teeth seemed to be all her own. She had taken off her hat. Her hair was prettily mousy.

'First time to do what?' said Hogg dourly.

'Oh, you know, go on one of these things. It's funny really, I suppose, but I know all about the moon yet I've never seen the Mountains of the Moon.'

'A stronger telescope,' said Hogg. He was leafing through a booklet, full of robes, skies of impossible blue, camels, palms, the wizened faces of professional Moorish beggars, which told him of the joys of Tangier.

'No, no, I mean the Mountains of the Moon in Africa.' She giggled.

Hogg heard the door of the aircraft slam. It did not slam properly. Charlie the dragoman, who now wore a little woolly highly coloured cap, helped the stewardess to give it a good hard slam, and then it seemed to stay shut. Engines and things began to fire and backfire or something. They were going to take off. Hogg felt safe for an instant, but then realised that there was no escape. They had things like Interpol and so on, or some such things. Spanish police, with teeth all bits of gold like John, waiting for him at Seville. But perhaps not, he thought with a little rising hope. Perhaps Spain would consider the murder of a pop-singer a very nugatory crime, which of course it was. Not really a crime at all if you took the larger view. Well then, landed in Spain, let him stay in Spain, *el señor inglés*. But how live there? With his little bit of money he could not, even in that notoriously cheap (because poverty-stricken) country, find a re-treat or lavatory that would accommodate him long enough to coax, like a costive bowel, the art of verse back. The Muse had still made no real sign. There was a poem still to be completed. And, besides, there was terrible repression in Spain, a big dic-tator up there in the Escorial or wherever it was, directing pha-langes of cruel bruisers (no, not bruisers; thin sadists, rather) with steel whips. No freedom of expression, poets suspect, for-eign poets arrested and eventually handed over to Interpol. No, better to go to a country full of men on the run and smugglers and (so he had heard) artistic homosexuals, where English, lan-guage of international shadiness, was spoken and understood, and where at least he might hide (even out of doors; the nights were warm, weren't they?) and work out the future. One step at a time.

'You haven't fastened your safety-belt,' said the woman. Hogg grumbled, fumbling for the metal-tipped tongues of dirty webbing. The airfield, his last view of England, was speeding as a grey blur back into the past. Speed increased; they were getting off the ground. You in that high-powered car. Perhaps an old-fashioned image, really. Hogg leafed through the Tangier brochure absently noticing little box advertisements for restaurants and bars. He frowned at one of these, wondering. It said:

AL-ROKLIF
English Spoken Berber Dances
Wide Range of Exotic Delights
A Good British Cup of Tea
'IN ALL THE ANTHOLOGIES!'

He wondered, he wondered, he wondered. Artistic, which included literary, homosexuals. The name, rationalised into mock-Arabic:

الروقليف

The slogan. Well. He began to breathe hard. If they caught him, and he would surely know if they were going to catch him, he would not be punished gratuitously. There was something very just but highly punishable he would do before Interpol dragged him off in handcuffs. When you came to think of it, Tangier sounded like just the sort of place a man of Rawcliffe's type would end up in. Moorish catamites. Drinking himself to death. Drinking was too slow a process.

Hogg came to to find the woman gently unclicking his safety-belt for him. 'You were miles away,' she smiled. 'And we're miles up. Look.' Hogg, mumbling sour thanks, surveyed without much interest a lot of clouds lying below them. He had seen such things before, travelling to Rome on his honeymoon. He gave the clouds the tribute of a look of weary sophistication. It was the Romantic poets really who should have flown; Percy Shelley would have loved to see all this lot from this angle. How did that thing go now? He chewed a line or two to himself.

'Did you say something?' asked the woman.

'Poetry,' said Hogg. 'A bit of poetry. About clouds.' And, as if to make up for his neglect of her, kind and friendly as she was, he recited, in his woolly voice:

'I silently laugh at my own cenotaph,
And out of the caverns of rain,
Like a child from the womb, like a ghost from the
tomb,
I arise and unbuild it again.'

'Oh, I do love poetry,' this woman smiled over the engines. 'It was a toss-up whether I did literature or astronomy, you know. But it was the moon that won.'

'How do you mean,' asked Hogg carefully, 'it was the moon that won?'

'That's what I do,' she said. 'That's what I lecture in. The moon. Selenography, you know.'

'Selene,' said learned Hogg. 'A fusion of Artemis and Hecate.'

'Oh, I wouldn't know about that,' she said. 'Selenography is what it's called. I'd better introduce myself, I suppose. My name's Miranda Boland.'

Miranda: a wonder to her parents: poor woman, all alone as she was. 'Well,' said Hogg cautiously, 'my name—'

Charlie the dragoman suddenly boomed through a crackling speaker. 'My name,' he announced, 'is Mr Mercer.' No familiarity, then; he was no longer to be thought of as Charlie. 'My job,' he said, 'is to look after you on this cruise, show you around and so on.'

'Come wiz me to ze Kasbah,' said the rubbery man. He had made it, then. It was his début as resident comedian. 'Shut up, George,' his wife said, delightedly. Members of the party grinned and made their bottoms and shoulders more comfortable. The holiday was really beginning now.

'I hope you will enjoy this cruise,' crackled Mr Mercer. 'Lots of people do enjoy these cruises. They sometimes come again. And if there's anything you don't like about this cruise, tell me. Tell *me*. Don't bother to write a letter to Panmed. Let's have it out at once, man to man, or to woman should such be the case. But I think you'll like it. Anyway, I hope so. And so does Miss

Kelly, your charming air-hostess, and Captain O'Shaughnessy up front. Now the first thing is that we can expect a bit of obstruction at Seville. It's this Gibraltar business, which you may have read about. The Spanish want it and we won't let it go. So they get a bit awkward when it comes to customs and immigration and so on. They try and delay us, which is not very friendly. Now it's quicker if I show your passports all in one lump, so I'm coming round to collect them now. And then Miss Kelly here will serve tea.'

Miranda Boland (Mrs? Miss?) opened a stuffed handbag to get her passport out. She had a lot of things in her bag: tubes of antibiotics and specifics against diarrhoea and the like. Also a little Spanish dictionary. That was to help her to have a good time. Also a small writing-case. This put into Hogg's head an idea, perhaps a salvatory one. Hogg, without fear, produced his own passport.

'Miss Boland?' said Mr Mercer, coming round. Miss, then. 'Quite a nice photo, isn't it?' And then: 'Mr Enderby, is it?'

'That's right.' Mr Mercer examined a smirking portrait of an engaged man, occupation not yet certain at that time but given as *writer;* a couple of official Roman chops: in and then, more quickly, out again.

'And what do *you* do, Mr Enderby?' asked Miss Boland.

'I,' said Enderby, 'am a poet. I am Enderby the Poet.' The name meant nothing to this poetry-loving selenographer. The clouds below, Shelley's pals, were flushed with no special radiance. 'The Poet,' repeated Enderby, with rather less confidence. They pushed on towards the sun. Enderby's stomach quietly announced that soon, very soon, it was going to react to all that had happened. Delayed shock said that it would not be much longer delayed. Enderby sat tense in his seat, waiting for it as for an air-crash.

3

One

'COPERNICUS,' Miss Boland pointed. 'And then a bit to the west there's Eratosthenes. And then further west still you get the Apennines.' Her face shone, as if she were (which in a sense she really was) a satellite of a satellite. Enderby looked very coldly at the moon which, for some reason to do with the clouds (Shelley's orbéd maiden and so on), he had expected to lie beneath them. But it was as high up as it usually was. 'And down there, south, is Anaxagoras. Just under the Mare Frigoris.'

'Very interesting,' said Enderby, not very interested. He had not himself ever made much use of the moon as a poetic property, but he still thought he had more claim on it than she had. She behaved very familiarly with it.

'And Plato, just above.'

'Why Plato?' They had had not only tea but also dinner, spilt around (hair fallen over her right eye and her tongue bitten in concentration) by that Miss Kelly. It had not been a very good dinner, but Enderby, to quieten his stomach, had wolfed his portion and part of (smilingly donated; she did not have a very big

appetite) Miss Boland's. It had been three tepid fish fingers each,
with some insufficiently warmed over crinkle-cut fresh frozen po-
tato chips, also a sort of fish sauce served in a plastic doll's
bucket with a lid hard to get off. This sauce had had a taste that,
unexpectedly in view of its dolly-mixture pink and the dainty
exiguity of even a double portion, was somehow like the clank of
metal. And, very strangely or perhaps not strangely at all, the
slab of dry *gâteau* that followed had a glutinous filling whose
cold mutton fat gust clung to the palate as with small claws of
rusty iron. Enderby had had to reinsert his top teeth before eating, doing this under cover of the need to cough vigorously and
the bright pamphlet on Tangerine delights held to his left cheek.
Now, after eating, he had to get both plates out, since they
tasted very defiled and bits of cold burnt batter lodged beneath
or above them, according to jaw. He should really get to the
toilet to see about that, but, having first had doubts as to
whether this aircraft possessed a toilet and then found these dis-
pelled by the sight of the rubbery comedian called Mr Guthkelch coming back from it with theatrical relief, he felt then
superstitiously that, once he left the cabin, even for two minutes,
a stowaway newsboy might appear and distribute copies of a
late edition with his photograph in it, and then they would, Mr
Guthkelch suddenly very serious, truss him against the brutal arrest of the Seville police. So he stayed where he was. He would
wait till Miss Boland had a little doze or they got to moonlit Seville. The moon was a very fine full one, and it burnt framed in
the window to be tickled all over with classical names by Miss
Boland.

'I don't know why Plato. That's what it's called, that's all.
There's a lot of famous people commemorated all over the lunar
surface. Archimedes, see, just above Plato, and Kepler, and right
over there on the edge is Grimaldi.'

'The clown Grimaldi?'

'No, silly. The Grimaldi that wrote a book on the diffraction
of light. A priest I believe he was. But,' she added, 'I often
thought it might be nice if some *newer* names could be put up
there.'

'There are a lot of new Russian ones at the back, aren't there?'
said well-informed Enderby.

'Oh, you know what I mean. Who's interested in the Rabbi Levi and Endymion, whoever he was, any more? Names of great modern people. It's a daring idea, I know, and a lot of my colleagues have been, you know, aghast.'

'The trouble is,' said Enderby, 'that nobody knows who's really great till they've been a long time dead. The great ones, I mean. Dead, that is.' Mount Enderby. 'Like some of these Russian towns. One minute they're one thing and the next another. Stalingrad, I mean. Now it's something else.'

'Volgograd.'

'Yes, and that's another. You'd be having pop-stars up there perhaps, and then in ten years time everybody would be wondering who the hell they were.' Pop-stars. He shouldn't have mentioned that. He felt very and metallically sick. Then it passed. 'Sorry I said "hell",' he said.

'People who give pleasure to the world,' said Miss Boland. And then: 'There's Hell on the moon, did you know that? A bit old-fashioned really, but that's true of a lot of lunar nomenclature, as I say.' And then: 'Of course, you being a poet wouldn't like pop-stars much, would you? I can quite see that. Very inferior art, you'd say. I know.'

Enderby wished he could get his teeth out and then back in again. But he said quickly: 'No, no, no, I wouldn't say that. Some of them are very good, I'm sure. Please,' he begged, 'don't consider me an enemy of pop-culture.'

'All right, all right,' she smiled, 'I won't. All these long-haired young singers. It's a matter of age, I suppose. I have a nephew and niece who are mad on that sort of thing. They call me a kvadrat.'

'Because I'm not, you see.'

'But I was able to say to them, you know, that this special idol of theirs seemed very unkvadrat, if that's the right expression, publishing this book of quite highbrow verse. Now that ought to change your opinion of pop-artists, if not of pop-art. I take it you saw the book? One of our junior English lecturers was quite gone on it.'

'I've got to get out,' said Enderby. She looked surprised. This was not, after all, a bus. 'If you'll excuse me—' It wasn't just a matter of teeth any more; he really had to go. A fat beaming woman was just coming away from it now. 'A matter of some urgency,' Enderby explained and prepared to go into further, plausible, details. But Miss Boland got up and let him out.

The stewardess, Miss Kelly, was sitting at the back with Mr Mercer. Mr Mercer still had his woolly cap on but he was sleeping with his mouth open. Miss Kelly seemed totally content with an expression and posture of sheer vacancy. Enderby nodded grimly at her and entered the toilet. Why hadn't he known these things—kvadrats and so on and that lout publishing a book of verse, and who blasted Vesta had got married to? He had read the *Daily Mirror* every day with positively adenoidal attention. Very little had got home, then: his rehabilitation had never had a hope of being perfect. He quietened his stomach via his bowels and, the while, rinsed his clogged teeth under the tap and scrubbed them with the nailbrush. Then he reinserted them and, with hands gently folded on his bared lap, cried bitterly for a minute or two. Then he wiped his eyes and his bottom with the same pink paper and committed both lots of wrapped ex- creta to the slipstream, as he supposed it was called. He blinked at himself in the little mirror, very recognisable Hogg. If he had still had that beard which, in the intensive phase of personality change, he had been made to grow, he could be shaving it off now, having borrowed a razor from somebody, perhaps even Miss Boland, who must surely have one for leg-hair and so on in her crammed bag. Ha ha, you and the start of a holiday make me feel quite young again: I can't wait to divest myself of this fungus, ha ha. But that beard had had to go when he became a barman. So there was nothing between him and the urgently telegraphed photographs (straight from Holden's bloody secret- police dossier) now being handled by swarthy Interpol Span- iards. Nothing except the name. But damnable and treacherous Wapenshaw would already be talking away, baling out what were properly secrets of the confessional. And tomorrow morn- ing copies of the *Daily Mirror,* which was notoriously on sale before other newspapers, as if unable to wait to regale egg- crackers with the horrors of the world, would be circulating among British holidaymakers on the Costa Brava or whatever it was called. There would be a stern portrait of Hogg on the front page, under a very insulting headline. On the back page would be great air disasters and bombs in Vietnam and avalanches and things. But on the front page would be the murderer Hogg. He did not, it seemed, read the *Daily Mirror* closely enough, but he had a sufficient appreciation of its editorial philosophy.

He re-entered the long dozing cabin with its little sprays of ceiling light blessing bald and dyed heads. Miss Boland seemed to be counting moon-craters with a puzzled finger: perhaps something new had got up there since her last going-over with a telescope. Enderby said with sudden fierceness to Miss Kelly: 'This woman in charge of pop-singers and so on. Who was it she married?'

Miss Kelly seemed unsurprised by the question. It seemed that pride in her ability to answer the question overcame such surprise as she ought properly to be showing. 'Vesta Wittgenstein? Oh, she married this man called Des Wittgenstein who ran the Fakers and the Lean Two, but now she runs them and a lot more besides. She'd been married before, to the racing-driver Pete Bainbridge, but he got himself killed. Very tragic, it was in all the papers. Then there was something about her marrying a middle-aged man and that did not bring her true happiness and it lasted less than a year, just imagine. But now she's found true happiness with Des Wittgenstein and they've both got pots of money. You ought to see her clothes. I was on an aircraft she flew on once, coming back from Rome. That's when she was very ill with this unhappiness, but she was still terribly smart."

Enderby nodded a casual thank-you, as if for some pedestrian information about time of arrival. Miss Kelly smiled conventionally and went into a vacant relapse. Enderby thought he would now write a letter on some of Miss Boland's stationery, so he went back to his seat purposefully, like a man with something other to do than merely be flown to Seville. She welcomed him as if he had been a long time away and even said: 'Feeling all right now?'

'I've got to write,' said Enderby at once. 'A matter of some urgency.' He felt he had perhaps used those words before. 'If you could oblige me with the wherewithal.'

'A poem? How thrilling. What do you mean by the wherewithal? You want me to pay you for it? I will if you like. This is the first time anybody's ever said they'd write a poem for me.'

Enderby looked sternly at her. She seemed to be teasing. It was possible she did not believe that he was a poet. Her eyes were, he noted with gloom, what might be termed merry.

'Paper is what I want,' he said. 'And an envelope, if you can spare it. Two envelopes,' he amended.

'Dear, dear, you do want a lot.' She took out her writing materials gaily. Enderby said:

'I'll write you a poem tonight. When we get there.'

'I'll hold you to that.'

Enderby took out his ballpoint and wrote to John the Spaniard: 'You know I didn't do it. Pass this note on to you-know-who. I shall be in you-know-where. Your brother. That fat dog place you mentioned. Keep in touch. Yours—' He didn't know how to sign himself. At last he wrote PUERCO. Then he took another piece of paper and addressed it from In The Air. He wrote: 'To Whomsoever It May Concern. It was not me who shot that pop-singer, as he is called. It was—' He was damned if he could remember the name. To Miss Boland he said once more: 'I've got to get out. I've forgotten something.' She let him out, mock-sighing and smiling. He kept paper and ballpoint in his hands. He went back to Miss Kelly, still in a trance of vacancy. Mr Mercer was lip-smacking, ready to surface. A monitor in his sleep had perhaps warned him that soon they would be starting to drop towards Seville. Enderby said:

'That one that used to be with Mrs Einstein's lot—'

'Mrs Wittgenstein.'

'That's right. The one that got out and became unsuccessful and goes round the clubs now.'

'Jed Foot, you mean.'

'That's it.' He wrote the name in standing. He might forget it again if he waited till he got back to his seat. Might spill it on the way. He nodded thanks and went back now, and Miss Boland, letting him in, said:

'You *are* a busy little bee.'

Enderby wrote: 'He handed me the gun and I took it without thinking. I panicked and ran. Pick him up and get him to confess. I am innocent.' Then he signed that abandoned pseudonym. He addressed one envelope to The Authorities and the other to Mr John Gomez, Piggy's Bar, Tyburn Towers Hotel,

W.1. He licked and folded and arranged. Then he sighed. Finished. He could do no more. He thought he had better shut his eyes and get ready for Seville. That would stop Miss Boland teasing him further. Miss Boland, he noticed, was looking something up in her little Spanish dictionary. She was grinning. He didn't like that. It was too small a dictionary to have anything to grin at in it. He killed her grin with his eyelids.

Two

Enderby slept, though without dreaming, as though the recent materials made available for dreams were far too shocking to be processed into fantasy. He was shaken awake by Miss Boland, who smiled on him and said, for some reason, 'Dirty.' He said: 'Eh?'

'We're there,' she said. 'Sunny Spain, though it's the middle of the night and it's been raining. The rain in Spain,' she giggled.

'What do you mean, dirty? Did I do something I shouldn't? In my sleep, that is?' He wondered what incontinent act might have overtaken him.

'That's what it says. Come on, we're to get out.' People were passing down the aisle, some yawning as after a boring sermon. Miss Boland smiled as if she were some relative of the vicar. 'Also,' she said over her shoulder, 'it says nasty and foul.' Enderby saw wet-gleaming tarmac under dim lamps. There was something he had to worry about. He said:

'What does?'

'Oh, come on.' She was getting her raincoat and overnight satchel from the rack. Enderby had nothing to get. Feeling naked, he said:

'I'll carry that if you like.' And then his fear smote him and his hand shook.

'That's sweet of you. Take it then.' He could hardly get his hand through the straps of the bag, but she didn't notice: she had arrived in non-sunny, not even moony, Spain. Mr Mercer seemed as nervous as Enderby himself; it was as though he had to introduce Seville like his wife and, perhaps being on the menopause, she might do something embarrassing. This was it, En-

derby thought, this was it. He was cold and sober and ready and
he would bluff it out to the end. He looked coldly and soberly
on Miss Boland and decided that she must, in a manner, help
him. He would laugh down the steps with her, linked, as if she
were his wife. They were looking for a single desperate fugitive,
not a laughing married man. But, as they smiled and Enderby
nodded at Miss Kelly, standing at the aircraft exit, he saw that
the stairway was very narrow and that he must go down un-
linked. Miss Kelly beamed at everybody as if they had all just
arrived at her party, which was being held in the cellar. Enderby
heard Mr Guthkelch ahead, singing 'The Spaniard who blighted
my life,' doing his job.

'He shall die! He shall die! He shall die tiddly iddly eye tie tie
eye tie tie tie!'

In very bad taste, Enderby thought. Stepping out into moist
velvet warmth, he saw at the stair-bottom only Mr Mercer with
an armful of passports chatting quite amiably, though in the
loud and slow English needful when speaking to a foreigner, to
a foreigner. It was a uniformed Spaniard in dark glasses. He had
both hands in his trousers pockets and seemed to Enderby to be
playing the solitaire game known as pocket billards. He looked
up at Miss Kelly, blowing up sparks from his cigarette at her like
impotent signals of desire. He was not, Enderby was sure, from
Interpol.

Miss Boland descended before him. As soon as he had reached
damp tarmac, Enderby skipped up to her and took her arm. She
seemed surprised but not displeased; she pressed Enderby's arm
into her warm side. There seemed, and Enderby's knees liquefied
in relief as he saw that there seemed, to be no raincoated men
waiting anywhere for him on the passage over the tarmac to the
airport building. There seemed to be only very lowly workmen,
thin and in blue, leaning against walls, smoking vigorously, and
eyeing the tourists with the hungry look of the very poor. The
airport itself, despite its being very late at night, was busy.
There was an aircraft with Arabic letters on it preparing to take
off and there was one called IBERIA taxiing in. There were men
in overalls pulling carts around and chugging about in little
tractors. Enderby approved of all this bustle, especially the
passenger-bustle that was evident in the building they now

approached. He saw himself being chased and hiding behind people. But no, he was safe for the time being. Miss Boland said:

'There's no *luna.* That's what it's called, isn't it? *Luna.* Better than "moon." Lunar. Lunation. Endo-lunar. I thought the *luna* would be here to meet me. Never mind.'

'You've had plenty on the way,' said Enderby in a slightly chiding tone. 'You'll get plenty while you're here. On holiday, I mean. But I thought perhaps you'd want to get away from it.' A fellow-tourist walking near them gave Enderby a suspicious look. 'The *luna,* I mean,' Enderby said.

'You can't get away from it,' said Miss Boland. 'Not if you've given your whole life to it, as I have.' And she squeezed Enderby's arm with hers. She was very warm. 'Where did you learn Spanish?' she asked.

'I never did. I don't know any Spanish. Italian, yes, a bit. But not Spanish. They're similar, though.'

'You're very mysterious,' said Miss Boland mysteriously. 'You intrigue me rather. There seems to be a lot you're holding back. Why, you haven't even brought a raincoat. But I suppose that's your business, not mine. And no overnight bag of your own. You give me the impression of a man who had to get away in a hurry.'

'Oh, I had to,' palpitated Enderby. 'What I mean is, I'm a man of impulse. I think of a thing and then I do it.' She squeezed his arm again and said:

'You can call me Miranda if you like.'

'A very poetical name,' said Enderby in duty. He couldn't quite remember who wrote that poem. A big Catholic winy man in a cloak. 'The fleas that tease in the high Pyrenees,' he quoted. And then: 'Never more, Miranda, never more. Only the some-thing whore.'

'Pardon?'

'And something something something at the door.' They had now entered the airport building. It was small, dark, and smelt faintly of men's urinals, specifically foreign ones, a garlic-scented effluent. There was a big photograph of General Franco, dressed as a civilian, a bald man with jowls and parvenu lifted eyebrows. There were also yellowing notices, probably forbidding things.

Mr Mercer was already there, having perhaps been given a lift in one of those tractors. All the cruise members clustered round him, as for protection. Enderby saw that his arm was still in Miss Boland's. He disengaged it by saying he had to post a letter.

'Mysterious again,' she said. 'You're no sooner here than you have to post a mysterious letter. Signed with a mysterious name.'

'What?' squawked Enderby.

'I'm sorry. I couldn't help seeing it. You left it on the seat. Do forgive me. It was with those brochures and things, and I picked them up to look at them and there was your letter. But it's no good my pretending that I don't know your first name now, is it? Or nickname it must be.'

'Oh, no.'

'It *must* be. I've never seen the name Puerco before.' She pronounced it *Pure co*. 'And then, since it looked foreign, I looked it up in my Spanish dictionary, and, lo and behold, there it was. Meaning "dirty".'

'Actually,' Enderby improvised in delirium, 'it's an old border name. Welsh border, I mean. My family came from near Shrewsbury. That's a coincidence, that is, the Spanish business, I mean. Look, I've *got* to post this letter. I'll be back.' As soon as he had clumsily pushed his way through the crowd that was round woolly-capped Mr Mercer, he realised he had behaved foolishly in being willing to leave her if only for five minutes. She wouldn't believe that story about Puerco being an old border name; she'd look it up again in her Spanish dictionary and she'd find more than dirty and filthy and so on. She was bound to. He hesitated at a door that led on to a dismal wet garden, beyond it a kind of restaurant all made of big dirty windows. He would have to get that dictionary away from her, tear out the dangerous page or lose the whole book. Or should he now, with his five-pound notes and anthology of exotic *pourboires*, get out there into the great rainy windy peninsula, lose himself in cork-woods, later became dried up like a raisin tramping the hot white country roads? He thought not. A lean poor man was standing by the door, opposing cigarette-sparks to the dull damp night. It was possible, thought Enderby, that

Spanish John's hispaniolising of his mother's maiden name represented a historical phase of the word, long superseded. But if, of
course, it was the same as Italian and—Enderby said to this
man:

'*Amigo.*' The man responded with a benison of sparks. Enderby said: 'In *español. L'animal.* What's the *español* for it?' He
snorted and snuffed the air all around at chest-level as though
rooting for truffles. Then he saw that a man in smart uniform,
just behind him, was watching with some interest. The lean poor
man said:

'*Entiendo. Un puerco.*'

That was it then, Enderby thought grimly. He stood wavering,
letter in hand. The thin poor man seemed to be awaiting further
charades from Enderby. The uniformed man frowned, very
puzzled. The thin poor one whinnied and said, '*Un caballo.*'
Enderby said, '*Sí,*' then tripped over the uniformed man's left
boot as he went in again, letter unposted.

'My goodness, you were quick,' said Miss Boland.

'It's the language,' Enderby said. 'I don't know the language,
as I said. Perhaps if I could borrow your little dictionary—'

'Right,' Mr Mercer was now saying. 'Everybody please stand
round there where the baggage is.' They'd got it out pretty
quickly, Enderby thought distractedly: no spirit of *mañana* here.
'As you know, they have customs here same as everywhere
else—'

'Old Spanish customs,' cried Mr Guthkelch.

'—But only a few of you will have to open your bags—'

'As long as nobody has to drop 'em,' cried Mr Guthkelch,
perhaps going too far.

'—It's a sample, you see, what you might call a sample check-
up.'

'I don't suppose,' said Miss Boland to Enderby, 'that you've
got anything so bourgeois as luggage, have you? I suppose you'll
be sleeping in your shirt or in the altogether.' Her eyes glistened
when she said that, as though excited by it. Enderby was disgusted; he said:

'You'll soon see whether I've got anything or not. I'm no different from anybody else.' The man who had looked at him suspiciously on the way across the tarmac now did the same thing

again. 'In the sense, that is,' expanded Enderby, 'of personal possessions and the like.'

'This is a bit like an identification parade, isn't it?' giggled Miss Boland. 'Very thrilling.' They were all there near the pile of luggage, and an official with a peaked cap did a caged-tiger walk up and down in front of this squad of pleasure-seekers, hands folded behind his back. Enderby saw who it was: that man out there who had frowned at his pig-snorting. The man now halted and faced them. He had jowls not unlike those of his Caudillo and even allomorphs of those eyebrows; perhaps a lowly relative for whom the régime had had to find a job. He sternly pointed at people. He pointed at Enderby. Enderby at once looked round for the man with the overweight luggage. He found him and said:

'Where is it?'

'What? That? Why can't you show him your own?'

'Reasons,' Enderby said. 'Things nobody must see.'

'Thought there was a catch in it. Right liberty, I call it. Anyway, I've got nothing to fear.' And he showed where the supernumerary bag was. Enderby lugged it to the customs-counter. The official was already delicately rooting in a pair of very clean white cotton gloves. He was perfunctory about most passengers' luggage; with Enderby's supposed he was thorough. At the bottom of the bag he found, under that man's Bermuda shorts, the three garish paperbacks that had looked quite harmless in the London air terminal. Here, in a repressed and repressive Catholic country that discharged its extramarital lust in bull-fights, they suddenly seemed to flare into the promise of outrageous obscenity. Miss Boland, though not of the luggage-opening elect, was nevertheless by Enderby's side. She saw; 'Dirty,' she said, grinning. The official held up the three books very nearly to the level of the portrait of the Caudillo, as if for his curse. Mr Guthkelch said: 'Who'll start the bidding?' The covers blared three allotropes of mindless generic blonde, in shock and undress. The official pronounced: '*Pornográficos.*' Everybody nodded, pleased that they could understand Spanish. And then, straight at Enderby, he snorted and gave back Enderby's own mime of snout-truffling, adding: '*Puerco.*'

'I see, I see,' said Miss Boland, quietly gratified, pressing into

Enderby's flank. 'So that's how you pronounce it. And it means "pig" too. Stupid of me, I should have seen that. They know you here then. You *are* a dark horse. Pig, I mean, a dark pig.'

From one of the upheld books two flat square little packets dropped out. They fell on to the exposure of somebody's sensible white underwear. All the men at once knew what they were, but one elderly woman, evidently sheltered from the world, said: 'Sort of rings. What are they for then?' The man who could best tell her was heard groaning: those objects were obviously ferial, not marital, equipment. The official wiped one cotton-gloved hand against another, made an extravagant gesture of disgust and dismissal, and turned his back on the lot of them. *'Ipocritico,'* murmured Enderby. The official did not hear, or else the Spanish was different from the Italian.

'It pays to be straight,' the overweight man was whining. 'I've learned my lesson, that I have.' His wife looked out, dissociated from him but there would be hell tonight in a foreign bedroom, into wet dark Seville, Don Juan's town. 'Let me down, you have,' he said unreasonably to Enderby. Everybody else frowned, puzzled, not quick on the uptake. Even Miss Boland. Miss Boland took Enderby's arm, saying: 'Come on, Piggy.' A very liberalising influence the moon, Enderby bitterly thought. Mr Mercer called them, in a fatigued voice, to the waiting bus.

Three

An hour later, Enderby lay exhausted on his hotel bed. He had posted that letter in the box in the hotel lobby, having found some pesetas in his little treasury of tips and been able to buy stamps from the moustached duenna yawning with dignity at the reception desk. None of the hotel staff, admittedly tired and proudly resentful of the late-arriving guests, seemed even minimally agitated by news of the death of a British pop-singer. So things were all right so far. But soon they would not be. A lot of course depended on the chief guardian of the true identity of Hogg, namely bloody Wapenshaw; much depended on the Hogg-photograph in tomorrow's newspapers; a little depended on Miss Boland's semantic investigations into the word *puerco*.

Soon, when he was less exhausted, he would go and see Miss Boland. She was on this floor of the hotel, which was called the Hotel Marruecos; she was just a couple of doors down. Soon. Enderby had had sent up a bottle of Fundador and a glass. He knew Fundador from Piggy's Sty: it was a kind of parody of Armagnac. He was drinking it now for his nerves. He lay on the bed, whose coverlet was the colour of boiled liver. The wall-paper was cochineal. There were no pictures on the walls. It was all very bare, and he had done nothing to mitigate that bareness. Nothing in the wardrobe, no suitcase on the luggage-stand at the bed's bottom. The window was open, and a hot wind had started blowing up, one which seemed to match the cochineal walls. This hot wind had scattered the clouds and disclosed what was now a Spanish moon, a Don Juan stage property. Miss Bo-land, in a sensible dressing-gown, would now be putting curlers in her hair, looking at the moon. *Luna.* Perhaps she would be checking the word in her handbag dictionary.

Painfully Enderby got up and went to the bathroom. He could hear, through the wall, in the adjoining bathroom, the man with overweight luggage being rebuked bitterly by his wife. Libidi-nous wretch. Condom-carrier. Thought he'd have a nasty sly go at the *señoritas* or *bintim* did he? Words to that effect, anyway. Best years of her life slaving away for him. Enderby, sighing, micturated briefly, pulled the chain and left his room buttoning, sighing. Leaving his room, he met Miss Boland coming to his room. Quite a coincidence, really.

'I've come,' she said, 'for my poem.' She looked rather like a woman who was coming to collect a poem, not a bit the lecturer in selenography. Her dressing-gown was far from sensible: it was diaphanous black, billowing in the hot wind from the window at the corridor's end, and under it was a peach-coloured nightdress. Her pretty mousy hair had been brushed; it crackled in the hot wind; a peach-coloured fillet was binding it. She had put on cochineal lipstick, matching the hot wind. Enderby gulped. Gulping, he bowed her in. He said:

'I haven't had time yet. To write a poem, that is. I've been unpacking, as you can see.'

'You've unpacked *everything?* Goodness. A bit pointless, isn't it? We're only here for the night. What's left of it, that is. Ah,' she said, billowing in the hot wind over to the window, 'you have the *luna* too. My *luna* and yours.'

'We must,' Enderby said reasonably, 'be on the same side of the corridor. The same view, you see.' And then: 'Have a drink.'

'Well,' she said, 'I don't usually. Especially at this hour of the morning. But I am on holiday after all, aren't I?'

'You most certainly are,' Enderby said gravely. 'I'll get a glass from the bathroom.' He went to get it. The row was still going on next door. Uncontrollable lust in middle age. Comic if it was not disgusting. Or something like that. He brought back the glass and found Miss Boland sitting on his bed. 'Mare Imbrium,' she was saying. 'Seleucus. Aristarchus.' He poured her a very healthy slug. He would make her drunk and have a hangover, and that would distract her tomorrow morning from *puerco* business. Soon he would go to her room and steal her dictionary. Everything was going to be all right.

'You've been thorough,' she said, taking the glass from him. 'You've even packed your suitcase away.'

'Oh, yes,' he said. 'It's a sort of mania with me. Tidiness, that is.' Then he saw himself in the dressing-table mirror—unshaven since early this morning in London (he had written *Londra* on the envelope; was that right?) and with shirt very crumpled and trousers proclaiming cheapness and jacket thin at the elbows. He gave himself a grim smile full of teeth. They looked clean enough, anyway. He transferred the smile to Miss Boland. 'You poor man,' she said. 'You're lonely, aren't you? I could see that when you got on the bus in London. Still, you've no need to be lonely now. Not for this holiday, anyhow.' She took a sip of the Fundador without grimacing. 'Hm. Fiery but nice.'

'*Mucho fuego*,' said Enderby. English man no *fuego:* he remembered that.

Miss Boland leaned back. She wore feathery slippers with heels. Leaning back, she kicked them off. Her feet were long and clean and the toes were unpainted. She closed her eyes, frowned, then said: 'Let me see if I can remember. *A cada puerco* something-or-other *su San Martín*. That means: Every dog has his day. But it should be "every hog" really, shouldn't it? The dictionary says hog, not pig.'

Enderby sat down heavily on the other side of the bed. Then

he looked with heavy apprehension at Miss Boland. She seemed to have lost about two stone and fifteen years since embarking at London. He tried to see himself imposing upon her a complex of subtle but vigorous amation which should have an effect of drowsy enslavement, rendering her, for instance, totally indifferent to tomorrow's news. Then he thought he had perhaps better get out of here and find his own way to North Africa: there must surely be something hopping over there at this hour. But no. Despite everything, he was safer in Mr Mercer's party—a supernumerary, fiddled in with a wink, no name on the manifest, waved through by officials who were waved back at by Mr Guthkelch. Moreover, Mr Mercer had returned everybody's passport, and Enderby's was snug once more in its inside pocket. He was not going to let it go again, unless, in final desperate abandonment of identity, to the fire of some Moorish kebab-vendor. He saw this man quite clearly, crying his kebabs against the sun, brown and lined and toothless, opposing his call to the muezzin's. That was the poetic imagination, that was.

'And,' Miss Boland was now saying, having helped herself to more Fundador, 'Mother and Dad used to take me and Charles, that was my brother, to see Uncle Herbert when he lived in Wellington—Wellington, Salop, I mean; why do they call it Salop? Oh, the Latin name I suppose—and we went up Bredon Hill several times—'

'The coloured counties,' Enderby said, doing an estimate of her for seduction purposes and realising at the same time how purely academic such a notion was, 'and hear the larks on high. Young men hanging themselves and ending up in Shrewsbury jail. For love, as they call it.'

'How cynical you are. But I suppose I've every right to be cynical too, really. Toby his name was—a silly name for a man, isn't it?—and he said I had to choose between him and my career—I mean, more the name for a dog, isn't it, really?—and of course there was no question of me abandoning my vocation for the sake of anything he said he had to give. And he said something about a brainy wife being a bad wife and he wasn't going to have the moon lying in bed between us.'

'A bit of a poet,' said Enderby, feeling himself grow drowsy. The hot wind puppeteered the window-curtains and plastered

Miss Boland's nightdress against her shin.

'A bit of a liar,' Miss Boland said. 'He lied about his father. His father wasn't a solicitor, only a solicitor's clerk. He lied about his rank in the Royal Corps of Signals. He lied about his car. It wasn't his, it was one he borrowed from a friend. Not that he had many friends. Men,' she said, 'tend to be liars. Look at you, for instance.'

'Me?' said Enderby.

'Saying you're a poet. Talking about your old Shropshire name.'

'Listen,' said Enderby. And he began to recite.

'Shrewsbury, Shrewsbury, rounded by river,
    The envious Severn like a sleeping dog
That wakes at whiles to snarl and slaver
    Or growls in its dream its snores of fog.'

'That's yours, is it?'

'Lover-haunted in the casual summer:
    A monstrous aphrodisiac,
The sun excites in the noonday shimmer,
    When Jack is sweating, Joan on her back.'

'I was always taught that you can't make poetry with long words.'

'Sick and sinless in the anaemic winter:
    The nymphs have danced off the summer rout,
The boats jog on the fraying painter,
    The School is hacking its statesmen out.'

'Oh, I see what you mean. Shrewsbury School. That's where Darwin went to, isn't it?'

'The pubs dispense their weak solution,
    The unfructified waitresses bring their bills,
While Darwin broods upon evolution,
    Under the pall of a night that chills—'

'Sorry, I shouldn't have interrupted.'

'—But smooths out the acne of adolescence
    As the god appears in the fourteenth glass

And the urgent promptings of tumescence
  Lead to the tumbled patch of grass.'

'A lot of sex in it, isn't there? Sorry, I won't interrupt again.'
'This is the last bloody stanza,' Enderby said sternly. 'Coming
up now.

  "Time and the town go round like the river,
    But Darwin thinks in a line that is straight.
  A sort of selection goes on for ever,
    But no new species originate."'

They were silent. Enderby felt a spurt of poet's pride, and
then exhaustion. It had been a terrible day. Miss Boland was
impressed. She said: 'Well, you *are* a poet, after all. If that *is*
yours, that is.'

'Of course it's mine. Give me some more from that bottle.'
And she glugged some out for him gladly, handmaiden to a
poet. 'That's from my early volume, *Fish and Heroes*. Which
you haven't read. Which nobody's read. But, by God,' said Enderby, 'I'll show them all. I'm not finished yet, not by a long
chalk.'

'That's right. Don't you think you'd be more comfortable with
your shoes off? Don't bother—leave it to me.' Enderby closed
his eyes. 'And your jacket too?' Enderby soon lay on one half of
the bed in shirt and trousers; she had had his socks off too and
also his tie, which was in the hotel colours of red, white, and
blue. The hot wind was still there, but he felt cooler. She lay
next to him. They had a cigarette apiece.

'Associations,' Enderby found himself saying. 'Mind you, everybody's done it, from that Spanish priest right up to Albert Camus,
with Kierkegaard somewhere in the middle.'

'Who's Kierke-whatever-it-is?'

'This philosopher who made out it was really like God and the
soul. Don Juan using women and God using man. Anyway, this
is his town. And I was going to write a poetic drama about a
Don Juan who bribed women to pretend that he'd done it to
them because really he couldn't do it, not with anybody. And
then poetic drama went out of fashion.' His toenails, he decided,
could really do with cutting. The big toenails, however, would
have to be attacked with a chisel or something. Very hard. He

had not changed all that much, after all. A bath, after all, was a tank for poetic drafts. He felt a new poem twitching inside him like a sneeze. A poem about a statue. He looked rather warmly on Miss Boland. *The final kiss and final*—If only he could get that one finished first.

'And who was this barber of Seville?'

'Oh, a Frenchman invented that one, and there's a French newspaper named after him. A sort of general factotum, getting things for people and so on.' Enderby nodded off.

'Wake up.' She was quite rough with him; that would be the Fundador. 'You could have a play in which this barber was really Don Juan, and he did horrible things with his razor. In revenge, you know.'

'What do you mean? What revenge?'

'I said nothing about revenge. You dropped off again. Wake up! I don't see why the moon couldn't be a proper *scientific* subject for a poem instead of what it is for most poets—you know, a sort of lamp, or a what-do-you-call-it aphrodisiac like the sun in your poem. Then you could have as many nice long words as you wanted. Apogee and perigee and the sidereal day and ectocraters and the ejecta hypothesis.'

'What did you say about ejectors?'

She hadn't heard him. Or perhaps he'd said nothing. 'And the months,' she was now saying. 'Synodic and nodical and sidereal and anomalistic. And isostasy. And grabens and horsts. And the lunar maria, not seas at all but huge plains of lava covered in dust. Your body is a horst and mine a graben, because horst is the opposite of graben. Come on, let's get out of here and wander the streets of Seville as we are, in our night clothes I mean. But your night clothes are the altogether, aren't they? Still, it's a lovely night though the moon's setting now. Feel that warm wind on your flesh?' That was not true about the moon setting. When they were walking down the *calle* outside the hotel, Enderby totally bare, his little bags aswing, the moon was full and huge and very near. It was so near that an odour came off it—like the odour of cachous from old evening bags, of yellowing dance-programmes, of fox-fur long laid in mothballs. Miss Boland said: 'Mare Tranquillitatis. Fracastorius. Hipparchus. Mare Nectaris.' She had brought the moon right down to the

Seville housetops so that she could go burrowing into its maria.
She disappeared temporarily into one of those, and then her
head, its mousy hair become golden Berenice's and flying about,
popped through the northern polar membrane. She seemed to be
agitating this hollow moon from the inside, impelling it towards
Enderby. He ran from her and it down the *calle*, back into the
hotel. The old hall-porter yawned out of his *hidalgo* lantern jaws
at Enderby's twinkling nakedness. Enderby panted up the stairs,
once getting his toe caught in a carpet-hole, then cursing as a
tack lodged in his calloused left heel. He found his room blindly
and fell flat on the bed, desperate for air. There was not much
coming from the open window. What was coming in by that
window was the moon, much shrunken but evidently of consid-
erable mass, for the window-frame creaked, four unwilling tan-
gents to the straining globe, bits of lunar substance flaking off
like plaster at the four points of engagement. Miss Boland's head
now protruded at a pole which had become a navel, her hair still
flying in fire. Enderby was stuck to that bed. With one lunge she
and the moon were on him.

'No,' he grunted, waking up. 'No, you can't do that, it isn't
right.' But she and her heavy lunar body held him down. That
left heel was fluked by one of her toenails; the staircarpet-hole
turned out to be a minute gap between the fabric of her dressing-
gown and its lacy border. There was no real nakedness, then:
only exposure, things riding up and pulled down.

'Show me then, show me what's right. *You* do it.'

He rolled her off, so that she lay expectant on her back now,
and with desperate agility he trampolined his buttocks away
from the punished mattress. This was springier than he had
thought, for he found himself on his feet looking sternly down at
her. 'If,' he said, 'you want that sort of a holiday there'll be
plenty to provide it. Gigolos and whatnot. Little dark-skinned
boys and so on. Why pick on me?'

She started to whimper. 'I thought we were going to be
friends. You're unnatural, that's what you are.'

'I'm *not* unnatural. Just very very tired. It's been a terrible
day.'

'Yes.' She wrapped her dressing-gown round her body and
looked up at him, hard but tearfully. 'Yes, I'm sure it has.

There's something not quite right about you. You've got things on your mind. You've done something you shouldn't have done. You've got away in a hurry from something or other, I can tell that.'

This wouldn't do at all. 'Darling,' creaked Enderby, holding out his arms and advanced, smirking.

'You can't get round me that way.'

'Darling.' Enderby frowned now, but with his arms still out.

'Oh, take your non-pyjamas out of your non-suitcase and get to bed after your terrible terrible day. There's something very fishy about you,' said Miss Boland. And she started to get up from the bed.

Enderby advanced and pushed her back again somewhat roughly, saying: 'You're right. I *have* run away. From her. From that woman. I couldn't stand it any longer. I got out. Just like that. She was horrible to me.' A back cinder in Enderby's raked-out brain spurted up an instant to ask what was truth and niggle a bit about situation contexts and so on. Enderby deferred to it and made an emendation: 'I ran away.'

'What woman? Which woman?' Woman's curiosity had dried her tears.

'It was never really a marriage. Oh, let me get to bed. Make room there. I'm so desperately tired.'

'Tell me all about it first. I want to know what happened. Come on, wake up. Have some more of this brandy stuff here.'

'No no no no. Tell you in the morning.' He was flat on his back again, ready to drop off. Desperately.

'I want to know.' She jerked him as roughly as he had pushed her. 'Whose fault was it? Why was it never really a marriage? Oh, *do come on.*'

'Hex,' said Enderby *in extremis.* And then he was merrily driving the rear car of the three, a red sports job, and arms waved jollily from the Mercedes in front. It was a long way to this roadhouse type pub they were all going to, but they were all well tanked-up already though the men drove with steely concentration and insolent speed. The girls were awfully pretty and full of fun. Brenda had red hair and Lucy was dark and small and Bunty was pleasantly plump and wore a turquoise-coloured twin-set. Enderby had a college scarf flying from his neck and a pipe clenched in his strong white smiling teeth. 'You wait, Bunty old girl,' he gritted indistinctly. 'You'll get what's coming to you.' The girls yelled with mirth. Urged on by them hilariously, he fed ever greater speed with his highly-polished toecap to the growling road-eating red job, and he passed with ease the other two. Waves of mock rage and mock contempt, laughter on the spring English wind. And so he got to the pub first. It was a nice little pub with a bald smiling barman presiding in a cocktail bar smelling of furniture polish. He wore a white bum-freezer with claret lapels. Enderby ordered for everybody, telling the barman, called Jack, to put a wiggle on so that the drinks could be all lined up waiting when the laggards arrived. Bitter in tankards, gin and things, an advocaat for Bunty. 'That'll make you bright-eyed and bushy-tailed, old girl,' winked Enderby. And then the watery signal from within. As Frank and Nigel and Betty and Ethel and the others roared into the bar, Enderby at once had to say: 'Sorry, all. Got to see a man about a dog.' Bunty giggled: 'Wet your boots, you mean.' At once the urgency roared in his bladder, drowning the roaring of his pals, but he did not run to the gents: he walked confidently, though he had never been in this pub before. But, seeing it at the end of a corridor, he had to run. Damn, he would only just make it.

He would only just make it. He jumped out of bed and made for the toilet, fumbling cursing for the light-switch. Pounding his stream out, he grumbled at the prodigality of dreams, which could go to all this trouble—characters, décor and all, even an advertisement for a beer (Jason's Golden Fleece) which didn't exist—just so that he would get out of bed and micturate in the proper place. He pulled the chain, went back to bed and saw, by the bathroom light he had not bothered to put out, that there was a woman lying in it. He remembered roughly who it was, that lunar woman he'd been flying with (why flying?) and also that this was some foreign town, and then the whole lot came back. He was somewhat frightened that he wasn't as frightened as he should be.

'What, eh, who?' she said. And then: 'Oh. I must have dropped off. Come on, get in. It's got a bit chilly now.'

'What time is it?' Enderby wondered. His wrist-watch had stopped, he noticed, squinting in the light from the bathroom.

Somewhere outside a big bell banged a single stroke. 'That's a lot of help,' said Enderby. Funny, he hadn't noticed that bell before. They must be near a cathedral or town hall or something. Seville, that was where they were. Don Juan's town. A strange woman in bed.

'So,' she said. 'Her name was Bunty, was it? And she let you down. Never mind, everybody gets let down sometime or other. I got let down by Toby. And that was a silly name, too.'

'We were in this car, you see. I was driving.'

'Come back to bed. *I* won't let you down. Come and cuddle up a bit. It's chilly. There aren't many clothes on the bed.'

It was quite pleasant cuddling up. *I've been so cold at night.* Who was it who had said that? That blasted Vesta, bloody evil woman. 'Bloody evil woman,' muttered Enderby.

'Yes, yes, but it's all over now. You're a bit wet.'

'Sorry,' Enderby said. 'Careless of me.' He wiped himself with the sheet. 'I wonder what the time is.'

'Why? Why are you so eager to know what the time is? Do you want to be up and about so soon? A night in Seville. We both ought to have something to remember about a night in Seville.'

'They lit the sun,' said Enderby, 'and then their day began.'

'What do you mean? Why did you say that?'

'It just came to me. Out of the blue.' It seemed as though rhymes were going to start lining up. Began, plan, man, scan, ban. But this other thing had to be done now. She was not a bit like that blasted Vesta, spare-fleshed in bed so that she could be elegant out of it. There was plenty to get hold of here. He saw one of his bar-customers leering, saying that. Very vulgar. Enderby started to summon up old memories of what to do (it had been a long time). The Don himself seemed to hover above the bed, picking his teeth for some reason, nodding, pointing. Moderately satisfied, he flew off on an insubstantial hell-horse and, not far from the hotel, waved a greeting with a doffed insolent feathered *sombrero* at a statue of a man.

'They hoisted up a statue of a man,' mumbled Enderby.

'Yes, yes, darling, I love you too.'

Enderby now gently, shyly, and with some blushing, began to insinuate, that is to say squashily attempt to insert, that is to say.

A long time. And now. Quite pleasant, really. He paused after
five. And again. And again. Pentameters. And now came an ejac-
ulation of words.

> What prodigies that eye of light revealed!
> What dusty parchment statutes they repealed,
> Pulling up blinds and lifting every

A sonnet, a sonnet, one for a new set of *Revolutionary Sonnets*,
the first of which was the one that bloody Wapenshaw had
raged at. The words began to flood. He drew the thing out,
excited.

'Sorry,' he said. 'I've got to get this thing down. I've got to
get some paper. A sonnet, that's what it is.' There was, he
thought, a hanging bulby switch-thing over the bed-head. He
felt for it, trembling. Seville's velvet dark was jeered out by a
sudden coming of light. She was incredulous. She lay there with
her mouth open, shocked and staring. 'I'll just get it down on
paper,' promised Enderby, 'and then back on the job again.
What I mean is—' He was out of bed, searching. Barman's pen-
cil in his jacket-pocket. Paper? Damn. He dragged open drawers,
looking for that white lining-stuff. It was all old Spanish newspaper, bullfighters or something. Damn.

She wailed from the bed. Enderby dashed into the bathroom,
inspired, and came out swathed in toilet-paper. 'This will do
fine,' he smiled. 'Shan't be long. Darling,' he added. Then he
sat at the dressing-table, horridly undressed, and began to
write.

> Pulling up blinds and lifting every ban.
> The galaxies revolving to their plan,
> They made the coin, the conch, the cortex yield
> Their keys

'You're hateful, you're disgusting. I've never in my whole life
been so insulted. No wonder she—'

'Look,' said Enderby, without turning round, 'this is important. The gift's definitely come back, thank God. I knew it
would. Just give me a couple of minutes. Then I'll be in there
again.' In the bed, he meant, raising his eyes to the dressing-
table mirror as to make them tell her, if she was in that mirror,

precisely that. He saw her all right. He ought, he knew, to be shocked by what he saw, but there was no time for that now. Hell has no fury. Better not let other poems get in the way. Besides, that quotation was wrong, everybody always got it wrong.

> And in a garden, once a field,
>   They hoisted up a statue of a man.

'Finished the octave,' he sang out. 'Shan't be long now.'

'You filthy thing. You sexless rotter.'

'Really. Such language.' Mirror, terror, error. Pity there was no true rhyme for *mirror*, except that bloody Sir Launcelot thing Tennyson pinched from the pincher Autolycus. 'And you a seleno-whatever-it-is.'

'You won't get away with this. You wait.' And, dressing-gown decently about her, she was out through that door, to Enderby's mild surprise, and was gone, slamming it.

'Look here,' Enderby said feebly. And then the mirror, holding out its English name, told him to get on with the sestet.

Four

The sestet. It was all right, he thought. He told the Spanish dawn he thought it was all right. Then he had a swig of Fundador. Not all that much left. She'd put her name into it, that one, Miss whoever-it-was, moon-woman. He told the sestet to his reflection like an elocutionist:

> 'Of man, rather. To most it seemed a mirror:
> They strained their necks with gazing in the air,
> Proud of those stony eyes unglazed by terror.
> Though marble is not glass, why should they care?
> There would be time for coughing up the error.
> Someone was bound to find his portrait there.'

And the meaning? It seemed pretty clear, really. This was what happened in a humanist society. The Garden of Eden (and that was in the other sonnet, the one that had rendered bloody Wapenshaw violent) was turned into a field where men built or

fought or ploughed or something. They worshipped themselves
for being so clever, but then they were all personified in an auto-
cratic leader, like this Franco up there in Madrid. Humanism
always led to totalitarianism. Something like that, anyway.

Enderby was moderately pleased with the poem, but he was
more pleased with the prospect of a bigger structure, a sequence. Some years before he had published the volume called
Revolutionary Sonnets. The book had contained things other
than sonnets, but the title had derived from that opening group
of twenty, each of which had tried to encapsulate—exploiting
the theme and countertheme paradigm of the Petrarchan form
—some phase of history in which a revolution had taken place.
He felt now that it might be possible to wrest those twenty sonnets from that volume and, by adding twenty more with the co-
operation of the Muse, build a sizeable sequence which would
make a book on its own. A new title would be needed—
something more imaginative than the old one, something like
Conch and Cortex or something. So far he had these two
sonnets—the Garden of Eden one and the new one about man
building his own world outside the Garden. Somewhere at the
back of his mind there pricked the memory of his having started
and then abandoned, in a very rough state, another sonnet that,
nicely worked up and carefully polished, would make a third. It
was, he thought, really an anterior sonnet to these two, an image
of the primal revolution in heaven—Satan revolting, that sort of
thing. Lucifer, Adam, Adam's children. Those would make the
first three. He felt that, with a certain amount of drunkenness
followed by crapulous meditation, that sonnet could be teased
back to life. He was pretty sure that the rhymes, at least, would
come marching back, in U.S. Army soft-soled boots, if he left the
gate open. Octave: Lucifer fed up with the dead order and unity
of heaven. Wants action, so has to conceive idea of duality. Sestet: he dives, creates hell to oppose heaven. Enderby saw him
diving. An eagle dropping from a mountain-top in sunlight. Out
of Tennyson, that. The wrinkled sea beneath him crawls. Alls,
balls, calls. Was that one of the sestet rhymes?

He felt excited. He toasted himself in the last of the Fundador. That bloody woman. But there was time for shame now and
for the desire to make amends. He thought he had better go now

to her room and apologise. He saw that it was not perhaps really all that polite to get out of bed and so on with a woman in order to write down a poem. Especially on toilet-paper brought in like triumphal streamers. Women had their own peculiar notion of priorities, and this had to be respected. But he had no doubt that she would see his point if properly explained. Suppose, he might say, she had suddenly spotted a new lunar crater while so engaged, would she not herself have leapt up as he had done? And then he could read his sonnet to her. He wondered whether it was worth while to dress properly for his visit. The dawn was mounting and soon the hotel would stir with insolent waiters coming to bedrooms with most inadequate breakfasts. But she might, thoroughly mollified by the sonnet, bid him back to bed again, her bed now, to resume what had, so to speak, that is to say. He blushed. He would go, as a film Don Juan he had once seen had gone, in open-necked shirt and trousers.

He went out on to the corridor, his sonnet wrapped round his wrist and one end secured with his thumb. Her room was just down there, on the same side as his own. When they had all, with Mr Mercer leading and Mr Guthkelch crying: 'Keep in step there, you horrible lot,' marched up together, he had definitely seen her allotted that room there. He went up to it now and stood before it, taking deep breaths and trying out a plenidental smile. Then he grasped the door-handle and boldly entered. Dawn-lit, the curtains drawn back, a room much like his own though containing luggage. She was lying in bed, possibly asleep, possibly—for every woman was supposed to be able to tell at once when there was an intruder, something to do with the protection of honour—pretending to be asleep. Enderby coughed loudly and said:

'I came to tell you I'm sorry. I didn't mean it. It just came over me, as I said.'

She started awake at once, more surprised, it seemed, than angry. She had changed her nightdress to demure cotton, also the colour of her hair. It was the aircraft's stewardess. Miss Kelly was the name. Enderby frowned on her. She had no right—But perhaps he had entered the wrong room. She said:

'Did you want something? I'm not really supposed to be available to passengers, you know, except on the flight.'

'No, no,' frowned Enderby. 'Sorry. I was after that other woman. The moon one. Miss Boolan.'

'Miss Boland. Oh, I see. It's your wrist, is it? You've got that thing round your wrist. You've cut your wrist, is that it? All the first-aid stuff's on the aircraft. The hotel people might be able to help you.'

'Oh, no, no, no,' Enderby laughed now. 'This is a poem, not an improvised bandage. I had to get up and write this poem, you understand, and I fear I annoyed Miss Boland, as you say her name is. I was going to apologise to her and perhaps read out this poem as a kind of peace-offering, so to speak. It's what's known as a sonnet.'

'It's a bit early, isn't it?' She slid down into her bed again, leaving just her head and eyes showing. 'I mean, everybody's supposed to be still asleep.'

'Oh,' Enderby smiled kindly, 'it's not that sort of poem, you know. You're thinking of an aubade—a good-morning song. The Elizabethans were very fond of these. Hark hark the lark, and so on. When all the birds have matins said, and so forth. A sonnet is a poem in fourteen lines. For any occasion, I suppose.'

'I know what a sonnet is,' her voice said, muffled but sharp. 'There's a sonnet in that book by Yod Crewsy.'

Enderby stood paralysed, his own sonnet held forward like a knuckleduster. 'Eh?' Thought fell in at a great distance and, in British tommies' clodhoppers, advanced steadily at a light infantry pace.

'You know. You were asking about pop-singers on the plane. Vesta Wittgenstein you were asking about too, remember. Yod Crewsy did this book of poems that won the prize. There's one in it he calls a sonnet. I couldn't make head nor tail of it really, but one of the BOAC ground-hostesses, educated you see, she said it was very clever.'

'Can you,' faltered Enderby, 'can you remember anything about it?' Like Macbeth, he began to see that it might be necessary to kill everybody.

'Oh, it's so early. And,' she said, a girl slow on the uptake, sitting up again, things dawning on her, 'you shouldn't be in here really at this hour. Not at any hour you shouldn't. Nobody asked you to come in here. I'll call Captain O'Shaughnessy.' Her voice was growing louder.

'One line, one word,' begged Enderby. 'Just tell me what it was about.'

'You're not supposed to be in here. It's taking advantage of being a passenger. I'm not supposed to be rude to passengers. Oh, why don't you go?'

'About the devil and hell and so on? Was that it?'

'I've had enough. I'm going to call Captain O'Shaughnessy.'

'Oh, don't bother,' groaned Enderby. 'I'm just going. But it's liberty after liberty.'

'You're telling *me* it's taking a liberty.'

'First one thing and then another. If he's dead I'm glad he's dead. But there'll be other heads rolling, I can tell you that. Did it have something about an eagle in it? You know, dropping from a great height?'

Miss Kelly seemed to be taking a very deep breath, as though in preparation for shouting. Enderby went, nodding balefully, closing the door. In the circumstances, he did not much feel like calling on Miss Boland. Women were highly unpredictable creatures. No, that was stupid. You could predict them all right. He had thought he would never have to see blasted treacherous Vesta again, but he obviously had to confront her before he did her in. The future was filling itself up horribly. Things both monstrously necessary and sickeningly irrelevant. He wanted to get on with his poetry again.

4

One

Cᴀʟᴍ, calm. Enderby reflected that it was morning and he was up and there was nothing to prevent his engaging Seville in the doing of what had to be done. First, a question of pesetas. Unshaven, dirty-shirted, otherwise respectable, he asked the day-porter of the hotel, yawning to his duty, where sterling might be changed. He asked in Italian, which, thanks to the Roman Empire, the porter clearly understood. Enderby had some idea that it was forbidden by the British government, treacherously in league with foreign bankers (even Franco's fiscal thugs), to present naked pounds in any Continental place of official monetary transaction. They found you had more pound-notes on you than you ought, by law, to have, and then, by various uncompassionate channels, they reported you to the Chancellor of the Exchequer, an insincerely smiling man Enderby had once seen with a woman in Piggy's Sty. In Italy that time, on his brief and dummy honeymoon, it had been traveller's cheques, which were all right. The porter, in mime and basic Romance, told Enderby that there was a barber round the corner who gave a very good rate of exchange. Enderby felt a little ice cube of pleasure, soon to be pounced on and demolished by the hot water he was in. He needed a shave, anyway. A barber of Seville, eh? 'Figaro?' he asked, momentarily forgetting his actual, and other people's proleptic, trouble. Not Figaro, said the unliterary and literal porter. He was called Pepe.

This barber breathed hard on Enderby as he shaved him, a sour young man smelling of very fresh garlic. He seemed not unwilling to change fifty pounds of Enderby's money, and Enderby wondered if the suspiciously clean pesetas he got were genuine. The world was terrible really, full of cheating and shadiness, as much in low as in high places. He tested his pesetas in a dirty eating-den full of loud dialogue (the participants as far away from each other as possible: one man tooth-picking at the door, another hidden in the kitchen, for instance). Enderby asked for *ovos* which turned out to be *huevos,* and for *prosciutto,* not cognate with *jamón.* He was learning essential words: he would not starve. He changed a big note with no trouble, receiving back a fistful of small dirty rags. Then, on the counter, he saw a copy of a newspaper called *Diario Pueblo.*

How often had he, on the day of publication of a volume of his verse (or the day before, if publication day had been Monday), gone to the quality papers as to a condemned cell, his stomach sick and his legs pure angelica. Usually there was no review, poetry being left to accumulate in literary editors' offices until there was enough of it for one expert to do a single clean sweep in a grudging brief article, everybody—Enderby, poetesses, poetasters, Sir George Goodby—all fluffed up together. But once, surprisingly, there had been a prompt solus of condemnation, all for Enderby, in a very reputable paper. Since then, the smell of newsprint had always made him feel slightly giddy. The fear he felt now was strong enough, since it was to do with his appearance in a context of action, but it was mitigated somewhat by the fact of the newspaper's foreignness. It seemed a very badly put together newspaper, with a lot of news items boxed in thick black, as though they were all obituaries. 'Scusa,' he said to the curled dark youth who took his money. And then he looked for news of himself.

He did not have far to look. It was on the front page. There

was, thank God, no photograph, but there were frightful succinct words, as though from some sensational foreign novel.
Chocante. Horroroso. Come, that was going too far. *Delante del
Primer Ministro Británico.* They had to bring that in, make it
political. *Banquete para celebrar* something or other. And then
Yod Crewsy, cuadrillero de los Fixers. Was he dead, then? What
was 'dead'—*morto?* No, Enderby concluded from both his
Spanish pseudonym and his eggs, now repeating violently, it
must be *muerto.* References to a *revólver,* very clear that, and to
a *tiro* and—what the hell was this?—an *escopetazo.* And then it
said: *El víctima, en grave estado, fué conducido al* some *hospital* or other, English name of it all messed up. Not *muerto* yet,
then. Enderby was horrified at feeling cheated. All this upset for
just *en grave estado.* Still, that might be pretty bad. Then it said
something about *Scotland Yard buscando* something something
un camarero. He knew what that was: Spanish John had once or
twice been hailed by that title facetiously by men and women
who had been to the Costa del Sol. John had always responded
readily, gleaming in complaisant dentition, all of gold. And now
it was he, Enderby, who was the *camarero.* He was wanted, the
paper said, to *ayudar* the *policía* in their *investigación.* Well,
he'd already helped, hadn't he? He'd sent them the name of the
true attempted *matador,* or whatever it was. And now the newspaper gave Enderby's own abandoned other name, or a version
of it. *Hagg.* That was hardly fair to that barely imaginable sweet
woman.

Un camarero quien se llama Hagg. He now felt somewhat better, the eggs settling down, the reality of the thing confirmed, no
bad dream. So he went out now, nodding politely to various
walnut-skinned early-morning coffee-suckers, and looked on the
calle for a general outfitter's shop. The cathedral bell banged
once at him, as to announce that the fight was on. So he went
and bought himself a drip-dry green *camisa,* a pair of cheap
grey *pantalones,* and a very light *americana* or jacket of fawn
Moygashel. Also a tie or *corbata* of rather mouth-watering lime.
He changed into these in a dark breadcrumby cubbyhole at the
rear of the shop. He also bought a black Basque beret (ah, that
took him back, back to the old gusty seaside days when he had
fed the ungrateful gulls every perishing morning; happy days,

before the horrible outside world's impinging, pressing, over-powering). Also a little overnight bag to put his Hogg clothes in. *Hagg*, indeed. He couldn't help laughing. Also a razor and blades. And a kind of superstructure of plain anti-sun lenses to clip on to his spectacles. Then he sat outside a café and drank Spanish gin and tonic while a shoeblack blacked his shoes. He counted what money he had left in sterling and pesetas. Not a lot, really, though the shoeblack seemed to think so: his hands performing busily away, he gave money-counting Enderby close attention, as if he were a conductor. And then Enderby saw her, Miss Boland, walking down the *calle* with arms full of little toys and dolls bought from street-vendors.

Of course, she had as much right to be here as he had, if not more. And so had various other members of the tour who were walking down this main street (the hotel just around the cor-ner), probably newly released from breakfast. There was even Mr Guthkelch over there on the pavement opposite, full of gummy fun though inaudible because of the traffic. Enderby stood up, one foot still on the cleaner's box, and shyly waved at her with both arms. She recognised him, despite his new smart-ness, and looked grim. She seemed fifteen years older than last night, also very thin, as though wasting away. Her summer dress was suitable for the warm southern autumn, but very dowdy—a blue flowery sack with a string defining her waist. Having given Enderby a filthy look, she was prepared to walk on, but Enderby cried:

'It was inspiration, that's what it was, inspiration. Can't you see that? That hadn't happened to me for years. And I came round to your room, but the door was locked, and I—'

'Don't shout,' she hissed. 'Don't shout at me. For that matter, don't speak to me. Do you understand? I don't want to see you again. Ever. I want to make that clear, here and now. I don't know you and I don't want to know you.' She prepared to move on. Enderby put pesetas on the table, leaving their apportion-ment to waiter and shoeblack, and then grabbed her arm. He said:

'I know precisely how you must feel.' He found he had left his overnight bag on the table, so he went back to get it. 'How you must feel,' he panted, 'but just think,' panting to keep up with her long strides. 'It was you who brought the gift back. You. The excitement. I didn't dare lose that poem. It meant so much. It was you. The poem was you.' He marvelled at himself. 'I knew you'd understand.' She shook her body impatiently, as to shake him, Enderby, away, and a small clockwork goose, with articulated neck, fell from her arm to the pavement. Enderby picked it up and the beak came off. He panted worse than ever. He said: 'In my bag. Put those things in my bag. See, I bought this bag this morning. I got up early and bought things, including this bag. But I'll take my things out, if you like, and you can use the bag for putting your things in.'

She began to cry, still walking down the *calle*. A swarthy man saw her tears and looked with distaste on Enderby. 'Oh, you're horrible,' she said.

'I'll buy you another goose,' promised Enderby. 'Though it wasn't my fault it broke,' he added, justly. 'Look, give me those dolls and things and they can all go in my bag.'

She wanted to dry her eyes but couldn't, her arms being full of toys. Who were they for? Perhaps a maternal lust had welled up in her suddenly, thought Enderby with fear. Perhaps she was looking ahead. Perhaps any man would do. He had read of such matters. She was buying playthings for children yet unborn. Enderby said eagerly:

'I wanted to read you the poem, but I couldn't get in.' Then he saw that that particular poem, with its tabloid history, would not have done. He was slow in learning about women. Only a love poem could placate her. Had he anything in stock? 'See,' he said, 'look. There's a horse and carriage thing.' A *coche* was creaking along, drawn by a glossy sugar-fed mare. 'We'll go for a drive in that, and you can tell me how horrible I am.'

'Oh, leave me alone, go away.' But she wanted to wipe her cheeks. The coachman, a lined, knowing, very old man, had stopped in response to Enderby's eager look.

'Get in,' Enderby said, pushing her. A small tin tortoise prepared to dive from her arm. Enderby saved it and made it nest in his bag, along with the goose. Life was terrible, really. 'Go on, get in,' he said, more roughly. And then: 'I've told you I'm sorry. But you can't get in the way of a poem. Nobody can.' So then, sniffing, she got in. 'The way of a poem,' Enderby said, 'passes all human understanding.' The cathedral bell clanged a sort of amen. And so they were trotted off gently, and she was able to dry her eyes.

'It could have waited,' she said. She began to look plumper again; she was becoming near-mollified. They turned right down a narrow street of pleasant yellow houses with balconies, empty, at this hour, of coy serenaded señoritas.

'A kind of sprung rhythm,' said Enderby. He now thanked God, or *Dios* as He was here, that some crude lines from an apprentice poem came wriggling back. 'Listen.' He gave her them in counterpoint to the jaunty bouncing crupper with its blue-ribboned tail:

> 'I sought scent, and found it in your hair;
> Looked for light, and it lodged in your eyes;
> So for sound: it held your breath dear;
> And I met movement in your ways.'

'I see what you mean.' She was quick to forgive, a bit too quick. She was thinking of her holiday; Enderby was primarily for holiday use. And on holiday my dear I met this poet. Really? A poet, just imagine. 'But even so.'

'That time will come again, often.' Oh no, it bloody well wouldn't. The ghost of Juan was in the sunlit streets, approving his proposed desertion. 'Whereas the time for paying homage— to your beauty, that is—'

'Oh, you *are* a pig, aren't you?' She came up close to him. 'A dirty pig, a *puerco puerco*. Piggy.'

'Don't call me that.'

'Hog, then. Hoggy.' Enderby sweated. 'Perhaps,' she said, 'we could get off soon and have a drink. I'm terribly thirsty.'

'It's the crying that does it. A big thirst-maker is crying.' He remembered his stepmother jeering at him when she'd clouted his earhole and made him howl: *Go on, cry more and you'll pee less.* 'A loss of liquid, you see. It needs replacing.'

Two

They had lunch at an open-air café place, and of course it had to be paella. She had read about this in some coloured supplement as being one of the glories of the Spanish cuisine, but Enderby considered that never in his life had he been served with anything so insolent. It was warm sticky rice pudding embedded with strips of latex and small gritty seashells. Before it they had cold tomato soup full of garlic. She giggled and said: 'It's a good thing we're both having garlic.' Enderby choked on that, but later he choked harder on both a seashell and her saying: 'Oh, look, there's a little man selling newspapers. Do let's have a Spanish newspaper. I've got my little dictionary with me.' He choked so frightfully at the vendor that the vendor went off.

'Has something gone the wrong way? Have a drink of your nice wine.' It was *not* nice wine: it tasted of ink and alum and eels and catarrh. 'Oh, I did so want a newspaper.'

'Lies,' snarled Enderby. 'Spanish bloody lies. All propaganda and censorship. You're not to have one, do you hear?'

'Darling Hoggy. Quite the heavy husband, aren't you? Perhaps there was fault on both sides.'

'What do you mean?'

'Your wife.'

'Oh, her.' He sourly tongued wine-lees from his palate. 'She's got a lot to answer for. Plagiarism, apart from anything else.' As soon as he got to Morocco he would get hold of that book. Some effete expatriate writer would probably have it.

'Plagiarism?'

'Oh, never mind.' He had gone too far, or nearly had. 'I don't want to talk about it.'

'Perhaps she didn't like your poem-writing habits.' Miss Boland had had too much of this adenoidal wine-substitute. Enderby scowled at her. 'No poems tonight, hm?'

'That,' said Enderby, with a kind of reproving leer, 'I can promise.'

'Oh, good heavens, look at the time. There won't be any tonight at all if we don't get back to the hotel. The coach leaves at one-thirty.'

Enderby paid the bill, leaving no tip. It had been a horrible meal and it was a horrible place, full of eroded statues and stunted trees. She squeezed his arm, linking him, as he went to the pavement's edge to call at any vehicle that looked like a taxi. One taxi already had Miss Kelly and two uniformed men, pilot and co-pilot probably, in it. Miss Kelly clearly recognised Enderby but did not smile or wave. A damned silly girl. Enderby thought he would mention that business of the wrong room to Miss Boland, but then he decided not. The female temperament was a strange one.

At last a taxi took them to the Hotel Marruecos, where tour-members were already assembling at the entrance, luggage all about them. Miss Boland had to rush to her room to see about hers, not quite finished packing. Enderby saw another news-paper-seller hovering and gave him a five-peseta note to go away. Things would be all right, but for God's sake let things be hurried up. Mr Guthkelch had bought a pair of castanets and was fandangoing clumsily, clumsily clacking them. The man with the condoms in his luggage looked very tired, but his wife was erect, in rude health. Mr Mercer counted and re-counted and stopped counting when Miss Boland appeared, flushed and panting, a porter bearing her bags. And then the coach came and then they were off.

The airport was full of gloomy British travellers from Gibral-tar, and they were being punished for that by being made to wait a long time for customs clearance. So, anyway, their courier whined to Mr Mercer, whom he seemed to know as an old pal in the game. And then Mr Mercer's lot marched across the tarmac and Miss Boland, God be praised, was a little sleepy after the wine. There was Miss Kelly waiting to welcome them all aboard again, but she had no welcome for Enderby. Mr Mercer came round with immigration forms, and they took off. It was a lovely golden Spanish afternoon.

Courteously, Enderby gave Miss Boland the window-seat he had had on the first leg of the journey. She slept. Enderby slept. Enderby was awakened. A uniformed man, pilot or co-pilot, was bending over him. He was a thick man, not old, jowled with good living, hangoverishly bloodshot. 'Is your name,' he said, his rather hairy hand on Enderby's shoulder, 'Enderby?'

Enderby could do no more than feebly nod. So, then, radio messages were crackling all over the world's air. Wapenshaw had talked, killing in childish spite his own handiwork.

'I'm the pilot of this aircraft. You'll appreciate I have certain responsibilities.' O'Shaughnessy then, but it was not an Irish voice. Enderby said, voicelessly:

'I'll come quietly. But I didn't do it. I just took his gun without thinking.'

'Well, perhaps it might be better if you *did* think a bit, man of your age. She's my responsibility as a member of my crew. I won't have passengers taking advantage.'

'Oh, that. You mean that.' Enderby's relief was vented in a cough of laughter.

'It may be just a bit of a holiday lark to you, but this is our work. This is what we do for a living. We take our work seriously, but you don't help much with that sort of liberty-taking.'

'I took no liberty,' Enderby said with heat. 'I made a mistake. I went to the wrong room. The room I meant to go to was the room of this lady here.' He jerked his eyes and thumb at Miss Boland and saw she was awake.

'Make a habit of going to ladies' rooms, do you? Well, if it was a mistake you took long enough apologising for your mistake. She said something about you spouting poetry about putting the devil in hell and whatnot. Now, I may be only an ignorant pilot, as you'd think me I suppose, but I've read that thing about putting the devil in hell. The Cameron it's called.' There were many passengers straining to listen, but the engines were loud. But Captain O'Shaughnessy was becoming loud too.

'The Dee Cameron,' said Enderby. 'Look, she's been telling you lies.'

'We've never had any complaints before about passengers' behaviour. I don't want to be nasty, but it's my duty as pilot of this aircraft to give you fair warning. Any more of this interfering with Miss Kelly and I must ask you to leave the tour. I'm sorry, but there it is.'

'It's a tissue of lies,' said flushed Enderby. 'I demand an apology.'

'There it is. I take full responsibility. So no more messing about. Is that clear?'

'I'll give you messing about,' cried Enderby. 'If I could get off now I would. But I'm getting off at Marrakesh anyway. It's an insult and an injustice, that's what it is.' Captain O'Shaughnessy jerked a salute at Miss Boland and went back to his engines. 'That's what one's up against all the time,' said Enderby to Miss Boland. 'It makes me sick.'

'All the time,' said Miss Boland. 'It makes you sick.'

'That's right. It was the wrong room, as I said.'

'As you said. And now would you kindly sit somewhere else? Otherwise I shall scream. I shall scream and scream and scream. I shall scream and scream and scream and scream and scream.'

'Don't do that,' said Enderby, very concerned. 'Darling,' he added.

'How dare you. *How dare you.*' She pressed the little bell-push up above.

'What did you do that for?' asked Enderby.

'If you won't go you must be made to go. I'm defiled just by sitting next to you.' Miss Kelly, wisely, did not come to the summons. Mr Mercer came, sad and troubled in his woolly cap. 'You,' said Miss Boland. 'Make this man sit somewhere else. I didn't come on this tour to be insulted.'

'Look,' said Mr Mercer to Enderby. 'I didn't say anything about that other business. It's the captain's responsibility, not mine. But this sort of thing is something that I'm not supposed to let happen. I made a big mistake having you on this, I did that. Now will you be told?'

'If you won't do something,' said Miss Boland, 'I'll scream.'

'Don't worry,' said Enderby. 'I'll go. I'll go into that lavatory there.' He got up and took his bag and beret from the rack. There were toys still in the bag. Enderby gravely dropped them into Miss Boland's lap—tortoise, beakless goose, flamenco doll, cymbal-pawed clockwork brown bear. She at once became thin and evil and ready to throw these things at Enderby, crying:

'He's hateful. No woman is safe with him. Throw him out.' Many of the passengers looked on with interest, though not well able to understand, or even hear, what was proceeding. Behind, the condom overweight man and his wife sat stiffly, still not on speaking terms. They refused to be interested in the Miss Boland-Enderby trouble, though it was just in front of them, since showing interest would have drawn them into a common area of attention, which would have been rather like, or indeed might have led to, being on speaking terms again. Enderby stood stony in the corridor, swaying with the plane in a slight air turbulence (the Mountains of the Moon perhaps, or something), waiting for instructions. To the condom man's wife, who was in the outer seat, Mr Mercer said:

'I wonder if you'd mind, Mrs er, changing places with this er. It's only for a short while, really. We're not all that far from Marrakesh now.'

'Men on holiday. Brings the beast out as you might call it. *I know*. I have no objection if she there hasn't.' And, getting up, she gave Enderby a murderous look which he considered unfair, since he had, after all, been the instrument of disclosure of her husband's beastliness, meaning the truth. As she sat down grunting next to Miss Boland, Enderby saw that she had an English newspaper folded to what looked like a simple crossword puzzle. She had a ballpoint, but she did not seem to have filled anything in yet. He leaned across her bosom to squint at the date and saw that, as far as he could judge, it was yesterday's. That was all right, then. Before that lot happened. And then he saw that it was the *Evening Standard* and it was not all right. He said to this woman, leaning over more deeply:

'Where did you get that? Give it me, quick. I must have it. Something I've got to see.'

'Right,' said Mr Mercer. 'Go and sit down quietly behind next to this lady's husband. We don't want any more trouble, do we now?'

'Cheek,' said the woman. 'It was left in the ladies at the airport by one of them Gibraltar people. I've as much right to it as what he has.'

'Oh, please go on now,' said Mr Mercer in distress. 'If you can't hold it you shouldn't take it. A lot of this foreign stuff's stronger than what many are used to.'

'*She* may be drunk,' said Enderby, shoulder-jerking towards Miss Boland, 'but I'm not, thank you very much. All I want to see is that paper. Something in it. A book review, very important. And then I'll go to that lavatory and sit in there quietly.' Seeing Miss Boland gasp in a lot of air to revile him further, he made a grab for the newspaper. The condom man's wife strengthened her hold.

'For God's sake,' said Mr Mercer, uncourierlike, 'let him see what he wants to see and then let's get him out of the way.'

'I want to find it myself,' said Enderby. 'I don't need her to show it me.'

'And who's *her* when she's at home?' said the woman. Miss Boland looked cunning and said:

'Let *me* see. There's something very fishy about all this. Running away from his wife, so he said.'

'Really? Told you, did he?'

'Let *me* see.' And Miss Boland, unhandily in the manner of all women with a newspaper, unfolded the *Evening Standard*, and the safe backwater of small ads and cartoons and crossword gave place, after a rustling tussle, to the horrid starkness of front page news. There it was, then. Enderby gulped it all in like ozone.

'Oh,' said the woman, 'I never seen that. Oh terrible, that, oh my word.'

'Yes,' said Miss Boland. 'Terrible.'

A screaming banner announced the shooting of Yod Crewsy. In hour of triumph. In Premier's presence. Waiter believed assailant. There was a large blurred photograph of Yod Crewsy with stretched gob or cakehole, but whether shot or just singing was not indicated. There was also a still photograph of the Prime Minister looking aghast, probably taken from stock. No picture, thank God, of waiter believed assailant. But Miss Boland was reading avidly on. Enderby had to now or never. He leaned over the condom man's wife and grabbed. The paper did not tear: he got the thing whole. He said:

'Very important review. Book page, book page,' rustling tremulously through. 'Oh, stupid of me. Wrong day for book page.' And then, as though an issue without the book page were an insult to the literate, he crumpled the *Evening Standard* into a ball.

'That's going too far,' said Mr Mercer.

'You mannerless thing,' said the woman. 'And that poor lad dead, too.'

'Not yet,' said Enderby unwisely. 'Not dead yet.'

'Hogg.' That was Miss Boland.

'Eh?' Enderby looked at her with bitter admiration. He had been right, then; he had known all along this would happen.

'Hogg. *Puerco*. That's why you're on the run.'

'She's mad,' Enderby told Mr Mercer. 'I'm going to the lavatory.' He began to unball the paper and smooth it out. She had

seen the name Hogg; the only thing to do now was to insist that
he was not Hogg. There was no point in hiding the fact that
Hogg was wanted to assist in a police enquiry. If, that is, one
were oneself not Hogg. And one was not, as one's passport
clearly showed. Enderby nearly drew out his passport, but that
would look too suspiciously eager to prove that he was not
Hogg. A lot of people were not Hogg, and they did not have to
keep presenting their passports to prove it.

'The police,' said Miss Boland. 'Send a radio message to the
airport. He did it. That's why he's run away.'

'I don't have to put up with all this, do I?' said Enderby with
a fine show of weariness.

'He said all the time that he hated pop-singers.'

'That's not true,' said Enderby. 'All I said was that you
mustn't necessarily regard me as an enemy of pop-culture.'

'Jealousy,' said Miss Boland. 'A bad poet jealous of a good
one. And what was that you said just then about a gun? I'm
quite sure I didn't dream it.' She seemed very calm now,
glinting, though breathing heavily.

'I'll give you bad poet,' said Enderby, preparing to shout. 'If
there's any good in that book of his, it's because it's been
pinched from me. That bitch. Plagiarism. I hope he dies, because he deserves to die.'

'Look,' said Mr Mercer, 'we don't want any trouble, right?
This is supposed to be for pleasure, this cruise is. Will you both
stop shouting the odds? If there's anything to be seen to I'll see
to it, right?'

'If you don't,' said Miss Boland, 'I will. I will in any case. He
killed him, no doubt about it. He's as good as admitted it.'

'Who's a bitch?' said the condom wife, belatedly. 'Who was
he saying was a bitch? Because if he was meaning me—'

'I'm going to the lavatory,' said Enderby. Mr Mercer did not
attempt to stop him; indeed, he followed him. The crumpled
Evening Standard had somehow reached Miss Kelly. She was
spelling all that front page out, reserving her reaction till she
had taken everything in. Just by the lavatory door Mr Mercer
said:

'What's going on with her down there? Is she potty or what?'

'A matter of sex,' Enderby said. 'I spurned her advances. I

don't think it's decent the way she carries on, and me with my mother dying in Marrakesh.'

'Look,' said Mr Mercer without sympathy. 'You shouldn't rightly be on this plane at all, as you well know, and I'm bloody sorry I let you come on it. It was a bit of a fiddle, and I think I've learned my lesson now about that sort of thing. Now she's going on about you being a dangerous criminal, which sounds to me like a load of balls. You've not been killing anybody, have you?'

'I have enough on my hands,' said Enderby gravely, 'with a dying mother.'

'Right then. I'll get her calmed down and I'll tell her that I'm doing whatever has to be done. The police and that. The customers have got to be satisfied, that's laid down in the rules. Now it won't be long to Marrakesh now, so I'll tell you what I'll do with you. You nip off before everybody else, see, because I'll let you.'

'Thanks very much,' said Enderby.

'I'll keep them all back till you have time to get away. I don't want her on the job again, howling murder and upsetting the other mugs,' said Mr Mercer frankly. 'So you'll find three taxis laid on specially for the tour. They take one lot to the Hotel Maroc and then keep coming back for the rest. Well, you get into one and get the driver to drop you wherever it is you want to be dropped and then send him back to the airport, right? How far is it you have to go?'

'Near that place where Winston Churchill used to stay,' said Enderby with sudden inspiration.

'Not too far then, that isn't. And then,' said Mr Mercer, 'that'll be the end as far as you and me and everybody else is concerned. Got that?'

'That suits me well enough,' said Enderby.

'You'd better get in there, then. Look, she looks like getting up to start asking for immediate action. Summary execution and that. You thrown out into the bleeding slipstream. You sure you done nothing wrong?'

'Me,' said Enderby, 'with a dying mother?'

'You don't look the type, anyway. Get in there. If anybody else wants to go I'll have to tell them to let it bake till we get to

Marrakesh. I wish,' said Mr Mercer with large sincerity, 'I'd never bloody well set eyes on you.' Enderby bowed his head. 'Mysterious fascination for women, eh? Now get yourself locked in there.'

It was better in the lavatory, an interim of most delectable peace and quiet. All Enderby could hear was the engines except for a brief phase of shock and howling from Miss Kelly. She was, it seemed, sorry that Yod Crewsy had been shot. Then she appeared to have got over it.

Three

Mint, mint, mint. It was too easy to think that, though the immigration official waved him through when he cried: '*Ma mère est mortellement malade,*' though the leading taxi opened up smartly for him when he mentioned *Monsieur Mercer,* he was destined for the butcher's block. The sun was about half way down the sky, but it was still up to Regulo Mark 4 and there was all this mint. The memory fumed in of his once trying out a small leg of fatty New Zealand in Mrs Meldrum's gas oven. It had emerged not well-cooked, and he had made a stew out of it. You could not really go wrong with a stew. There had been a lot of grease to skim off, though. The driver, a Moor as Enderby took him to be, was stewy in the armpits—no, more like a tin of Scotch Broth. But he was fumigating himself and his cab with a home-rolled cigarette that reeked of decent herbs, though possibly hallucinogenic. He also rolled his eyes. Soon, Enderby considered, the time must come for jettisoning his Enderby passport. Miss Boland would soon be uncovering aliases to the police. He could not be Hogg, he could not be Enderby. The nasty world outside had succeeded in taking pretty well everything away from him. Except his talent, except that.

A well-made road with trees, probably bougainvillea and eucalyptus and things. And plenty of mint. Also people in turbans, caftans, nightgowns with stripes, and what-you-call-them djebalas. The driver drove with the automatism of a pony pulling a trap, though much faster, his being not to reason why Enderby had to reach the tour hotel before everyone else. It was time to tell him some other place to go. Enderby said:

'*Je veux aller à Tanger.*'

'*Demain?*'

'*Maintenant.*'

'*Impossible.*'

'*Regardez,*' Enderby said, 'I'm not going to that bloody hotel. *Une femme. Une question d'une femme. Il faut que j'évite une certaine femme.*'

With care the driver steered his cab round the next corner and stopped by the kerb. His hand-brake ground painfully. '*Une femme?*' It was a pleasant little residential avenue full of mint. But down it a bare-legged man in Sancho Panza hat and loose brown clouts urged a laden donkey. '*Tu veux une femme?*'

'Just the opposite,' said Enderby, frowning at the familiarity. '*J'essaie à éviter une femme, comme j'ai déjà dit.*'

'*Tu veux garçon?*'

'Let's get this straight,' cried Enderby. 'I want to get away. *Comment puis-je* get to bloody Tangier?'

The driver thought about that. '*Avion parti,*' he said. '*Chemin de fer—*' He shrugged. Then he said: 'You got money, Charlie?'

'I thought it would come to that,' said Enderby. He brought out his small bundle of old international tips. What was the currency here? There were a couple of notes with a bland capped and robed ruler on them. *Banque du Maroc* and a lot of Arabic. What were these? Dirhams. He had, it seemed, ten dirhams. He didn't know how much they were worth. Still, resourceful Enderby. Ready cash for all emergencies of travel. The driver was quick to grab the ten dirhams. He pushed them, as if he were a woman, into his unbuttoned hair-whorled brown breast. Then he cheerfully started up his cab again. 'Where are we going?' Enderby wanted to know. The driver didn't answer; he just drove.

Enderby was past being uneasy, though. After all, what was he trying to do except borrow time against the inevitable? If Yod Crewsy died, well then, he, his supposed murderer, could only be put in jail for a long period, the death penalty having kindly been abolished. And in jail poetry could be written. There would be ghastly stews, but he knew all about those. Great things had been written in jail—*Pilgrim's Progress, De Profundis,* even *Don*

Quixote. Nothing to worry about there. Slops out. Here's your skilly, you horrible murderer, you. Snout-barons. What you in for, matey? I murdered a practitioner of foul and immoral art. You done a good job, then, you did. But, sheep for a lamb (all this mint, mint everywhere), he had things to do first. They had to catch him first, and it was up to him, rules of the game, to make things difficult. They drove down a great smooth highway, then turned right. It was all French colonialism, with decent official buildings, green lawns, palms. Little Moroccan girls were coming out of school, gaily shrieking, and some were sped off home to their mint tea, as Enderby supposed, in haughty squat automobiles. But soon the road changed its character. Instead of shooting cleanly along an artery, the cab began to engage a capillary that was pure, and dirty, Moorish.

'Where are we going?' asked Enderby again.

'*Djemaa el Fna,*' said the driver. This meant nothing to Enderby. They were now honking among fruit-barrows, donkey-whippers, brown and black vociferators in pointed hoods and barmcake turbans and even little woolly caps like Mr Mercer's. The faecal-coloured houses and windowless shops (loaves, strangled fowls, beads, eggplants) bowed in towards each other at the top. Somebody wailed about Allah in the near distance. It was what was known as very picturesque, all laid on for Winston Churchill as amateur painter. Then, shouted at through gold or no teeth, the cab-flanks resonantly fisted, they drove into a great square which was full of robed people and very loud. There seemed to be native shows going on: Enderby glimpsed a fire-swallower and a man who let snakes crawl all over his person. Then, above the heads of the crowd, a small black boy went up into the air, wiggled his fingers from his ears, then sailed down again. Enderby did not really like any of this. The driver stopped and, with a vulgar thumb, pointed to where Enderby should go. It seemed to be a soft-drink stall, one of many set all about the square. He shooed Enderby out. Enderby got out, bag on arm, groaning. The driver did an urgent and insolent turn, butting bare shins with deformed fenders and, cursed at by some but greeted toothily and, Enderby presumed, with ribaldry by others, probed the crammed barefoot alley whence he had come. He honked slowly among thudded drums and weak pipe-skirls, fowl-squawks and ass-brays, then was smothered by nightshirts and most animated robes, pushing his way back to a world where an airport, complete with waiting Miss Boland, might be possible. Enderby encountered blind men howling for baksheesh. He brutally ignored them and made his shoes pick their way among great splay brown feet towards this soft-drink stall that had been thumbed at him. He would have a soft drink, anyway. No harm in that. And that climbed hill of an act would show the next one. But just by the stall, newly disclosed by a small mob that came away chewing things, probably nasty, he saw a patriarch tending a small fire. A little boy, his head shaven as for ringworm, was threading rubbery gobs of what Enderby took to be goat meat on to skewers. Enderby nodded in awed satisfaction. His imagination had not failed him, then. It was time to get rid of that passport.

He stood by the fire, the passport in his hands open, mumbling to himself the liturgy of its shards of autobiography. There were still so many blank pages of travelling Enderby to be filled, and they would not now be filled. He must appear, he thought, like some Zoroastrian missionary to these who skirted him warily in robes and yashmaks: murmuring a late afternoon office to the fire. And then, as he prepared to drop the well-bound document in, the act was, as by an Oriental miracle, arrested. A bony tanned wrist gripped his chubbier whiter one, pulled, saved. Enderby looked from wrist to shoulder, meekly surprised. Then up to face above that. A white man, though brown. Lined, crafty, the eyes blue but punished. The straight hair as though bleached.

'I was,' said Enderby with care, 'just getting rid of it. No further use, if you catch my meaning.'

'You cracked? You skirted? You got the big drop on? Grandmother of Jesus, I never seen.' The man was not old. His accent and vernacular were hard to place. It was a sort of British colonial English. One hand still gripped Enderby's wrist; the other hand snatched the passport. The man then let go of Enderby and began to pant over the passport as if it were a small erotic book. 'Holy consecrated grandad of Christ Jesus Amen,' he said. 'And this is you too on it and the whole thing donk and not one little bit gritty. The genuine, and you ready to ash it up. If you don't want it, others as do. A right donk passy. Feel his uncle, O bastard daughters of Jerusalem.'

Enderby almost smiled, then felt cunning creeping along his arteries. 'I tried to sell it,' he said. 'But I could find no buyers. All I wanted was a trip to Tangier. No money, you see. Or not very much.'

'You better come over,' said the man. 'Ariff's got a swizer of that-there at the back.' And he led Enderby across to the very soft-drink stall that had been thumbed to him by that driver.

'Funny,' Enderby said. 'This man who brought me wanted me to wait there or something. I wondered what for.'

'Who? One of the cab-nogs? Ahmed, was it?'

'Don't know his name,' said Enderby. 'But I told him I had to get away.'

'You on the out, then? How did he know it was tonight? Some shitsack's been on the jabber.' He mumbled strange oaths to himself as he led Enderby over. The drink-stall was a square wooden structure covered in striped canvas. There was a counter with cloudy glasses and bottles of highly coloured liquids. There were oil-lamps, blind at the moment, since the sun had not yet gone down. A few Moors or Berbers or something were downing some sticky yellow horror. Behind the counter stood a lithe brown man in an undervest, snakes of veins embossed on his arms. Crinkled hair rayed out, as in shock, all over his bullet-head. 'Right,' said this British colonial man, 'swing us two bulgies of arry-arry.'

'Where do you come from?' asked Enderby. 'I can't quite place the accent. No offence,' he added hurriedly.

'None took. Name of Easy Walker. Call me Easy. Your name I know but I won't blart it. Never know who's flapping. Well now, you'll have heard of West Rothgar in New Sunderland. Fifty or so miles from the capital, boojie little rathole. Had to blow, see the great wide open. And that. And other things.' As if to symbolise the other things, he stretched his left mouth-corner, as also the left tendon of his neck, and held the pose tremulously. This, Enderby seemed to remember, was known as the ki-yike. Easy Walker then scratched his right ear with Enderby's passport and said: 'You sound to me like from back.' Enderby stared. Easy Walker snarled a full set in impatience. 'Great

Dirty Mum,' he explained. 'How shall we extol thee?'

'I beg your pardon?'

'Who were born of thee,' danced Easy Walker. 'Here it is, then. Down the upbum or,' he said, in a finicking uncolonial accent, 'the superior arsehole.' There were on the counter two tumblers of what looked like oily water. Easy Walker seemed to wrap his lips round the glass-rim and, with a finger-thud on the glass-bottom, drive the substance down as though it were corned beef hard to prise from its container. He smacked in loving relish. Enderby tasted what tasted of aniseed, lubricator, meths and the medicinal root his stepmother had called ikey-pikey. 'Similar,' Easy Walker told the barman. 'And now,' to Enderby, 'what's on? Why you on the out, brad?'

'You can't really say "similar" if it's the same again you want. "Similar" means something different. Oh, as for that,' Enderby recalled himself from pedantry that reminded him poignantly of those good seaside days among the decrepit, 'it's partly a matter of a woman.'

'Ark.' Easy Walker was not impressed.

'And,' Enderby bid further, 'the police are after me for suspected murder of a pop-star.'

'You do it?'

'Well,' said Enderby, 'I had the means and the motive. But I want to get to Tangier to see off an old enemy. Time is of the essence.'

This seemed reasonable to Easy Walker. He said: 'See that. Right right. Gobblers watching at the airport and on the shemmy. Clever bastard that cab-nog, then. Ahmed, must have been. Well,' he said, fanning Enderby with Enderby's passport, 'give me this and you can come on the lemon-pip by the long road. Fix you up in Tangey up the hill. No questions, get it? The gobblers leave it strictly on the old antonio. Wash me ends, though. Right up to you, brad. Never clapped mincers on you, get it?'

'Oh, yes,' Enderby said. 'Thank you very much. But,' he added, 'what are you on then, eh?'

'Well,' said Easy Walker, rolling his refilled tumbler. 'It's mostly Yank camps, junkies, had-no-lucks. See what I mean?'

'American troops in Morocco?' Enderby asked.

'Riddled,' said Easy Walker. 'All off the main, though. Forts,

you could call them. Very hush. Moscow gold in Nigeria I mean
Algeria. PX stuff—fridges mainly—for Casablanca and Tangey.
That's why I've got this three-ton.'

'A lorry? Where?'

'Up the road. Never you mind.'

'But,' said Enderby with care, 'what are you doing here,
then?'

'Well, that's the real soft centre,' Easy Walker said. 'See these
niggers here? Not the Marockers, more brown they are than the
others, the others being from more like *real* blackland.'

'The heart of darkness,' said Enderby.

'Call it what you like, brad. Berbers or Barbars. Barbar black
shit, but no offence is what I tell them. They bring the stuff up
with them for this here racketytoo.'

'What stuff? What is all this, anyway?'

'Everything,' said Easy Walker, with sudden lucidity, 'the
heart of darkness could desire. Tales of Ali Baba and Sinbad the
whatnot, and snake-charmers and all. Suffering arsehole of J.
Collins, the sprids they get up to in this lot. Hear them drums?'

'Go on,' said Enderby.

Easy Walker did a mime of sucking in dangerous smoke and
then staggered against the flimsy counter. The barman was light-
ing the lamps. 'Pounds and pounds of it, brad. I'm like telling
you this because you won't gob. Daren't, more like, in your state
of you-know-what. They grind up the seeds and nuts and it
burns cold, real cold, like sucking ice-lollies. The Yank junks go
bonko for it.'

'Drug addicts,' questioned Enderby, 'in army camps?'

'Drag too,' said Easy Walker calmly. 'Human like you and I,
aren't they? Loving Aunt Flo of our bleeding Saviour, ain't you
seen the world? What you on normal, brad? What you do?'

'I,' said Enderby, 'am a poet. I am Enderby the poet.'

'Poetry. You know the poetry of Arthur Sugden, called Ricker
Sugden because he played on the old rickers?'

'I don't think so,' said Enderby.

'I know him all off. You can have the whole sewn-up boogong
tonight on the road.'

'Thank you very much,' Enderby said. 'What time do we
start?'

'Moon-up. Crounch first. You crounch with me. Little stoshny I got up this street of a thousand arseholes. Up above Hassan the hundred delights. Know what those are? Glycerine like toffees with popseeds, stickjaw that'll stick to your jaw, shishcakes and marhum. And I mean a thousand arseholes. Not my creed. Yours?'

'I don't like anything any more,' Enderby said. 'I just want to get on with the job.'

'Right, too. Ah, here comes the old jalooty.' A sly black man came in. He grinned first then peered behind as though he feared he was being followed. He had a woolly cap on, a knee-length clout done up like a diaper, a stiff embroidered coat with food stains on it. He carried a grey darned gunnysack. Easy Walker tucked away Enderby's passport in the breast-pocket of his shirt, then from the back-pocket of his long but creaseless canvas trousers he pulled out a wallet. 'This,' he told Enderby, 'is as it might be like my agent. Abu.' The black man responded to his name with a kind of salivation. 'Mazooma for pozzy, as my dad used to say. Died at Gallipoli, poor old reticule. It's my Aunt Polly as told me he used to say that. Never clapped mincers on him myself. Abu grabs what per cent he has a fish-hook on. Leave it to him.' To this Abu Easy Walker told out what appeared to Enderby to be no more than fifty dirhams. Then he took the gunnysack and shushed Abu off like a fly. 'Now then,' he said, his hand on Enderby's arm, leading him out to the flared and oil-lamped sinister gaiety of the evening, 'time for the old couscous. You like couscous?'

'Never had it,' said Enderby.

'The best one of Ricker Sugden's,' said Easy Walker, as they walked among baskets and moonfruit in the reek of lights, 'is "The Song of the Dunnygasper." You not know that one, brad?'

'What,' asked Enderby, 'is a dunnygasper?' A youngish wom-an raised her yashmak and spat a fair gob among chicken-innards. Two children, one with no left leg, punched each other bitterly.

'A dunnygasper is a bert that cleans out a dunny. Now, the pongalorum of a dunny is that bad that you'd lay out a yard in full view if you drew it in in the way of normality. So he has to like under water hold his zook shut then surface for a gasp. You see that then?' An old man with a bashed-in turban tottered by,

crying some prayer to the enskied archangels of Islam. Easy
Walker started to recite:

> 'Gasping in the dunny in the dead of dark,
>   I dream of my boola-bush, sunning in the south,
> And the scriking of the ballbird and Mitcham's lark,
>   And bags of the sugarwasp, sweet in my mouth.'

'That's not bad,' said Enderby. 'Not much meaning, though.'
Meaning? Too much meaning in your poetry, Enderby. Arch-
devil of the maceration of good art for pop-art. Kill, kill, kill. He
could be calm at soul, whatever justice said.

> 'For here in the city is the dalth of coves,
>   Their stuff and their slart and the fell of sin,
> The beerlout's spew where the nightmort roves
>   And the festered craw of the filth within.'

A moustached man, the veins of his head visible under a dark
nap, called hoarsely at Enderby and, with flapping hands,
showed small boys in little shirts lined up behind the lamp in his
shop-front. A woman squatted on a step and scooped with a
wooden spatula the scum from a seething pot on a pungent
wood-fire.

'That drink,' belched Enderby, 'whatever it was, was not a
good idea.'

'Feel like a sack of tabbies when you've gooled up a pompey
of couscous.'

Graaarch, went Enderby. Perfwhitt.

> 'God's own grass for this porrow in my pail,
>   Surrawa's lake for this puke and niff,
> Prettytit's chirp for the plonky's nipper's wail,
>   And the rawgreen growler under Bellamy's Cliff.'

'Rawcliffe,' growled green Enderby. 'It won't (errrrgh) be
long now.'

Easy Walker stopped in his tracks. A beggar clawed at him
and he cleaned the beggar off his shirt like tobacco ash. 'You say
Rawcliffe, brad? Rawcliffe the jarvey you bid to chop?'

'Plagiarist, traitor (orrrph), enemy.'

'Runs a little beacho. Called the Acantilado something-or-the-next-thing. Not far from the Rif. Not there now, though. Very crookidy. Quacks pawing him all over on the Rock.'

'In Gibraltar? Rawcliffe? Ill?'

'Crookidy dook. He'll be back, though. Says if he's going to snuff he'll snuff in his own dung.'

'Rawcliffe,' said Enderby, 'is (orrrfff) for me.'

'We're there,' said Easy Walker. 'Up that rickety ladder. Niff that juicy couscous. Yummiyum. Then we hit it. Moon's up, shufti.' Enderby saw it with bitterness. Miss Boland seemed to rage down from it.

'This jarvey Rawcliffe,' said Easy Walker, leading the way up the ladder, 'is some kind of a big jarvey. Big in films and that. You sure you know what you're on, brad?'

'I (arrrrp) know,' said Enderby, following him up. A fresh beggar, wall-eyed, embraced his left leg passionately, shrieking for alms. Enderby kicked him off.

II

1

One

ALI FATHI sat on the other bed and pared his foot-soles with a table-knife honed to lethal sharpness on the window-sill. He was on the run from Alexandria, which he called Iskindiriyya, and was scornful of the Moors, whose language he considered debased. He himself spoke a sort of radio announcer's Arabic, full of assertive fishbone-in-the-throat noises and glottal checks that sounded like a disease. He was very thin, seemed to grow more and more teeth as time went on, and was always talking about food. '*Beed madruub*,' he said to Enderby now. He had a passion for eggs. '*Beeda masluugha*.' Enderby said, from his own bed:

'*Mumtaaz*.' He was learning, though not very quickly. It was hardly worth while to learn anything new. Soon, he saw, he must give up giving money to Wahab to buy the English newspapers that were sold on the Boulevard Pasteur. They were a terrible price, and money was fast running out. When the hell was Rawcliffe going to come back to be killed? He read once more the latest Yod Crewsy news. It could not be long now, they reckoned. Yod Crewsy was in a coma. Day and night vigils of

weeping fans outside the hospital. Stones hurled at windows of
No. 10 Downing Street. Probability of National Day of Prayer.
Mass of Intercession at Westminster Cathedral. In Trafalgar
Square protest songs, some of them concerned with the Vietnam
war. Attempted suttee of desperate girls in a Comprehensive
School.

'*Khanziir.*' That was not right, Ali Fathi being a Muslim, but
Enderby himself would not have minded a nice plate of crisply
grilled ham. His diet, and that of Ali Fathi and the other two
men, Wahab and Souris, was very monotonous: soup of kitchen
scraps and rice, boiled up by fat Napo in the snack-bar below,
the odd platter of fried sardines, bread of the day before yesterday. Enderby was now sorry that he had exchanged his passport
for a mere jolting trip from Marrakesh to Tangier. He had dis-
covered that British passports fetched a very high price on the
international market. Why, this Ali Fathi here had looked at Enderby as if he were mad when he had been told, in French,
what small and uncomfortable (as well as to him hazardous)
service in lieu of money Enderby had been willing to take in exchange for a valuable document. If he, Ali Fathi, had it he
would not be here now. He would be in Marseilles, pretending
to be an Arabic-speaking Englishman.

'*Beed maghli.*' He was back on eggs again. Well, that valuable document, with its old identity razor-bladed and bleached
out and new substituted, was now at its charitable work in the
world of crime and shadiness. It was saving somebody from
what was called justice. It could not, nor could its former guardian (Her Majesty's Government being the avowed owner,
though it had not paid for it) ask better than that. Enderby
nodded several times. Encouraged, Ali Fathi said:

'*Bataatis mahammara.*' That meant, Enderby knew now, po-
tato crisps. An inept term, soggy-sounding. It had been, Enderby
admitted to himself, a boring trip on the move under the moon
(courtesy of Miss treacherous bloody Boland), with Easy
Walker reciting the collected works of Arthur Sugden, called
Ricker Sugden because he had used, when composing his verses,
to clash out the rhythm with the castanetting bones once a per-
cussive staple of nigger, christy rather, minstral shows. Easy
Walker had given Enderby not only a reprise of 'The Song of

the Dunnygasper' but also 'The Ballad of Red Mick the Pran-
cerprigger,' 'The Shotgun Wedding of Tom Dodge,' 'Willie
Maugham's Visit to Port Butters,' 'My Pipe and Snout and
Teasycan,' and other specimens of the demotic literature of an
apparently vigorous but certainly obscure British settlement.
'*Kurumba.*' Some vegetable or other, that. Cabbage, probably. And then these American camps, off the main north-south
motor route, with torches flashing through the Moorish dark, a
rustling in the shadows and whispers as of love (money and
goods changing hands), the loading—Enderby cajoled to help
—of refrigerators, huge cans of butter, nitrited meatloaf, even
military uniforms, all on to Easy Walker's truck. And then more
of Ricker Sugden—'The Ditty of the Merry Poddyman,' 'Wal-
lop for Me Tomorrow Boys,' 'Ma Willis's Knocking Shop
(Knock Twice and Wink for Alice)'—till the next call and, finally, what Easy Walker knew as Dear Old Tangey. Well, Easy
Walker had at least found him what seemed a safe enough re-
treat off the Rue El Greco (many of the streets here were named
for the great dead, as though Tangier were a figure of heaven)
—no passports needed, no questions asked of guests or tolerated
of casual visitors to bar below or brothel above, but, on the
other hand, too much cash demanded in advance, too little to
eat, the bedclothes never changed, not enough beds.

'*Shurbit tamaatim,*' watered Ali Fathi, still slicing thin shives,
as of restaurant smoked salmon, from a foot-sole. At once, as
though he had spoken of the source of gingili or benne oil, the
door-handle began to turn. He poised that knife at the ready.
The door opened and Wahab came in. Smiling teeth popped and
rattled as the two men embraced, full of loud throaty crooning
greeting, yum yum yum and the voiced clearing of phlegm from
pharyngeal tracts. Enderby looked with distaste on this, not
caring much for sex of any kind these days really, for himself or
for anybody else. Ali Fathi hugged his friend, knife still clutched
in a hand that knuckled his friend's vertebrae, all his teeth dis-
played in glee to Enderby. Enderby said coldly:

'*Le patron de l'Acantilado Verde, est-il revenu?*'

'*Pas encore,*' said Wahab's back. Wahab was a Moor, hence
his mind was despised by Ali Fathi, but his body was apparently
loved. He had fled from trouble in Tetuan and was lying low till

things cooled. He spent much of the day trying to steal things. Now, as evening prepared to thud in, tally-hoed on by the punctual muezzin, he grinningly pushed Ali Fathi temporarily away, then took off his long striped nightshirt with hood attached. He was dressed underneath in blue jeans and khaki (probably American army) shirt. He had a marsupial bag knotted round his waist, and from this he produced his spoils, neither choice nor lavish, holding them up for Ali Fathi to admire. He was not a very good thief; it was evident that he was not on the run for thievery; perhaps he had merely spat on the King's picture. On the bed he placed, with a smile that was meant to be modest, a couple of gritty cakes of the kind dumped with the coffee on outside café tables, also a single Seville. Then he produced a small round tin labelled in English. Enderby could read that it was tan boot-polish, but Ali Fathi seized it with a kind of gastronome's croon, probably believing it to be a rare (hence the exiguity of the tinned portion) pâté.

'*Pour les bottines,*' said Enderby helpfully. '*Ou pour les souliers. Pas pour manger, vous comprenez.*' Soon Ali Fathi and Wahab saw that this was so, and then they started a kind of married wrangle. Enderby sighed. He hated these public homosexual carryings-on. Shortly Ali Fathi would have Wahab down on the bed, and they would perhaps indulge in the erotic refinement they called *soixante-neuf*, which reminded Enderby of the Pisces sign on newspaper horoscope pages. Or else there would be plain howling sodomy. And to them Enderby was only a piece of insentient furniture—the only piece indeed, save for the two beds, in the whole room. Souris, the other man, would not come in till very much later, often when Ali Fathi and Wahab were already in bed, and then what took place took place, mercifully, in the dark. The bed was not big enough for three of them, so there was a lot of crying and writhing on the floor and, if a synchronised triple crisis was reached, which happened occasionally, the window rattled and the beds, one of them with tired but sleep-deprived Enderby in it, shook from the legs up. Souris was not a murine man. He was very gross and he sweated what looked like crude oil. He had hurt somebody very badly on the outskirts of Casablanca—a totally unwilled act, he swore frequently, an ineluctable side-issue of a process designed mainly for pleasure. When the three of them had completed their Laocoon performance, they would sometimes (Enderby had seen this in the moonlight, Miss Boland also grimly seeming to look down from the moon) shake hands, though not heartily: it was like the end of a round in a wrestling bout, which in a sense it was, though three were involved and there was no purse. Once or twice, Souris had then tried to get into bed with Enderby, but Enderby would have none of that. So Wahab, the youngest, was often made to sleep in his robe on the floor, as though it were the desert. He would sometimes cry out in his uneasy sleep, seeming to roar like a camel. This was no life for anyone.

'*Moi*,' said Enderby, pocketing the tan boot-polish, '*j'essayerai à le vendre ou, au moins, à l'échanger pour quelquechose de comestible.*'

'*Tu sors?*' said Ali Fathi, who already had Wahab round the neck.

Enderby did not like this familiarity. He nodded frowning. Yes, he was going out. The time had come to find out what was going on with respect to himself as regards the impending death of Yod Crewsy. For nobody back there in Scotland Yard seemed to be doing anything. There was the usual odd statement about investigations still proceeding, but most of the newspaper concentration now seemed to be on Yod Crewsy as a dying god, not one of the daily victims of common murderous assault. The butcher had become somehow shadowy and august, a predestined and impersonal agent of the dark forces, proud and silent in a Frazerian grove. But the police back there in England were brought up on Moriarty, not Frazer, and Enderby felt sure they were slyly about something. They might be grilling Jed Foot in under-river cellars. Or they might be here, raincoated, holding on to their hats in the Tangerine sea-wind. It was time to go to this Fat White Doggy Wog Place and see if John the Spaniard had sent a letter to Enderby through his brother Billy Gomez, if Enderby had remembered the name right.

There were two other bedrooms on this floor, and these comprised the brothel part of the establishment, though, on busy nights, cubicles in the bar below were curtained off for the more urgent and perfunctory clients, and fat Napo's kitchen had once or twice been used, since it had a stout table for table-corner specialists. The room that Enderby shared with Ali Fathi, Wahab, and Souris had not, so far as Enderby knew, ever been desecrated by acts of a heterosexual nature, but it was understood that, normally in the late morning, an occasional sharp act of commercial pederasty might be consummated there, Enderby and Ali Fathi (who were not supposed to leave the premises, Napo apparently not trusting them not to be caught) going into the backyard with the scrawny hens, there to smoke a soothing marijuana fag or two, given to them by Napo as a little reward for temporarily and gratuitously leasing lodgings for which they had paid in advance.

Out now on the landing, which had a naked light-bulb and a portrait of the King of Morocco, Enderby saw disgustedly that one of these other bedrooms had its door open. A couple of laughing male friends, both of a Mediterranean complexion, were preparing to engage houris—whose giggles agitated their yashmaks—on adjacent beds. Enderby angrily slammed their door on them, then went down the carpetless stair grumbling to himself. A scratchy record of popular Egyptian music was playing in the bar—the same theme over and over again in unison on a large and wasted orchestra. Peering through a hole in the worn curtain of dirty Muslim pink, Enderby saw Napo behind his counter. A man grosser than Souris, he had modelled himself on the Winston Churchill he had once, he alleged, seen painting in Marrakesh, but the baby-scowl sat obscenely on a face bred by centuries of Maghreb dishonesty. He was now arguing about the magical properties of certain numbers with a customer Enderby could not see: something to do with a lottery ticket.

Enderby went loudly to the lavatory by the kitchen, then tiptoed through the kitchen to the back door. It was a blue evening but rather gusty. In the little yard the hens had gone to roost in the branches of a stunted tree that Enderby could not identify. They laid on a quiet crooning protest chorus, all for Enderby, and their feathers ruffled minimally in the wind. Enderby frowned up at the moon, then climbed to the top of the low wall by means of an empty Coca-Cola crate and a couple of broken-brick toeholds. He dropped easily, though panting, over the other side. It was an alley he was in now, and this led to a street. The street went downhill and led to other streets. If you kept going down all the time you eventually came to the Avenue d'Espagne, which looked at the plage. That dog place was down there, not far from the Hotel Rif.

It was very steep and not very well lighted. Enderby teetered past a crumbling theatre called the Miguel de Cervantes then, finding that the next turning seemed to take him some way up-hill again, tried a dark and leafy passage which went unequiv-ocally down. Here a little Moorish girl cried when she saw him, and a number of house-dogs started to bark. But he went gamely on, supporting himself by grasping at broken fences. Precipitous: that was the word. At last he emerged from the barking dark, finding himself on a street where a knot of Moorish boys in smart suits called to him:

'You want boy, Charlie?'

'You very hot want nice beer.'

'For cough,' said Enderby, in no mood for foreign nonsense, and a boy riposted with:

'You fuck off too, English fuckpig.' Enderby didn't like that. He knew that this place had once belonged to the English, part of Charles II's Portuguese queen's dowry. It was not right that he should be addressed like that. But another boy cried:

'You fucking German. Kaput heilhitler.' And another:

'Fucking Yankee motherfucker. You stick chewing-gum up fucking ass.' That showed a certain ingenuity of invective. They were very rude boys, but their apparently indifferent despication of foreigners was perhaps a healthy sign, stirring in sympathy a limp G-string in his own nature. He nodded at them and, more kindly, said once more:

'For cough.' They seemed to recognise his change of tone, for they merely pronged two fingers each in his direction, one or two of them emitting a lip-fart. Then they started to playfight, yelping, among themselves. Enderby continued his descent, com-ing soon to a hotel-and-bar on his left called *Al-Djenina*. The forecourt had bird cages in it, the birds all tucked up for the night, and Enderby could distinctly see, through the long bar-window, middle-aged men drunk and embracing each other. Those would, he thought, be expatriate writers. He was, of course, one of those himself now, but he was indifferent to the duties and pleasures of sodality. He was on his own, waiting. He

had written, though. He was working on things. The wind from
the sea upheld him as he tottered to level ground. Here it was
then: the Avenue d'Espagne, as they called it.

He turned left. A fezzed man outside a shop hailed him, showing rugs and saddles and firearms. Enderby gravely shook his
head, saying truthfully: *'No tengo bastante dinero, hombre.'* He
was becoming quite the linguist. A gormless-looking boy, thin
and exhibiting diastemata in the shop-front lights, offered him
English newspapers. This was different. Enderby drew out dirhams. He tried to control his heavy breathing as he looked for
news. The wind breathed more heavily, seeming to leap on the
paper from all four quarters, as though it was all the news Enderby could possibly want. Enderby took his paper into the
doorway of the rug-and-saddle shop. The fezzed man said:
'You man like good gun. I see.' That was not a discreet thing
to say, and Enderby looked sharply at him. 'Bang bang bang,'
added the man, indicating his rusty Rif arsenal of Crimean rifles
and stage-highwayman pistols. Enderby read. *All Hope Abandoned,* a headline said Dantesquely. The end was very near
now, a few days off at most. He was in a coma. Where the hell
then, Enderby wondered, had that bullet struck him? Police
would be treating case as murder, the paper said. Redoubling
efforts, acting on valuable information, Interpol on job, arrest
expected very soon. The wind pushed, with a sudden whoosh,
those words into Enderby's open mouth. Enderby pushed back
and then looked at the date of the newspaper. Yesterday's. He
might be dead already, his gob, money-coining but not golden,
shut for ever. The shopkeeper now showed a real golden mouth,
like Spanish John's (and, there again, how far was *he* to be
trusted?), as he softly placed, on the newsprint Enderby held
tautly at chin-level like a communion cloth, a specimen pistol for
his inspection and admiration. Enderby started and let it drop in
the doorway. One of its fittings clattered free and the shopman
got ready to revile Enderby. *'No quiero,'* Enderby said. 'I said
that before, bloody fool as you are.' And then he entered the
wind, looking troubled at flickering lights on headlands. He
didn't need his newspaper any more, so he threw it into the
wind's bosom. The wind, like a woman, was clumsy with it.

The sea. *La belle mer.* Why had he never realised that that was the same as *la belle-mère*, which—with some kind of French irony—had been forced into meaning 'stepmother'? Well, he had come back to her for a brief time, belching and grousing over there, brewing strong green tea all day long, groaning in her bed at night. She had seen him taken off by a woman, and soon it would be by the police. Which was Rawcliffe's place? Street-lamps showed the Sun Trap, with a kosher inscription, and the Well Come. They were in the dark; people moved inland with the night, to fat belly-dancers and bottles of alum Valpierre. There it was: *El Acantilado Verde*, a tatty yellowish place. Rawcliffe had had, apparently, several little Tangerine bars and tea-shops. This would be his last.

Enderby mastered his breathing before entering the bar-restaurant that had a shagged dog sign swinging, with its lamp of low wattage, in the paper-ravaging wind. The crossword, pathetically unsolved, rode and span briefly on the air at Enderby's eye-level as he made for the closed door. There were deserted metal tables with chairs on top of them stretching along the pavement. From within came piano music. He pushed the door open.

The piano was an upright, in tone tinny, scarred in appearance, on a platform made of old beer-crates, and the man who played seemed to be a North European. He played slow jazz with sad authority, sadly chewing his lips. He had suffered, his blank face said, but had now passed beyond suffering. An American, Enderby decided. All Americans, he thought, looking shyly round: it was to do with sitting postures of insolent relaxedness. There was a herbal smell on the air, an autumn smell. *Herbst* was the German for autumn, was it not? A poem, like the transient randiness felt when coming upon a gratuitous near-nude set in the pages of a magazine article one finds absorbing, twitched. These Americans would call it the fall. A fall of herbs, of grace, herb of grace. No, there were other things to think of and do, and he already had a poem on the forge. Still, he sniffed. Drugs, he tingled; something stronger than that harmless marijuana (Mary Jane, that meant: a mere kitchenmaid of narcotics) he had been given to smoke. A very thin young man in dark glasses mouthed and mouthed in a trance. A white-haired cropped man, also young, sat reading a thin, or slim, volume. 'Shit,' he kept

judging. Nobody took any notice; nobody took any notice of Enderby. There was a man in the corner in a skin-tight costume as
for ballet practice writing words shakily on a blackboard. *Brain-
goose*, he wrote, and, under it, *Rape of Lesion*. Enderby nodded
with tiny approval. Literary exiles of a different sort. Which reminded him: that bloody book of that dying yob; here might
they know? 'Shit,' said the white-haired man, turning a page,
then laughed.

There seemed to be no waiter about. There was a wooden bar
in the distant corner, its lower paint ruined by feet, and three
bar-stools were empty before it. To get to it Enderby had to get
past a dangerous-looking literary man who had arranged three
tables about himself like an ambo. He had shears with which he
seemed to be busy cutting strips out of newspaper-sheets, and he
looked frowning at Enderby while he pasted some of these, apparently at random, on a pawed and sticky piece of foolscap. He
looked like an undertaker, mortician rather; his suit was black
and his spectacles had near-square black rims, like the frames of
obituary notices in old volumes of *Punch*. Enderby approached
diffidently, saying: 'Pardon me—' (good American touch there)
'—but can anybody?'

'If,' said the man, 'you mean aleatoric, that only applies to
the muzz you embed the datum in.' He sounded not unkind, but
his voice was tired and lacked nuances totally.

'What I meant really was a drink, really.' But Enderby didn't
want to seem impolite; besides, this man seemed engaged on a
kind of literature, correcting the sheet as he started to now with
a felt-tipped inkpencil; he was a sort of fellow-writer. 'But I
think I see what you mean.'

'There,' said the man, and he mumbled what he had stuck
and written down, something like: 'Balance of slow masturbate
payments enquiries in opal spunk shapes notice of that question
green ass penetration phantoms adjourn.' He shook his head.
'Rhythm all balled up, I guess.'

'I'm really looking,' Enderby said, 'for the waiter you have
here. Gomez his name is, I believe.' A man came out, somewhat
dandyishly tripping, from behind a curtain of plastic strips in various primary colours. He had a greenish shirt glazed with never
having been, for quite a time anyway, taken off, and thin bare

legs that were peppered with tiny holes, as with woodworm. His face was worn to the bone and his hair was filthy and elflocked. To the scissored man he said:

'He reckons he's through on the hot line now.'

'Any message?'

'Fly's writing it down. May I enquire whom you are?' he then said to Enderby.

'Something about Gomez, I guess,' said the mortician.

'Later.' The other dabbled his fingers in air as in water. 'He's off till *un poco mas tarde.*' The pianist was now working on some high-placed old-time discords, school of Scriabin. 'Crazy,' the dabbler said.

'I'll have a drink,' said Enderby, 'if I may.'

'British,' nodded the mortician. 'Guessed so. Goddamn town's lousy with British. Out here to write about tea with Miss Mitford, rose gardens in rectory closes, all that crap.'

'Not me.' Enderby made a noise which he at once realised was like what the cheaper novels called a gay laugh. He must be very ill-at-ease then. 'I'll have a Bloody Mary, if you have it, that is.' He clanked out a few dirhams. The tomato-juice would be nourishing; he needed nourishment.

'*Sangre de María,*' shrugged the filthy-shirted man, who seemed to own this place, going to behind the bar. Enderby went to climb a stool.

'Very baroque, that is,' he pronounced. 'They all call it that, I believe. They lack a knowledge of English history, naturally, the Spaniards, I mean, so they make a kind of Crashaw conceit out of it, though, of course, the Crashavian style derives, so they tell me, from Spanish models. Or that statue of St Teresa, I think it is, with the dart going through her. But this, of course, is the Virgin Mary, bleeding. A virgin, you see: blood. The same sort of thing, though. Professor Empson was very interested in that line of Crashaw—you know: "He'll have his teat ere long, a bloody one. The mother then must suck the son." Two lines, I mean. Baroque, anyway.' All who were not in a drug-trance looked at Enderby. He wondered why his nerves babbled like that; he must be careful; he would start blurting everything out if he wasn't. 'And your Gomez,' he said, 'is, I am credibly informed, something of an expert on Spanish poetry.'

'Gomez,' said the mortician, 'is an expert only on the involutions of his own rectum.'

The man with the blackboard shakily wrote *Comings in the skull*. The white-haired reader said, very seriously: 'Now, this, I reckon, is *not* shit. Listen.' And he read out:

'Society of solitary children—
Stilyagi, provo, beat, mafada,
Nadaista, energumeno, mod and rocker—
Attend to the slovos of your psychedelic guides—
Swamis, yogins and yoginis,
Amerindian peyote chiefs, Zen roshis.
Proclaim inner space, jolting the soft machine
Out of its hypnosis conditioned by
The revealed intention of the Senders—'

'But,' said Enderby unwisely, dancing the bloody drink in his hand, smiling, 'we don't have mods and rockers any more.' He had read his *Daily Mirror*, after all, to some purpose. 'That's the danger, you see, of trying to make poetry out of the ephemeral. If you'll forgive me, that sounded to me very old-fashioned. Of course, it isn't really clear whether it *is* actually poetry. Back to the old days,' he smiled, 'of *vers libre*. There were a lot of tricks played by people, you know. Seed catalogues set out in stanzas. Oh, a lot of the *soi-disant avant-garde* were taken in.'

There were low growls of anger, including, it appeared, one from a man who was supposed to be in a trance. The white-haired reader seemed to calm himself through a technique of rhythmic shallow breathing. Then he said:

'All right, buster. Let's hear from you.'

'How? Me? You mean—?' They were all waiting.

'You know the whole shitting works,' went the mortician. 'You've not quit talking since you came in. Who asked you to come in, anyway?'

'It's a bar, isn't it?' said Enderby. 'Not private, I mean. Besides, there's this matter of Gomez.'

'The hell with Gomez. Crap out with your own.'

The atmosphere was hostile. The owner air-dabbled from behind the bar, sneering. The pianist was playing something deliberately silly in six-eight time. Enderby said:

'Well, I didn't really come prepared. But I'm working on something in the form of an Horatian ode. I've not got very far, only a couple of stanzas or so. I don't think you'd want to hear it.' He felt doubt itching like piles. All that stuff about swamis and inner space. A sonnet, yet. Horatian ode, yet. He was not very modern, perhaps. A critic had once written: 'Enderby's addiction to the sonnet-form proclaims that the 'thirties are his true home.' He did not like the young very much and he did not want to take drugs. He was supposed to have killed a quintessential voice of the new age. But that voice had not been above garbling Enderby's own work and getting a fellowship of the Royal Society of Literature for it. Enderby now recited stoutly:

'The urgent temper of the laws,
That clips proliferation's claws,
 Shines from the eye that sees
 A growth is a disease.

Only the infant will admire
The vulgar opulence of fire
 To tyrannise the dumb
 Patient continuum

And, while the buds burst, hug and hold
A cancer that must be controlled
 And moulded till it fit
 These forms not made for it.'

Out of a trance somebody farted. 'That last couplet,' Enderby said trembling, 'needs a bit of a going over, I see that, but I think you'll get the general idea.' In confusion he swigged his Bloody Mary and presented the flecked glass (splash of some small slaughtered animal on a windscreen) for another. When Enderby had been a boy he had gone to sleep on the upper deck of the last tram of the night and had wakened in the tramshed. Leaving in shame he had noticed uniformed men looking at him in the quiet wonder which was the proper tribute to an act of an imbecile. He seemed to be getting that same look now. He said: 'I stand for form and denseness. The seventeenth-century tradition modified. When is this man Gomez coming in?' The mortician resumed snipping and gumming, shaking his head, grinning like a clown. The white-headed cropped man hid his own grin in a new slim volume. The entranced offered the loudest criticism, great lip-farts cometing through inner space. 'Well,' said Enderby, growing angry, 'what about that bloody act of plagiarism of bloody Yod Crewsy?'

A man came limping from behind the blackboard (which now had, very vulgar, *My cuntry is the yoniverse* scrawled on it) and said: 'I'll tell you about that, friend.' He was totally bald but luxuriantly bearded and spoke in an accent Enderby had hitherto associated with cowboy films on television. 'That was pure camp. Is, I guess. A new frame of awareness. It's not the poems as such so much as how he looks at them. Like you get these good pictures with shitty Victoriana in them, a frame inside a frame. Man, it's called the Process.'

'I'd very much like to see—' Enderby's nausea was complicated. And if that sonnet-draft was in there, the Satan one. And, whether it was there or not, could he control himself, handling richly rewarded flagrant sneering theft?

'You can learn any place,' said the bald bearded man. 'You'll find it in the john library.' He pointed beyond the curtain of many-coloured plastic strips with a finger that seemed half-eaten, a kindly man really. 'And as for plagiarism, everything belongs to everybody. Man, that's called the Lesson.' He returned to behind the blackboard, limping. On the blackboard was now written *Vinegar strokes through magnified sebacities.* Enderby went, his heart fainting, towards the john. There was a dark passage, sibilant with the wind, and crunchy rubbish underfoot. In a kind of alcove a man lay on a camp-bed under a dull bulb, another man beside him with a notebook. The supine man, on a drugged trip, sent reports up from the unconscious. Down there ghostly scissors were at work on newspapers out of eternity. It was a lot of nonsense.

The lavatory was small and dirty, but there was a red light of the kind used in electric log-fires. There were a lot of books, many of them eaten by mould. Enderby sat heavily on the hollow seat and disturbed the books with a paddling right hand, panting. That sinful volume was not too far from the top. The title was *Fixes;* there was a bold leering portrait of the pseudo-author. The sixteenth impression, Enderby noted with gloom. He noted too that many of the poems were not his own; it was a case of multiple theft, perhaps, unless bloody Vesta or that Wittgenstein man had written some of them. Enderby found six unpublished poems by himself and, a small mercy in a world of filth, not one of them was that sonnet. There was, as Miss Kelly had said, a poem entitled 'Sonnet,' but that had twelve bad unrhyming lines and might well be something that Yod Crewsy himself had composed at his secondary modern school. Enderby read it shuddering:

> My mum plonks them on the table for Susie
>   and Dad and I
> Plonk plonk and dull clanks the sauce bottles
> And Susie reads their names to herself
> Her mouth is open but that is not for reading
>   aloud
> The fact is that her nose is stopped up like
>   those sauce bottles are
> Like OK and HP and A1 and FU and CK and O
> I mean oh red red tomato
> And I dream while the frying goes on and Dad
>   has his mouth open too at the TV
> How I would like catsup or ketchup splattering
> All over the walls and it would be shaken from
>   these open mouths
> And hers in the kitchen all her open mouths
> And it would be red enough but not taste of
>   tomato

'God,' said Enderby to his shrinking bowels. 'God God God.' So they had come to this, had they? And his own finely wrought little pieces desecrated by contact. He dropped the book on the floor; it remained open, but a sharp draught from under the far from snugly fitting door pushed at the erect fan of its middle pages and disclosed a brief poem that Enderby, squinting in the dim red light, seemed thumped on the back into looking at. Something or somebody thumped him: an admonitory goblin that perhaps lived wetly in the lavatory cistern. He had not noticed this poem before, but, by God, he knew the poem. He felt a terrible excitement mounting. He grabbed the book with both hands.

Then the door opened. Enderby looked, expecting to see the wind, but it was a man. Excited though he was, he began to deliver a standard protest against invasion of privacy. The man waved it away and said: 'Gomez.'

'The fact that the door isn't locked is neither here nor there. All right then, I've finished anyway.' Something in the spread sound of his words seemed to tell him that he was smiling. He felt his mouth, surprised. It was the excitement, it was the first rehearsal of triumph. Because, by God, he had them now. By the short hairs, as they said. But was he sure, could he be sure? Yes, surely he was sure. Or was it just a memory of having foreseen it in print? He could check, he was bound to be able to check, even in this bloody heathen place. There might be some really cultivated man here among the expatriate scribblers.

'Gomez. Billy Gomez.' He was a bit rodent-like and, so Enderby twitched at once, might be dangerous. But in what context? Gomez finned out his paws in a kind of cartoon-mouse self-depreciation. He had a dirty white barman's jacket on but no tie. He seemed also to be wearing tennis-shoes.

'Ah.' That other structure of urgency was suddenly reillu-minated. Heavy as an ivied tower, it crashed the blackness, decol-lated, to the sound of brass, like something in *son et lumière*. 'Sí,' Enderby said. '*Su hermano*. In London, that is. *Mi amigo*. Or colleague, shall I say. Has he sent anything for me?' That sonnet by Wordsworth, on the sonnet. Key becomes lute becomes trumpet. This book he now thrust into his side-pocket. Load of filthy treachery becomes, quite as improbably, sharp weapon of revenge.

'You come.' He led Enderby out of the lavatory down a passage that took them to stacked crates of empties and then to a garlicky kind of still-room, brightly lighted with one bare bulb. Enderby now saw Gomez very clearly. He had red hair. Could he possibly be the true brother of swarthy John? Gomez was a Goth or perhaps even a Visigoth: they had had them in Spain quite a lot, finishing off the Iberian part of the Roman Empire: they had had a bishop who translated bits of the Bible, but that was much later: coarse people but very vigorous and with a language quite as complicated as Latin: they were perhaps not less trustworthy than, say, the Moors. Still, Enderby was determined to be very careful.

In this still-room a small brown boy in a striped nightshirt was cutting bread. Gomez cuffed him without malice, then he took a piece of this bread, went over to a stove maculate with burnt fat, sloshed the bread in a pan of what looked like sardine-oil, folded it into a sandwich and, drippingly, ate. He took in many aspects of Enderby with darting pale eyes. The boy, still cutting bread, as it were clicked his eyes into twin slots that held them blazing on to Enderby's left ear. Enderby, embarrassed, changed his position. The eyes stayed where they were. Drugs or something. Gomez said to Enderby:

'You say your name.' Enderby told him what he had been called in his regenerate, barman's, capacity, but only in the Spanish version. Enderby said:

'He said he'd send a letter through you. *Una carta.* He promised. Have you got it?' Gomez nodded. 'Well,' said Enderby, 'how about handing it over, then, eh? Very urgent information.'

'Not here,' dripmunched Gomez. 'You say where you stay. I come with letter.'

'Ah,' Enderby said, with something like satisfaction. 'I see your little game.' He smiled, it seemed to him, and to his astonishment, brilliantly: it was that triumph pushing up. 'Perhaps it would be more convenient if we could go to your place and pick up the letter there. It would be quicker, wouldn't it?'

Gomez, who had eaten all his oiled bread and licked some fingers, now took an onion from a small sack. He looked at the boy, who still cut bread but whose eyes had now clicked back down to the operation, and seemed to relent of cuffing him, however unmaliciously. He stroked the boy's griskin, grinning. Spanish poetry, thought Enderby. This man was supposed to know all about it. Was a knowledge of poetry, even a nominal one, a sort of visa for entry into the small world of Enderby-betrayal? Gomez topped and tailed the onion with his teeth (*tunthus*, Enderby suddenly remembered for some reason, was the Gothic for a tooth, but this man would know nothing of his ancestral language), then, having spat the tufts on to the floor, he tore off the onion's scarf-skin and some of the subcutaneous flesh and started to crunch what was pearlily revealed. There was a faint spray of zest. It smelt delicious, just as chunks of grilled human flesh might smell delicious. Enderby knew he had to get out. Fast. Gomez said:

'Tonight I work. You say where you live.'

The boy left off bread-cutting (who the hell would want all that bread, anyway?) and ran the knife-blade across his brown thumb. Enderby said:

'It doesn't matter, after all. Thanks for your help. Or not help, as the case may be. *Muchas gracias,* anyway.' And he got out of the room, clanking loose bottles on the floor of the dark corridor. Gomez called after him something ending with *hombre*. Enderby passed the man on the couch and in the next world and the amanuensis who sat by him. Then he breasted the plastic strips and blinked into the bar. There was a new man there, a Scot apparently, for he talked of 'a wee bit fixie.' The man at the blackboard had just finished writing *Hot kitchens of his ass.* Salami, Enderby thought in his confusion, salami was made of donkeys. The white-cropped man was reciting:

> 'Archangels blasting from inner space,
> Pertofran, Tryptizol, Majeptil,
> Parstelin and Librium.
> And a serenace for all his tangled strings.'

Romantic, thought Enderby distractedly, better than that other stuff. Remembering that he had stolen a book from their john, he clapped his hand to his pocket. A dithery young man in dark glasses recoiled, pushing out his palms against the expected gunshot. Enderby smiled at everybody, thinking that he had ample cause to smile, even when carted off. But not yet, not just yet. He yearned towards solitary confinement as to a lavatory, but duty, like an *engaged* sign, clicked its message. The mortician did not smile back. The dithering young man had recovered: all a joke, his manic leer seemed to say. Enderby held that book in, as if it might leap out. Out, out. Into the windy Moroccan night.

It was a slow and panting climb, and Enderby had to keep stopping suddenly, holding himself in shadow against whatever wall offered, listening and watching to find out if he was being followed. It was hard to tell. There were plenty of little Moorish boys about, any one of whom could be that bread-cutting lad, but none seemed furtive: indeed, one pissed frankly in the gutter (but that might be his cunning) and another hailed a smartly dressed elderly Moor who was going downhill, running after him then, crying unheeded certain complicated wrongs. Enderby passed dirty coffee-shops and then came to a hotly arguing group of what seemed beggars at a street corner. They had thin though strong bare legs under swaddling bands and ragged European jackets, and all were turbaned. Enderby stood with them a space, peering as best he could between their powerful gestures. Things seemed to be all right; there was nobody following; he had given that treacherous Gomez the slip. Two treacherous Gomezes. That bloody John in London was, after all, the rotten bastard Enderby had always known him to be. Enderby, filling his lungs first like a dog running to the door in order to bark, turned left for a steeper hill. Half way up was a very loud cinema with what he took from posters to be an Egyptian film showing (an insincerely smiling hero like Colonel Nasser). He felt somehow protected by all that row, which was mostly the audience. A tooth-picking dark-suited young man by the pay-desk looked at Enderby. The manager probably. 'Alors, ça marche, hein?' Enderby panted. If anybody asked that man if he had seen an Englishman going that way he would say no, only a Frenchman. Now he said nothing, merely looked, tooth-picked. Enderby climbed on.

When, dying and very wet, he came to the Rue El Greco, he realised he was not too sure what would be the right back wall. Fowls, stunted trees: they all probably had them round here. He should have chalked a sign: he was new to this business. He would have to risk going in the front way. After all, there would be a lot of customers at this hour and fat Napo would be too busy hitting the rotten ancient coffee-machine to notice. Enderby caught a sudden image of El Greco himself, transformed into his own Salvador, peering down in astigmatic woe at the deplorable street that bore his name. There were some very nasty-looking places called snack-bars, as well as upper windows from which small boys thrust their bottoms, either in invitation or contempt. You could also hear very raucous female laughter

—wrong, wrong; should not Islam's daughters be demure?—
from down dark passageways. An old man sat by deserted and
boarded-up premises. Inside, Enderby saw with poetic insight,
would be rats and the memories of foul practices, the last fleshly
evidence of outrage being gnawed, gnawed; the man cried his
wares of tiny toy camels with here and there a dromedary.

Enderby gave his sweated spectacles a good wipe with his tie
before approaching *El Snack-Bar Albricias.* By conceiving an
image of fat Napo waiting for him on the doorstep, as a tyran-
nical father his precocious debauched son, he was able to
forestall any such reality. Indeed, scratched Cairo music was
coming out very loud, but not so loud as the noise of customers.
Enderby peered before entering and was satisfied to see Napo
fighting the coffee-machine before a thick and applauding bar-
audience. *'Pardon,'* said a bulky fezzed would-be entrant to Enderby, Enderby being in the way. *'Avec plaisir,'* Enderby said,
and was happy to use this man as a shield for his own ingress.
To be on the safe side, he tried to make himself look Moorish,
flattening his feet, imagining his nose bigger, widening his eyes
behind their glasses. There were girls, giggling, yashmaks up like
beavers, drinking the local bottled beer with real Moorish men.
Enderby tut-tutted like one in whom the faith burned hot. Then
he noticed something he had not seen before—little verse couplets hanging on the wall behind the bar. He had time to read
one only before going to the lavatory before going upstairs. It
said:

> *Si bebes para olvidar,*
> *Paga antes de empezar.*

That, thought Enderby, meant that if you drank to forget you'd
better pay before you began. Drinking and forgetting, that was.
Enderby felt a bit cold. Verse and treachery went together. He
hadn't thought of it before, but Napo had, in the nature of
things, to be a traitor. Fugitives had sooner or later to be kicked
out from upstairs; no criminal could afford to stay for ever; the
quickest way of getting rid of a guest who'd outstayed his welcome was to—But no, no. There had to be someone you could
trust. Wasn't Napo, especially when a customer gave him a
cigar, an admirer of Winston Churchill? But when you thought

of political coat-turning and the guns pointing the wrong way at Singapore and some rumour of ultimate perfidy in the Straits of Gibraltar—No, no, no. Napo was all right. Well in with the police, too. Enderby felt colder.

Two

He came to full wakefulness in the middle of the night, the Boland moon looking grimly in on him. He had gone to sleep early, so that his eyes could avoid a very complicated and laborious (with hand-spitting beforehand) bout of triple sodomy on the floor. He had had enough sleep, then, but his room-mates were hard at it, snoring, Wahab on his back, mouth open to the spiders, in his robe on the bare boards. But what really seemed to have jolted him awake was the Muse, pushing lines at him. It was a bit more of that Horatian Ode:

> And something something something can
> Take partners for a plonk pavane,
> The blinded giant's staff
> Tracing a seismograph.

Accompanying this was a burbling of unhappy tomato-juice, together with, in the throat, a metallic suspicion that it had not been all that fresh. And then. And then. The derision of that bloody merry crowd (ha) in that place at what had seemed to him, Enderby, and still seemed very respectable verses. Was it then possible that art that was good for one time was not good for another, the laughter justified, himself out of date? There was a Canadian professor who had once been in Piggy's Sty with fawning hosts, going on burringly about new modes of communication and how words were all finished or something and everybody was too much bemused by Gutenberg and not wide enough awake to the revolution in electronics, whatever that was. And there were also these people who, by taking drugs, were vouchsafed visions of the *noumenon*, and this made them scornful of art that used merely phenomenal subject matter. But what could you do about a noumenal medium, mused Enderby, putting his glasses on. The moon defined itself in sharper craters

and ridges, as though the spectacles themselves were in the service of Miss bloody Boland. And, while bloody came into things,
that Bloody Mary was dancing about very obscenely inside, and
that vodka had probably not been vodka at all but something
merely sold as vodka. Enderby winced on a sour vague image of
the *noumenon* behind the label. Diluted surgical spirit, home-
made potato-fire, meths. He had better get up and go to the
lavatory.

He was fully dressed, except for his shoes, which he now painfully put on. It seemed to him to be cold tonight, and he
shivered. He also, despite the shattering evidence that had been
granted him this evening, felt depressed. Was anything he
could now do as a poet of any value to the world or God the
ultimate *noumenon?* Graaarp, answered his stomach, like some
new mode of communication. Behind the door on a nail was
hanging the hooded nightshirt garment, djebala or whatever
they called it, that Souris, now snoring on top of Ali Fathi, wore
when he essayed the streets. Enderby took it and wrapped it
round himself, but he saw that his shivering came from the expense of body-fuel in the service of the visceral bubbling that
oppressed him. He went downstairs to the lavatory, hearing
nothing from either brothel-dormitory, calm of brerrrrgh mind
all aaaaarfph passion gockle spent.

But from below he heard quiet but somehow urgent talking,
and he saw that a dim lamp, apt for furtive colloquy, was on. He
tiptoed down, suppressing his inner noises by some obscure action of the epiglottis and diaphragm. When he got to the bottom
of the stairs, he saw, from shadow, that Napo was with a couple
of men in the pretentious uniform of the local police. These men,
lean, moustached, mafia-swarthy, crafty-eyed, were each taking
from Napo a glass of something gold and viscid in the lamplight.
Alcohol, against the tenets of the faith, they ought to be had up
for that, police and upholders of Islamic law as they were supposed to be. Enderby, flat against his dark wall, listened, but the
language was Moghrabi Arabic. It was a serious discourse,
though, evidently, and Napo's part in it sounded a bit breathy,
even whining. Enderby listened for certain illuminative international or crassly onomatopoeic words, but the only word that
was made much of was something sounding like *khogh*. It was,

as Enderby's viscera quietly attested, parroting and nipping him like a parrot, a very visceral sound. *Khogh*, the viscera went. And then, somewhat louder, *Genggergy*. Enderby suddenly saw, and then he panicked.

The police and Napo had heard. Enderby saw, in addition to who *Khogh* was, opened mouths and wide eyes turned on to his patch of dark. He thought he heard a safety-catch clicking off. His first instinct was to run to the lavatory, but they would, he knew, soon have that door shot open. Still, his insides, like spoilt cats demanding milk as lava begins to engulf the town and the cats with it, complained and switched on a kind of small *avant-garde* chamber piece for muted brass. Enderby, like, with that gown on his shoulders, a student late for a lecture, ran through the kitchen, sufficiently lighted by Miss bloody Boland, and out into the yard. The roosting fowls crooned at him, and the stunted tree raised, like some outworn Maeterlinck property, a gnarled fist. He got over the wall with agility he marvelled at and then panted a second or two in the alleyway. They were after him all right, though they seemed first to be, from a sudden meagre uprush of lunated feathers and a squawked track of conventional gallinaceous protest, abusing the fowls for letting him get away. Enderby ran a yard or two downhill and tried a back door on the opposite side of the alley. It was locked, so he padded, in frightful borborygms and breathlessness, to the next. This was open. He got in, finding himself alone with a tethered white ruminating goat who surveyed Enderby with no surprise, and closed the door, a very warped one, gently. Very usefully, a dog next door made a deep chest-bay once only, as though Enderby had entered a frame or two of his dream, and this sparked off a small violent yapper further up the hill and, further up again, what, very improbable, could only be a pet hyena. Towards these noises, Enderby could tell, four feet were now, with a sketch of urgency, proceeding. The voice of Napo, back at base, made a brief speech with elements of controlled Churchillian outrage in it, then turned into grumbling coughs going back to the kitchen. Good. This would do very well.

Enderby was, in a sense, pleased that a new phase was beginning, perhaps the last phase of the fugitive. It was all a question now of how long Rawcliffe would be in rendering himself available for death. And that was absurd, when one came to think of it, he, Enderby, killing Rawcliffe. But, if one accepted that killing was a legitimate and sempiternal human activity, authorised by the Bible, was there any better motive than Enderby's own? The State made no provisions for the punishment of the perversion of art; indeed, it countenanced such perversion. God, whose name had so often been invoked in the name of bad art, was, at bottom, a Philistine. So it was up to him, Enderby, to strike a blow for art. Was he not perhaps by some considered to have done so already? The popular press might be against him, but surely some letters, suppressed by editors, must have been written on his behalf? There might even be a fund started by Earl Russell or somebody to provide cates and art for him in prison and set him up on his distant release. He was, he was convinced, not alone. His stomach felt easier.

Watched by the chewing goat, Enderby put the djebala or whatever it was on properly, so that, what with the hood, he became a kind of capuchin. He had slept in his teeth as usual, fearing their theft if he did not, but now he removed and stowed them. Remembering the tin of boot-polish in his pocket, he allowed his heart to leap in awe at the poetry which existence itself sometimes contrived: the fusion, or at least meaningful collocation, of disparates—as, for example, a tin of tan boot-polish and himself, Enderby. He removed his spectacles and bedded them with his teeth. Now he disposed his hood in the academic position, pushed up all available sleeves to near the elbow, got out the tin and his handkerchief, then began to dye himself, all that was likely to be visible, by dipping his handkerchief in the tin and thinly spreading the polish. He did not forget nape and ear-crevices. The smell of the stuff was not unpleasant—astringent, vaguely military. Why, there had been that man Lawrence, colonel and scholar, got up like this. He had been viciously debauched by Turks, but his country had honoured him. He too, like Enderby, had had to change his name. He had died in lowly circumstances, riding a motorcycle.

What, when he had finished, he now looked like there was no means of finding out. In the moonlight his hands seemed of a richer colour than nature herself might allow, a richness that suggested dye, or perhaps thinly spread tan boot-polish. Still, it

would serve, sleeves well down, hood well over. The goat, with
the blessed impartiality granted to animals, saw no difference
between the two Enderbys. It took without gratitude the empty
polish tin and began to crunch it up roundly, its goatee wagging.
Enderby took his leave, Ali bin Enderbi or some such name.

Whither? The Boland moon, asked, would not answer. His
true place was that Kasbah, high up at the end of the town,
where beggars slept at night in the doorways of shark shops, all
Rif rifles from the iron-founding Midlands. But it was necessary
that he stay near Rawcliffe's beach-place, not to let his quarry
slip out of his tan-polished hands. It was not windy now, but it
was not warm. Autumnal Morocco. He could doze, all hunched
up, in the shadow of the *Acantilado Verde*. In the morning he
could drink coffee and eat a piece of bread (there was a dirham
or so still in his pocket) and then, an eye open for Rawcliffe, get
down to begging. There was a lot of begging here: no shame in
it. There were a couple of rich hotels near the *Acantilado Verde*
—the Rif and the Miramar: good begging pitches.

He padded gently down the hill-alley, silently rehearsing the
Koranic name of God. Properly enunciated, it could serve for
many things—disgust, gratitude, awe, admiration, pain. Enderby
had heard the name several times a day in his hideout: he
thought he could manage the gymnastics of its articulation. You
had to try to swallow the tip of your tongue, growling, then pretend you had to give up the attempt because you had to expel a
fragment of matter lodged in your glottis. Easy: *Allah*. He allahed quietly towards the sea under a frowning moon.

2

One

eart. He let himself get upset about something. Blowing his top. Ranting and raving. Carrying too much weight, of course. That's what comes of building up rugger-muscle in youth.'

'Where's he been sent?'

'That place of Otto Langsam's. Out in the wilds. Cut off from the great world. Not even a daily newspaper.'

'They say he was going on about some piece of pottery. Abusive. Lines written in a public lavatory. Obviously needed a rest. Good job they got him in time.'

'Oh, very good job. Look, *emshi emshi* or whatever the word is. All right, take this. Now bugger off and buy yourself a shave.'

'*Allah.*'

President of the moon's waning, Enderby was not too cold at night. He slept uncertainly, however, in the lee provided by the suntrap arena of *El Acantilado Verde*, a sandyard for torso-bronzing with a couple of umbrella-topped tables. The seaward-looking gate was easily climbed over. Crouched in an angle, he would see at first light two walls made of bathers' changing-cubicles, a corner of the kitchen, the back door of the bar-restaurant. Mercifully, so far, there had been no night rain. Raw-cliffe could bring the rain with him if he wished. Nobody seemed to be sleeping on the premises, and Enderby moved away at dawn. Dawn brought the diamond weather of a fine autumn. Skirring his fast-growing grey face-bristles with a tanned hand, Enderby would gum-suck his way to a small dirty shop off the esplanade, sticking out the other hand for alms (*Allah*) if any untimely European were about, and then take breakfast of coffee-in-a-glass and a fatty Moorish pastry. He feigned mostly dumb, except for the holy name. A holy man perhaps, above dirt and toothlessness, once granted a vision of the ultimate garden (houris, nectar-sherbet, a crystal stream) and then struck speechless except for the author's signature.

Up the cobbled street tottered the saint-eyed donkeys, most cruelly panniered, driven by bare-legged Moors in clouts, ponchos, and immense straw sombreros. Biblical women with ancient hard eyes and no yashmaks carried hashish-dreaming fowls in upside-down bundles, scaly legs faggoted together. They climbed, in a whirl of wind-blown feathers, up to the dirty small hotels for long haggling on the pavement outside, then the leisurely *halal* slaughter, blood sluggishly rolling downhill, the chickens dying on a psychedelic vision. And just along there was that treacherous White Doggy Wog place. Were its denizens right? Was it right that art should mirror chaos? What kind of art would it be proper for him to produce in his coming cell?

His brain, aloof from his begging hand, worked away at one poem or another. Was it perhaps a kind of holiness that gathered the disparate arbitrarily together, assuming that God or Allah—at the bottom of the mind's well, a toad with truth's jewel in its brow—could take care of the unifying pattern, that it was blasphemy for the shaping human mind to impose one of its own? Shatter syntax also, and with it time and the relationships of space. That Canadian pundit had said something about the planet itself, earth, becoming, as perceived by a new medium which would be no more than heightened consciousness, a kind

of work of art, so that every aspect would be relevant to every
other aspect. Fish, spit, toe, antenna, cognac, spider, perspex,
keyboard, grass, helmet. Helmeted in grass, the perspex spider
spits with toed antenna, a noise like fish, the cognac keyboard.
Too elegant that, too much like Mallarmé or somebody. Old-
fashioned too, really. Surrealist.

Allah.

Up there the white huddled Medina on the hill, once watchful
of the sea-invaders. Blood and buggery, the Koranic cry of teeth
as the scimitar slashed. And now a pretty cram of stucco for the
visiting painter. Donkeys, palms, the odd insolent Cadillac with
a sneering wealthy young Moor in dark glasses. This bilious sea.
There were not, thank Allah, many police about and, in any
case, they did not greatly molest beggars.

'Give him something, George, go on. Poor old man.'

And the plebeian tourist, in open-necked shirt and double-
breasted town suit, handed Enderby a tiny clank of centimes.
His wife, growing a lobster colour that was vulgarly Blackpool,
smiled in pity. Enderby bowed and allahed. It was really sur-
prising what you could pick up on this game—handfuls of small
tinkle that often added up to well over a dirham, filthy torn
notes that the donors probably thought carried plague, the
absurd largesse of holiday drunks. He was eating, if not sleeping,
well on it all. Arab bread with melon-and-ginger *confiture*,
yummiyum couscous (better than Easy Walker's), fowl-hunks
done with saffron, thin veal-shives in a carraway sauce—all at a
quiet fly-buzzing incurious shop near the little Souk or Succo, one
that had, moreover, a Western WC instead of a hazardous wog
crouch-hole. He was also drinking a fair quantity of mint-tea,
good for his stomach.

'*Pauvre petit bonhomme. Georges, donne-lui quelque chose.*'

It was a living. For occupation he had the working-out,
though not on paper (there would be paper in prison), of a sonnet concerned with the relationship of the Age of Reason and
the so-called Romantic Revival:

> Augustus on a guinea sat in state—
> The sun no proper study but each shaft
> Of filtered light a column: classic craft

Abhorred the arc or arch. To circulate
(Blood or ideas) meant pipes, and pipes were straight.
As loaves were gifts from Ceres when she laughed—

A difficult form, most exigent. Those drug-takers in the Doggy
Wog place didn't have all that to worry about: no octaves and
sestets in the free wide-open unconscious. A load of bloody rubbish, of course, but he couldn't quell his new self-doubt. As for
reading, he would glance shyly at foreign papers left on outdoor
café tables: there seemed to be nothing about Yod Crewsy.

And then, outside the Rif, he had heard these two men, talking loudly about someone who could only be Wapenshaw. The
Turkish Delight commercial doorman was whistling a taxi to
come over for them from the taxi-stand opposite the Miramar.
And one of the two men, his belly pushed out to keep up his
unbelted long shorts, had said to the other (both had spatulate
scrubbed and shaven-looking fingers): 'Heart. He let himself get
upset about something.' It was as they were climbing into their
petit taxi or *taxi chico* that the other one, oldish but thin and
strong like a surgical instrument, had said: 'Now bugger off and
buy yourself a shave,' handing Enderby a fifty-centime piece.
'*Allah.*'

Retribution, justice: that was what it was. Serve Wapenshaw
right. He had grinned and then seen his grin reflected in the
glass door of the Rif, the back of a fat woman in black rompers
making a temporary mirror-back. He had looked pretty horrible—a face without margins peering from the cave of the
capuchin hood, toothless. He could not see his grey whiskers, but
he felt them: skirr skirr. He grinned in horror.

At this moment another beggar, sturdy and genuine, had come
up to remonstrate loudly. He had been crouched in the entrance
to the hotel garage, but now, seeing the grin, he had risen, it
seemed, in reproach of one not taking the business seriously
enough. He was darker than Enderby, more of a Berber, and
had plenty of teeth. He gnashed these in execration, starting to
push Enderby in the chest. 'Take your hands off,' Enderby
cried, and a visitor in a Palm Beach suit turned in surprise at the
British accent. 'For cough,' Enderby added, preparing to push
back. But careful, careful; respectable beggary only: the police
might conceivably come. He saw then what the trouble was:

pitch-queering. 'Iblis,' he swore mildly at this colleague or rival. 'Shaitan. Afrit.' He had learned these words from Ali Fathi. And then, the real beggar calling terms less theological after him, he began to cross the road rather briskly. Perhaps he ought, anyway, to haunt the beach more, specifically that segment near El Acantilado Verde, even though so many people on it had their clothes off and locked away, able with a good conscience to grin (more kindly than Enderby had grinned) and show empty hands and armpits filled only, in the case of the men, with hair.

The restaurant part of Rawcliffe's establishment was glassed like an observatory. The rare eaters sweated on to their food, brought to them by an amiable-looking negroid boy in an apron and tarboosh. Windows were open, and Enderby would shyly squint in, but Rawcliffe did not seem to be about yet. He would justify the peering by shoving in a hand for alms, and, on the first day of this new pitch, he had had a squashy egg-and-salad sandwich plopped on to his paw. Palms, alms. Was there a poem there? But he gained also the odd bit of small change when customers—mostly German, needing a substantial bever between meals—paid their bills.

These last two days had yielded a sufficiency, and the fine weather held. Padding the sand, on which the sea, clever green child but never clever at more than a child's level, had sculpted its own waves, he breathed in salt, iodine, the sea's childish gift of an extra oxygen molecule, and thought in quiet sadness of old days—bucket and spade, feet screaming away from jellyfish, Sam Brownes of seaweed and the imperial decoration of a starfish (belly thrust out like that Wapenshaw-talking man, chest sloped to keep it on). And El Acantilado Verde reminded him of later days by the sea, betrayed and ruined by so many. 'Baksheesh,' he suggested now to a mild German-looking couple who, in heavy walking dress except for bare feet, drank the wind, strolling. They shook their heads regretfully. 'German bastards,' Enderby said quietly to their well-fed backs. The light was thicker, less heat was coming today from the piecrust cloud. There might be rain soon.

Here was a family that looked British. The wife was thin as from a long illness, the husband wore stern glasses, a boy and girl undressed for water-play chased and tried to hit each other.

'Daft old Jennifer!'

'Silly stupid Godfrey! You've got all sand in your tummy-button!'

Enderby addressed the father, saying, with begging hand: '*Allah allah. Baksheesh, effendi.*'

'Here,' said the man to his wife, 'is an example of what I mean. You have a good look at him and what do you see? You see a wog layabout in the prime of life. He ought to be able to do a decent day's work like I do.'

'*Allah,*' with less confidence.

'They should be made to work. If I had the running of this tinpot little dictatorship I'd make sure that they did.' He had a cheap-looking plastic-bodied camera dangling from a cord. His stare was bold and without humour.

'He's only a poor old man,' said his wife. She was, Enderby could tell, a woman much put upon; the children too would be insolent to her, asking *why* all the time.

'Old? He's not much older than what I am. Are you? Eh? Speak English do you? Old.'

'No mash Ingrish,' Enderby said.

'Well, you should learn it, shouldn't you? Improve yourself. Go to night-classes and that. Learn something, anyway. This is the modern world, no room for people that won't work, unless, that is, they've been thrown out of it through no fault of their own. Don't understand a blind bit of what I'm saying, do you? Trade, eh? Learn a trade. If you want money, do something for it.'

'Come on, Jack,' said the wife. 'There's a man there keeps looking at our Godfrey.'

Enderby had not previously met a response to mendicancy as hard-hearted and utilitarian as this. He looked grimly at this man of the modern world: a trade-union man, without doubt; perhaps a shop steward. He wore a dark suit with, concession to holiday, wings of open-necked shirt apparently ironed on to lapels. 'Trade,' Enderby said. 'I got trade.' The sky seemed to be getting darker.

'Oh, understand more than you let on you're able to, eh? Well, what trade have you got, then?'

'*Bulbul,*' Enderby said. But that might not be the right word.

'*Je suis*,' he said, '*poète*.'

'Poet? You said poet?' The man's mouth had opened into a square of small derision. He took from a side-pocket a ten-centime piece. 'You say some poetry, then. Listen to this, Alice.'

'Oh, let him alone, Jack.'

It might have been the word *bulbul* that did it. Suddenly Enderby, in a kind of scorn, found himself reciting a mock *ruba'iy*. Would those debauchees of the Doggy Wog laugh less at this than at his Horatian Ode?

> '*Kazwana ghishri fana kholamabu*
> *Bolloka wombon vurkelrada slabu,*
> *Ga farthouse wopwop yairgang offalflow*
> *Untera merb—*'

A voice behind him said: 'Better, Enderby. Much better. Not quite so obsessed with meaning as you used to be.' It was an eroded dyspneal voice. Enderby turned in shock to see Rawcliffe being helped, by two Moorish youths in new black trousers and white shirts, up the three steps that led to the door of his bar-restaurant. Rawcliffe paused at the top, waiting for the door to be opened. He panted down ghastlily at Enderby, his palsied grey head ashake. 'Thou art translated,' he wavered, 'but not so much.' The door opened, and its glass panels mirrored momentarily the thickening sea-clouds. '*Gracias*,' Rawcliffe said to the two Moors and trembled from his trouser-pocket a ten-dirham note for them. They hand-waved and grinned off. Then, to Enderby: 'Come and drink with one about to die.'

'All right,' said the trade-union man. 'You win. Take your ackers.' But Enderby ignored him and followed, with his own shaking, the broken frame of Rawcliffe from which an Edwardian suit bagged and hung. About to die, death, dying. That man Easy Walker had said something about his being crookidy dook. But was it rather that Rawcliffe, out of the vatic residuum of a failed poet's career, knew that he was going to be killed? Enderby then realised that he'd done nothing, despite this long wait, about getting hold of a weapon. God knew the shops had offered him enough. Not cut out for murder perhaps really. Not really his trade.

Two

Enderby climbed those three steps like a whole flight, shaking and panting. When he entered the bar he found that Rawcliffe, helped now by a dark and curly pudding of a young man, had not yet arrived at the place he was groaning and yearning to-wards—a fireside-type chair at the end of the room, facing the main door, with the back door near it open for air. There was too much glass here altogether: it was to bake the summer cus-tomers and make them drink more. But now, in the expected pathetic fallacy, the sky was darkening fast, rain on its way. The bar-counter was to the right, facing the doorless entrance to the eating-conservatory. The pudding young man got behind the bar before starting to shoo Enderby out. Rawcliffe, now heavily sit-ting, said: '*Oqué, oqué, Manuel. Es un amigo.*'

'That's not,' Enderby said, 'quite what I'd call myself.' There was an aloof interested inner observer, he was concerned to be interested to note, noting all this as possible material for a future poem, including the notation of the interest. That was not right: it was that inner observer, also creator, that had primarily been wronged. 'The enemy,' Enderby said. 'Come to get you. You know what for.' The inner observer tut-tutted.

'I knew you'd give it up, Enderby,' Rawcliffe said. 'You did bloody well, really. All those years writing verse when, by rights, you should have flitted to the tatty Olympus of remembered po-tency.' He wavered all this like an ancient don pickled in the carbon dioxide of his college rooms. Then he coughed bitterly, cursing with little breath. Recovering, he gasped: 'Brandy, Manuel. Large.'

'Doctor he say—'

'Curse the bloody doctor and you and every bloody body. Who's master here, God blast you? Brandy. Very very large.' Manuel, his eyes on Rawcliffe, slopped much Cordon Bleu into a lemonade glass. 'Bring it over, Enderby. Have one yourself.'

'How did you know it was me?' Enderby asked, interest much too active.

'I can see through things. Poetic clairvoyance. Bring that

brandy over.'

'I'm not here—'

'To be a bloody waiter. I know, I know. Bring it over just the same.' Enderby shambled to where Rawcliffe was and splashed the glass down on a small table by the chair. This table had a mass of personal trash on it, as, Enderby thought, in that poem by Coventry Patmore: to comfort his sad heart. A pile of old newspapers, a Woolworth watch, a couple of stones (ha) abraded by the beach, an empty bottle, no bluebells, cigarette packets. Beware of pity, however. Pity spareth many an evil thing. Rawcliffe took the glass and, in an aromatic brandy tempest, put it to his starved lips. Bleeding to death, Enderby saw; he was near the end of his blood. Pity causeth the forests to fail.

'Swine,' Enderby said as Rawcliffe drank. 'Filthy traitor and pervert.'

Rawcliffe surfaced from drinking. His face started to mottle. He looked up at Enderby from behind his Beetle goggles, his eyes bloodless like his mouth, and said: 'I grant the latter imputation, Enderby,' he said, 'if you call a search for pure love perversion.' As on cue, the negroid waiter in the tarboosh appeared from the kitchen, posed against the door-post, and looked in a sort of loving horror at Rawcliffe. 'There, my black beauty,' cooed Rawcliffe's abraded larynx. 'Anybody noshing in there? *Quién está comiendo?*' His head twitched towards the dining-room.

'*Nadie.*'

'Shut up bloody shop, Manuel,' coughed Rawcliffe. 'We're closed till further notice. The bloody *baigneurs* and *baigneuses* —and a fat pustular lot they are, Enderby—can do key-business at the scullery door.' Manuel began to cry. 'Stop that,' said Rawcliffe with a ghost of sharpness. 'As for,' he turned back to Enderby, 'being a filthy traitor, I've done nothing to contravene the Official Secrets Act. The beastly stupid irony of sending you out here as a spy or whatever it is you are. That *maquillage* is ridiculous. It looks like boot-polish. Get it off, man. You'll find turps in the kitchen.'

'To me,' Enderby said. 'A traitor to me, bastard. You grew fat on the theft and travesty of my art.' Pity slayeth my nymphs.

'I mean metaphorically fat.'

'Of course you do, my dear Enderby.' Rawcliffe finished his brandy, tried to cough and couldn't. 'Better. A mere palliative, though. And that's why you got yourself up like that, eh? My brain's fuddled, such of it as has not yet been eaten away by this encroaching angel. I fail to see why you should dress up as whatever it is you're supposed to be in order to tell me I've grown metaphorically fat on your whatever it is.' He grew suddenly drowsy and then shook himself awake. 'Have you locked those bloody doors yet, Manuel?' he tried to shout.

'*Pronto, pronto.*'

'It's a bit of a long story.' Enderby saw no way out of seeming to make an excuse. 'I'm hiding from the police, you see. Interpol and so on.' He sat down on a stackable chair.

'Make yourself comfortable, my dear old Enderby. Help yourself to a drink. You look sunken and hungry. There's Antonio sleeping in his kitchen, a very passable pastmaster of short-order cookery. We'll shout him awake and he will, singing his not altogether trustworthy Andalusian heart out, knock you up his own idiosyncratic version of a mixed grill.' He probed his throat for a cough but none came. 'Better. I feel better. It must be your presence, my dear old Enderby.'

'Murder,' Enderby said. 'Wanted for murder. Me, I mean.' He couldn't help a minimal smirk. The Woolworth watch ticked loudly. As in a last desperate gasp, the sun slashed the shelves of bottles behind the bar with fire and crystal, then retired. The clouds hunched closer. Bathers were running into Rawcliffe's arena, after keys and clothes. Manuel was there shouting at them, jangling keys. '*Cerrado. Fermé. Geschlossen.* Shut up bloody shop.'

'Like something from poor dear dead Tom Eliot,' said Rawcliffe. 'He always liked that little poem of mine. The one, you may remember, that is in all the anthologies. And now the rain laying our dust. No more shelter in the colonnade and sun in the Hofgarten.' He seemed ready to snivel.

'Murder,' Enderby said, 'is what we were talking about. I mean me being wanted for murder.'

'Be absolute for life or death,' said Rawcliffe, fumbling a dirty handkerchief from one of the many pockets of his jacket-face.

He gave the handkerchief to his mouth with both hands, coughed loosely, then showed Enderby a gout of blood. 'Better up than down, out than in. So, Enderby,' he said, folding in the blood like a ruby and stowing it with care, 'you've opted for the fantasy life. The defence of pretence. I can't say I blame you. The real world's pretty horrible when the gift goes. I should know, God help me.'

'It went but it came back. The gift, I mean. And now,' Enderby said, 'I shall write in prison.' He crossed one leg over the other, disclosing much of his European trousers, and, for some reason, felt like beaming at Rawcliffe. 'They don't have the death penalty any more,' he added.

Rawcliffe shook and shook. It was with anger, Enderby saw with surprise. 'Don't talk to me about the bloody death penalty,' Rawcliffe shook. 'Nature exacts her own punishments. I'm dying, Enderby, dying, and you burble away about writing verse in prison. It's not the dying I mind so much as the bloody indignity. My underpants filling with bloody cack, and the agony of pissing, and the smell. The smell, Enderby. Can you smell the smell?'

'I've got used to smells,' Enderby apologised, 'living as I've been doing. You don't smell any different,' he smelled, 'than that time in Rome. You bloody traitor,' he then said hotly. 'You stole my bloody poem and crucified it.'

'Yes yes yes yes.' Rawcliffe seemed to have grown tired again. 'I suppose the decay was always with me. Well, it won't be long now. And I shall infect neither earth nor air. Let the sea take me. The sea, Enderby, *thalassa, la belle mer.* Providence, in whatever guise, sent you, in whatever guise. Because, delightful though these boys could often be in my violet-enough-smelling though really Indian summer, days, they can't altogether be trusted. With me gone, a mere parcel of organic sludge yum-yumyummed away at by boring phagocytes, Enderby, the post-humous memory of my request will not move them to fulfil it. Oh, dear me, no. So that can be handed over to you with total confidence, a fellow-Englishman, a fellow-poet.' The boys could be heard in the kitchen, hearty Mediterranean lip-smacking, the rarer and more sophisticated ping of a fork on a plate, Moghrabi conversation, laughter escaping from munches. Not altogether to be trusted. The rain now came down, and Rawcliffe, as if pleased that a complicated experimental process were under way, nodded. Enderby suddenly realised that that was who he'd got his own nod from: Rawcliffe.

'Rawcliffe,' he said, 'bastard. I'm not here to do anything for you, bastard as you are. You've got to be killed. As a defiler of art and a bloody traitor.' He noticed that he still had one leg comfortably crossed over the other. He disposed himself more aggressively, hands tensely gripping knees, though still seated. That tan polish seemed to be sweating off, a bit streaky. He'd better do something about that before killing Rawcliffe.

'If you killed me,' Rawcliffe said, 'you'd be doing me a very large favour. There might be a small obituary in *The Times*. The triumph of that early poem might be recalled, the poem itself reproduced, who knows? As for a weapon, there's a till-protect-ing service revolver in that cupboard behind the bar. Or our steak-knives are pretty sharp. Or you could feed me, say, fifty sleeping-capsules, pellet by pellet. Oh, my dear Enderby, don't be a bloody bore. Let me expiate in nature's way, blast you.'

'That's not right,' Enderby started to mumble. 'Justice. What I mean is.' What he meant was that he'd been quite looking forward to a life sentence, a bit of peace and quiet, get on with his. 'I mean that if they're going to get me it'd better be for something real.' Then: 'I didn't mean that. What I meant to say was for a sheep as well as a lamb. Look, I will have a drink after all.'

'Better, Enderby, much better. There's a nice bottle of Strega behind the bar. Remember those brief sunny Strega-drinking days by the Tiber? Days of betrayal, you will say. Was I the only betrayer?' He sat up with sudden alertness. 'Do pass me that bottle of life-surrogate there, my dear Enderby. Cordon Bleu, a blue cordon to keep out that scrabbling crowd of clawers hungry for my blood. They must wait, must they not? We have things to see to, you and I, first.' Enderby went to the bar, handed shaking Rawcliffe his bottle, unwilling anyway to pour for the sod, then looked at all the other bottles, embarrassed for choice. 'Didn't go well, that marriage, did it, Enderby? Not cut out for marriage, not cut out for murder. Tell me all about that. No, wait. Dear Auntie Vesta. Married now to some sharp Levantine with very good suits. But she failed really, you know, failed despite everything. She'll never be in anybody's biography, poor bitch. You're a remarkable man, Enderby. It was in all the papers, you know, that marriage. There was a pop nuptial mass or something. Choreography round the altar, brought downstage for the occasion. A lot of bloody ecumenical nonsense.'

'That,' grudgemumbled Enderby, 'is just what I said. Not in that connection. I mean in the other one. That priest, I mean. The day it happened.' Fundador. Not too bad a drink, despite that blasted moon woman. Rawcliffe clanked and clanked out his slug, then drank. Enderby, ashamed at his quieter co-ordination, did a real professional barman's pour of his own. 'What happened was this,' he said, before drinking. 'This yob got shot, Crewsy that is, was, and someone put the gun in my hand. I ran, you see. You'd have done the same.'

Rawcliffe frowned, made a shot at his lips with his glass, sprayed and dribbled cognac, sucked in a fair amount, gasped. 'Let's get all this straight, Enderby,' he gasped. 'I read the papers. I read nothing else. I've been hanging on to life, you know. The ephemeral, I mean, the sad, pretty, awful, tragic everyday, not the transcendencies of great art. I shall meet the eternal soon enough. I shall get my chamber music without the trouble of having to attend to profundities squeezed sweating from sheepgut. Or there will be nothing, like Sam Beckett. I read the papers—the pipe-smoking dogs, the topless weddings, the assassinations of pop-singers. Yod Crewsy I know all about. Dying, soon to die. Perhaps we shall die on the same day, he and I. That will be fitting, somehow. A barman shot him. I don't remember the name. Wait: something porcine.'

'Hogg,' said Enderby with impatience. 'Hogg, Hogg.' There was a young wall-eyed man in a dirty apron, the cook Antonio probably, standing by the kitchen door, picking his teeth with a quill and frowning puzzled at Enderby's get-up. 'Hogg.'

'That's it. So you read the papers too. A poetical name, that I did know. A very Jacobitical poet, that one. Charlie he's my darling. Wha the deil hae we goten for a King but a wee wee German lairdie. I like that weewee bit. He spoke out, Enderby. He didn't give a worsted-stocking damn.'

'Listen,' Enderby hissed, coming from behind the bar with his glass of Fundador. 'That was me. Hogg. That was my mother's name. They turned me into a barman, Wapenshaw and the rest of them. Yes, yes, they did. A useful citizen, they said, poet no longer. You didn't know, nobody knew. *That* was never in the papers.' Rawcliffe was all rigidity now, staring. 'But,' Enderby said, 'I got away. As Enderby. I'd got my passport. And then that bloody woman found out that Enderby and Hogg were the same. So I had to get rid of the passport. It's a long story really.' He drank some Fundador and tasted again that night of the bloody woman. Bloody women.

'It must be, it must be. But,' said Rawcliffe, 'it's a man called Hogg they were looking for.' Enderby borrowed Rawcliffe's rigidity, staring. 'Oh yes. Nothing about may be travelling under an alias. Ill-known minor poet who mysteriously disappeared, nothing like that. Nobody blew the gaff, my dear Enderby.'

'She must have done. Selenographer, she called herself. The police scouring Morocco. Me in hiding. And then there's John the Spaniard.'

'Yes yes yes.' Rawcliffe spoke soothingly. 'The world's full of traitors, isn't it? But tell me, Enderby, why did you shoot him?'

'He deserved to be shot. Plagiarism. A travesty of art. He stole my poems. The same as you.'

'Oh, for God's sake,' said Rawcliffe with emphatic weariness, 'get it over with. Shoot everybody. Shoot the whole damned treacherous world, then get behind bars and write your bloody self-pitying doggerel.'

'Doggerel,' Enderby sneered. 'You're a right bastard to talk about me writing doggerel.'

'Wait, though, wait. Didn't you say something about not having shot him at all? About someone putting the smoking gun in your innocent paw? That figures, as the smoking gun films put it. Spaghetti Westerns. They had me writing those, Enderby. But I got out. I didn't do too badly out of *L'Animal Binato*. That was a bloody good idea of yours.' He shook himself back to the immediate topic. 'You're no killer, Enderby, be sure of that. You're not even the predestined victim. You wriggle out of the real striking of the blow by the operation of a time-warp or space-woof or something. You fall on your feet. You'll have to rename the *Acantilado Verde*, of course.'

'Eh?'

'Green cliff, raw cliff. You've got somebody on your side. Who? There you stand, absurd but vigorous. And Auntie Vesta is vanquished and poor Rawcliffe is dying. Is there anything more you want? Oh, yes. I shall dictate a letter to Scotland Yard—there's an old office Oliver in my bedroom behind the bar—and confess all. After all, Enderby, I could quite easily have done it. I even had an invitation. After all, I have been one of the great diluters, worthy to be asked. And I was in London, seeing the last of my head-shaking consultants. Very grave he was. Prepare to meet thy God. My Goddess, rather. Yes yes yes, the mockers and diluters and travestists deserve to die.' Enderby frowned, unsure whether this was all drunkenness or the start of terminal delirium. Rawcliffe closed his eyes, his head lolled, his trouser-fly darkened and then his crotch dripped. Enderby saw barman and waiter and cook all crammed in the kitchen doorway, open-mouthed.

'Get him to bed,' he ordered. 'Come on, jump to it.' Antonio crossed himself, quill still in his teeth. They did not exactly jump to it, but Manuel and the tarbooshed waiter grabbed each an oxter of Rawcliffe. Rawcliffe was dimly roaring. Enderby took the legs. He had done that before for Rawcliffe, he remembered. In Rome, honeymooning. Rawcliffe was lighter now than then. Antonio pointed where the bedroom was. The rain was easing a bit.

Three

'You one of his *friends,* then?' asked the doctor. 'Didn't know he had any *British* ones.' He looked at Enderby with little favour, despite the restored teeth and shaved pinkness (that tan stuff had been hard to get off, the solvents painful), hair scant but washed and brushed, serious spectacles catching the pale after-rain Tangerine light. He was also wearing one of Rawcliffe's neo-Georgian suits, grey and hairy and not too tight in the armpits. The three boys, who were growing pimples and mannerisms as Enderby got to know them better (the tarbooshed waiter had also grown a name—Tetuani, after his hometown

Tetuan), had been helpful with the restoration. They had even made up a sort of bed for him with the fireside-type chair and two or three stackable ones. It seemed to them to be a relief to have an Englishman around who was not dying.

'Not in that sense,' Enderby said sternly. 'A sort of friend, but not in the sense you mean.'

'What do you mean, in what sense I mean?' The doctor was an upright tall man in his hale sixties, with a lot of wavy silver hair; he looked like a military medical officer who, on the repatriation of a superior garrison, had elected to stay behind. Liked the place or something. But probably secrets of his own; shadiness. He was a bit too sharp with his 'What do you mean?'

'You know what I mean,' Enderby said, blushing. 'I'm finished with sex, anyway,' he blabbed, ill at ease, unhappy with doctors. As if this declaration were a clue to identity, the doctor said:

'Seen you before somewhere, haven't I?'

'My picture in the papers perhaps. Or rather,' Enderby emended with haste, 'the picture of a man who looks very much like me, or so I'm told. A man called Hogg.'

'I wouldn't know. Never read the papers. A lot of lies mostly. As for that sex business, I'm not all that interested in what people do in that line so long as they don't come moaning to me about the consequences. This one,' he said, shouldering towards Rawcliffe, who lay feebly snorting under a blanket, 'has favoured the dirty and diseased. But you know that, of course, being his *friend*. *Nostalgie de la boue*, if you know what that means. But what he's dying of could happen to anybody. To you,' he said. 'To your maiden aunt in Chichester or wherever it is.'

'I haven't got—'

'He's riddled with it, no respecter of persons. All we can do is to ease the end. You can pay me for the hypodermic and the morphine now if you like. And for this and two previous consultations. Call me in again when you think he's gone. I'll have to sign the death certificate.'

'The body,' said Enderby. 'There's the question of—'

'He should have done what most of the British do out here. Fifty quid or thereabouts for a patch at St Andrew's. Burial service, resurrection and the life, the lot. Told me once he was a conscientious hedonist, though. Pleasure the end of life, that means. Very unwise, look where it's got him.'

'But you said it could happen to—'

'He'll have to be interred at Bubana. I daresay they'll say a few words over the grave. Somebody from the consulate usually turns up. Leave all that to you.'

'Look here—'

'I usually get paid in cash. Out of the till.' He marched ahead of Enderby into the bar and, nodding at Antonio and Manuel, who were playing Spanish Scrabble, helped himself to what looked like forty-five dirhams.

'ELLA.'

'ELLAS.'

'He says,' Enderby said, 'that he wants to be dropped into the sea. It's in writing, signed and witnessed. That he's to be dropped into the sea. Is there any law against that?'

'Damned irregular,' the doctor said, helping himself to a snifter of Bell's. 'The thing ought to be done properly. What must they think of the white man here, I often ask myself. Pederasty, if you know the term, and drunkenness. Also drugs and writing. You're new here so you wouldn't know half that goes on. Keep away from that stupidly-named Dog place across the road. Americans of the worst type. Still, *autres temps autres moeurs*. I need not, I hope, translate. I leave everything to you, his *friend*. Don't neglect to get me on the blower when the time comes.'

'Enby.' It was Rawcliffe, very feeble.

'You'd better go in and see what he wants. Don't excite him. He's in your hands now.'

'Look here—'

'DIOS.'

'ADIOS.'

'Little poem in itself, that, you could call it I suppose,' said the doctor. He smacked off the last of his Bell's. 'Still, I leave poetry to you and your kind. I must be off now.'

'What do you mean by—'

'Enby.' Rawcliffe had pumped up a few extra teaspoonsful of painful air to strengthen his call. No compassion in his march,

the doctor let himself out. 'Bgr you Enby. Comere.' Enderby
went back into the sickroom. It was small but cool. Rawcliffe's
bed was a double mattress laid on a worn Bokhara; thrown
about all over the floor were local goat-skins, of different degrees
of off-whiteness; there were cheap ornaments from the bazaar
—a hand of Fatma, a cobra which was really an iron spring—it
throbbed and jumped and burred on the Moorish coffee table if
you touched it, a Rif saddle, a hubble-bubble, scimitars and
daggers on the walls. One wall was all books in army cartridge-
boxes disposed like shelf-units. Enderby had not yet had time to
look through those books: there might conceivably be a copy
of—The smell of dying Rawcliffe fought against an incense-
burner and an aerosol lavender spray. Rawcliffe, naked under his
blanket, said: 'Brandy. Vry lrge.'

'He said you're to have morphine,' Enderby said uneasily.
'Alcohol won't help the pain, he said.'

'Bgrim. Wanna talk. Bndy.' Enderby tried to harden his heart
against him, traitor, traducer, diluter, sinner against literature.
He went to get a new bottle of Cordon Bleu. Could Rawcliffe
cope with a lemonade glass?

'CACA.'

'CACAO.'

There was a china feeding-cup next to the iron cobra. Enderby poured cognac in, sat on Rawcliffe's bed and helped him
to drink. Rawcliffe spluttered, coughed, tried to say *Christ*, but
he got down what Enderby estimated to be about a bar quin-
tuple. He had once, in Piggy's Sty, had to serve one of those to a
Cabinet Minister: it had come to thirty shillings, taxpayers'
money.

'Better, Enderby, much better. Taken that letter to the post,
has he? Loiters on the way sometimes, wayward. Good funda-
mentally, though. A bottom of good sense. Dr Johnson or somebody said that, Enderby.'

'It was about a woman.'

'Woman, was it? Well, of course, that's more your line, isn't
it? God God God God, the bloody pain. The thing to do is to try
to see the bloody pain as working in something out there. The
body is not me. No transubstan. But Christ Christ, there's a hot
line to the brain. Snip the nerve-endings, is there a me still there

when all have been snipped? Psychoneural paral paral paral-
lelism ism. Very popular that, before the war. The new immortality.'
'There's this morphine here,' Enderby said.
'More your line. Two lines there, though, hot and cold. Sun
and moon. Moon's no power over you, Enderby. Me, I sinned
against the Muse, all woman, and she took her revenge. And
now to be sacrificed to her. But she'll be partly cheated, Enderby. New moon coming up about now. But eastward there are
tideless waters. Drop this exterior thing in the tideless waters,
Enderby. More brandy.'
'Do you think you—'
'Yes, I do. Got to tell you. Give instructions.' Enderby poured
more cognac into the feeding-cup. Obscene, somehow, that festive gold and heady vapour in bland invalid china. Rawcliffe
sucked more in avidly. 'There's a man called Walker, Enderby.
Useful sort of man, British colonial. His precise terry territory
uncertain. He's in Casablanca now. Get in touch with him, his
phone number's behind the bar. He knows how to get a small
aircraft, borrows it from Abdul Krim or somebody, bloody rogue
whoever he is. Bloody rogue. What was I saying? Tight, a bit,
that's the trouble. Empty stomach, that's the trouble.'
'I know this Walker. Easy Walker he calls himself.' And then:
'Can you eat something? An egg or something?'
'It's not your job to keep me alive, is it, Enderby? What's the
bloody use of nutriment to me? Listen. The money's in this mattress. For Christ's sake don't let anybody burn it. It's not that I
don't trust the banks. It's the buggers in the banks I don't trust,
Enderby. Tattle tattle tattle about how much he's got, then coming along for a loan, then beat you up in a back-alley if they
can't have it. I know them all too well. You know them all too
well. You know Easy Walker. Always said you'd fall on your
feet, Enderby. Get that bloody Antonio in here.'
'What for?'
'Tell him to bring his guitar. Want to hear. To hear. In all the
anthol. He sings it.'
Enderby went out to the bar and said: '*Antonio. Señor Rawcliffe quiere que tu, usted canta, cante,* subjunctive there somewhere, whatever it is. *Su canción, él dice.*' Antonio and Manuel

both looked up from a Scrabble board now nearly full of words, their eyes ready to brim. Enderby went back to Rawcliffe. 'That letter to Scotland Yard,' he said. 'It won't do any good. There must be a lot who send in letters like that.' And where was he to go, where? He had reconciled himself, hadn't he? But that was when it had seemed possible to be able to murder Rawcliffe. Rawcliffe's eyes were closed. He had started snorting again. His body writhed feebly. And then he started violently awake.

'You've no bloody idea,' he said with slow seriousness, 'of the bloody agony. You wouldn't think it possible. Don't leave it too long, Enderby.'

'Morphine?'

'Brandy. Insult to the brain. Poor Dylan. Kill me with bloody kindness.' Enderby sighed, then recharged the feeding-cup. Antonio came in, trying his strings, crying. 'Sing, blast you,' said Rawcliffe, spluttering out cognac. The smell of it was fast overcoming his own. Antonio sat on the Rif saddle and twanged his thumb from E to e, sniffing his tears back. It was a well-worn guitar; Enderby could see the abrasions of fingers that, in Andalusian style, had drummed its body. Antonio gave out a thrummed major chord that, with the smell of cognac, seemed to affirm life (sun, zapateados, death in the afternoon). He wailed:

'Per ap sa yamna tuonti diri seyed,
    Per ap sayid beter go,
Ji seyed. Mocionles jer ayis, jer jeyed,
    Seyin not yes, not no.'

'In all the anthologies,' Rawcliffe cried, then coughed and coughed. Antonio did not go on. 'Put that, death, in your bloody pipe,' said Rawcliffe more weakly when the racking had subsided. '*Exegi monumentum.* And what of yours, Enderby?' He was so faint that Enderby had to drop his ear towards him. 'Better to be the one-poem man. But she left me then. Opened up heaven of creativity and then closed it. All right, Antonio. Later, later. *Muchas gracias.*' Antonio blew his nose on his cook's apron. 'Read me something of yours, Enderby. They're there, your slender volumes, somewhere. I bought your books at least. Least I could do. I am not all badness.'

'Well, really, this is hardly—What I mean is—'

'Something appropriate. Something to one about to die or one dead.'

Enderby felt grimly in his left jacket pocket. He had transferred that stolen horror thither. 'I can,' he said, 'without going to your shelves.' But there was here at last, and his heart began to climb as with muscular pseudopodia, the chance of checking. Auntie Vesta. He strode over Rawcliffe's hidden feet towards the wall of books. A lot of cheap nasty stuff there: *Bumboy, Mr Wigg's Fancy, Lashmaster.* He thought, from the shape and size, he saw a copy of his own *Fish and Heroes,* but it turned out to be a small collection of glossy photographs: men and boys complicatedly on the job, with idiot eyes. But here it was, that other volume, the one the critics had trounced: *The Circular Pavane.* He flicked and flicked through the pages. There weren't many. And then. 'Right,' he said. Rawcliffe's eyes were closed again but he could tell Enderby was smiling. He said:

'Glee, eh? The creator's glee? You've found something that recalls the actual ecstasy of its making. Don't exass exacerbate my agony. Read it.'

'Listen.' Enderby tried to be gruff, but his reading made the poem sound sneering, as though the emotions of the mature were being mocked by some clever green child:

'They thought they'd see it as parenthesis—
    Only the naked statement to remember,
Cleaving no logic in their sentences,
    Putting no feelers out to the waking dreamer—

So they might reassume untaken seats,
    Finish their coffee and their arguments,
From the familiar hooks redeem their hats
    And leave, with the complacency of friends.

But strand is locked with strand, like the weave of bread,
    And this is part of them and part of time—'

'Oh God God,' Rawcliffe suddenly cried. 'Ugly hell gape not come not Lucifer.' He began to babble. 'And if the eternal finds its figures in the temporal then they can find their inferno here.' He screamed and then collapsed, his head lolling, his tongue out, blood coming from his left nostril. Antonio's guitar clanged gently superposed fourths and my-dog-has-fleas as he put it down. He made the sign of the cross and prayed weeping. 'A shot, Enderby, for Christ's sake.' Enderby stared: a test; see if he could really kill? 'A lot of shots.' He saw then and went over to the coffee-table and the syringe and the morphine ampoules in their box. He hoped he could cope. Those Doggy Wog people would be able to cope all right.

Four

Rawcliffe did not stay under for long. There was a powerful life-urge there, despite everything. 'Brandy,' he said. 'I'll beat them all yet, Enderby.' Enderby filled the cup: the bottle was near its end. Rawcliffe sucked it all in like water. 'What news?' he asked. 'What irrelevancies are proceeding in the big world?'

'There's nothing as far as I can see,' Enderby said. 'But we've only got the Spanish paper, and I can't read Spanish very well.'

Enough, though. When Tetuani came back from posting that air-letter, he brought with him a copy of *España*, which Enderby took with him to a bar-table. Rawcliffe unconscious, though roaring terribly from deep in his cortex, Enderby sat with a large whisky, breathing the prophylactic of fresh air from an open window. '*Quiere comer?*' Antonio asked. Enderby shook his head: he couldn't eat anything just yet, not just yet, *gracias* all the same. He drank his drink and looked at the paper. It was better that he read what he was undoubtedly going to read not in English: he needed the cushioning of a foreign tongue, with all its associations of literature and tourism, despite his fore-knowledge. Words had power of their own: *dead* would always be a horrible word. On the front page the Caudillo still howled for the Rock, and some Arab leader called vainly for the exter-mination of Israel. When, on the second page, he came to the headline YOD CREWSY MUERTO, his response was that of a printer who had set the type himself. The score was, say, 10-2, and you had to wait ten minutes, say, for the anticlimax of the final whistle. What it said under the headline was brief. It said, as far as Enderby could tell, that he had passed into a terminal coma after a moment of flickering his eyes open and that soon there were no further indications of cardiac activity. There would be a sort of lying in state somewhere and then a requiem mass at the Catholic Cathedral in London (they meant Westminster). Fr O'Malley would deliver the panegyric. Nothing about girls weeping, as over Osiris or Adonis or somebody. Nothing about Scotland Yard expecting immediate arrest.

'Nothing at all,' Enderby said.

What would Scotland Yard do about Rawcliffe's letter? Enderby had two-fingered it himself to Rawcliffe's dictation. It would do no good, Enderby had said, but Rawcliffe had insisted. Repentance, seeing the light, symbolic blow against anti-art. A guest (check guest-list) who had come with full cold-blooded intention of killing and then being arrested—dying of those encroaching claws, what had he to lose?—he had succumbed in reflex to panic and handed gun to an anonymous waiter. He was not sorry, oh no, far from it: so perish all art's enemies, including (but with him it was the fullest blackest knowledge: he knew what he did) himself. Rawcliffe's scrawl, two witnesses: Antonio Alarcón and Manuel Pardo Palma. Well, Enderby thought, it might resolve things one way or the other. It would welcome the police to one terminus or another. And your name, sir, señor? Enderby. Your passport, please, por favor. Well, a slight problem there, officer. Whispered consultation, sergeant calling inspector over, comparing photograph with. All right, Hogg then. I recognised the true murderer and pursued him. Doing the job of the police for them, really, in best fictional tradition. I say no more. All right, arrest me then. Obviously I say no more. No warning necessary.

He was indifferent, really. All he wanted was a small room and a table to write verse on and freedom from the necessity to earn a living. But there remained self-doubt. Was the Muse so generous now only because she was dispensing rubbish? The future, perhaps, lay with those Doggy Wog people. He didn't really know; he wanted to be told, shown. But was he being reserved for something? Why did not everybody know that Hogg was Enderby? Why had that moon-bitch been silent? If John the Spaniard had blown the gaff, why was Tangier not milling with Interpol, demanding to see all foreign passports, combing? What force had struck down Wapenshaw, if it was Wapenshaw they'd been talking about, and rendered him dumb?

Enderby wondered now, sitting on the Rif saddle, keeping away from the putridity, whether he should ask Rawcliffe (meaning the still not foundered intelligence in the penthouse above the demolition squads), as a dying man who had nothing to gain by mendacity, what he thought of his, Enderby's, work and (what he really meant) whether he should go on with it. But heaving and groaning Rawcliffe gave him an answer without being asked, without speaking. Go on with anything so long as you're alive; nothing matters except staying alive. Enderby could see that now, but had not always thought so. Rawcliffe said:

'Get on to Walker. It's going to be *it* soon, Enderby. Never mind what he asks. Money money money. All money these days. Fortunately it's stuffed in here, mine I mean, by my feet. No danger, Enderby, of ultimate incontinence fouling it. Clean money, most. The dirty part did not really harm my country. Hashish a harmless enough drug. More brandy.'

'I'll have to get a new bottle.'

'Get it then, blast you. What are those bloody boys doing?'

'The siesta.'

'Something in the Bible about that. What, could ye not watch with me one hour? This night, before the cock crow.' Rawcliffe took breath, rattling, and went feebly cocorico. Then he coughed and coughed. Blood bubbled from both nostrils and some trickled from his right mouth-corner. 'Good Christ,' he panted, 'I won't have this. Bewrayed, beshitten. Die in one's own bloody dung.' He tried to shift his body away from the new foulness but rolled back on to it. 'I'm getting up,' he said. 'I'm going to die on my feet. Help me, blast you, Enderby.'

'You can't, you mustn't, you—'

'Best to be shot, knifed, standing.' He threw his blanket off. He was naked except for a safety-pinned towel like a baby's diaper. 'I insist, Enderby, you bastard. I'll drink my terminal liquor in a bar, like a man. My viaticum, you swine.' He started, cursing, to get up. Enderby had to help, no way out of it. He went further than he'd gone for anybody. He pulled off Rawcliffe's diaper and wiped him clean with the clean part of it. He forgave his stepmother everything. There was a bathrobe on a nail be-

hind the door. He put his arm round bare shivering Rawcliffe
and shuffle-danced him towards it. 'Better, Enderby, better,' as
he was clothed in gay yellow and blue. 'Take me to the bar.
Wake those bloody boys. They must be my crutch.'

Pushing Rawcliffe before him, Enderby yelled. Antonio peered
out from the kitchen first, startled, naked as Rawcliffe had been.
He went back in to get the others, himself yelling. Rawcliffe
tried to yell but collapsed into coughing. He collapsed against
the bar-counter coughing, trying to curse. Soon Antonio and
Manuel were holding him up, an arm each about him, in dirty
white shirts; Manuel's trousers were already black. 'Now, Enderby,' Rawcliffe gasped at last. 'You say you've been a bloody
barman. Mix me something. A cocktail called *Muerte*. Stop that
blasted snivelling, you two.' Tetuani, tarboosh on, came out,
frightened.

And I will, thought Enderby. 'Leave it to me,' he said, adding, in desperate facetiousness, 'sir.' He took a large beer-glass
and slopped brandy in, then white rum, gin, whisky, vodka. The
bottles flashed in the fair afternoon light. It was like celebrating
something.

'No need for ice,' Rawcliffe gasped. 'Get that, maybe, soon.
That thing in bloody Shakespeare. Measure for measure, eh? Altogether fitting. Thrilling regions of ribbed ice. Top it, Enderby,
with something spumous. Asti, memories of Rome. Add, for old
time's sake, a dollop of Strega. Strega, a witch. Witchbitch. That
bloody man in Mallorca, Enderby, says the day of the moon
goddess is done. The sun goddess takes over.' Enderby found a
bottle of Asti on the shelf, very warm, favoured of the sun. He
cracked its neck against the counter-edge. 'Good, Enderby.'
There was a fine gush. The stench of Rawcliffe was now well
overlaid with powerful yea-saying aromas. But, admired Enderby, those boys' stomachs were strong. He gave the full spum-
ing glass to both Rawcliffe's claws. 'A toast,' Rawcliffe said.
'What shall it be, eh? *La sacra poesía*? The sun goddess? The
survival of the spirit? To the,' he began to droop, 'impending
dissolution,' to snivel; the strong-handed boys began to snivel
with him, 'of this, of this—' Enderby became stern: he didn't
like this snivelling. He cried:

'Ah, shut up. Get that bloody drink down and shut up.' It was strong fatherly talk; the medicine was wholesome; had not he, Enderby, once dared death, though dragged gurgling back? 'Get on with it, Rawcliffe. Bloody traitor.'

'Good, Enderby, good, good. No false compassion there. Excellent.' Rawcliffe braced himself, pumped air into his lungs like a parody of a dog's panting, then took his medicine. It spilled and rilled, the *mousse* got up his nose, he coughed some back into the glass, but he went gamely on to the dregs. Antonio put the flecked glass down for him. Rawcliffe gasped and gasped. 'Put. That. On. The.' He coughed, like payment, a coin of bloody sputum on to the counter. 'I mean. *Muerte*. The. Ult. Ult. Ultmte. Cktl.' He yearned towards his chair, feebly turning. The boys took him over, only his bare toes touching the floor. Rawcliffe collapsed next to his chairside table, full of toys. Coventry Patmore. 'Lil slp now.' He at once began to snore. The boys put his feet up on a stackable. Enderby thought he had better now telephone Casablanca.

Five

It was growing dark when Rawcliffe surfaced for the last time. Enderby had sent the boys out, sick of the hand-wringing and snivelling. He sat at the other side of Rawcliffe's chair, smoking the local cigarettes that were called *Sport*, not drinking. The thought of drink made him shudder. When Rawcliffe surfaced, it was with an accession—that condemned man's supper—of clarity and calm. He said:

'Who's that there?'

'Me. Enderby.'

'Ah yes, Enderby. Know your poetry well. Stole one of your ideas once, a bloody good one. No regrets. Now I give you something in return. My last poem. It came to me in sleep. Listen.' He cleared his throat like an elocutionist and intoned slowly but with vigour:

> 'The benison of lights and the
> Hides of asses and the
> Milk of the tide's churns.

> She should not have
> Rejected me like any copulative
> Of the commonalty.

Too much light, Enderby. Turn one of those lights off.'
There were no lights on. 'I've done that,' Enderby said.
'Good, Now where was I? Ah, I know. Listen.

> At length I heard a ragged noise and mirth
> Of thieves and murderers. There I him espied,
> Who straight, *Your suit is granted,* said, and died.'

'That,' Enderby said, 'is George Herbert.'
Rawcliffe suddenly began to rage. 'It's not it's not it's not you
fucking swine. It's me. Me.' In the dusk his head rolled. Quietly,
'Your suit is granted,' he said, and died. With the conventional
accompaniment of rattle and postlude of rictus and liquidity.

3

One

'A ND,' Easy Walker cried above the engine, 'real donk dirt-
bibles. Got a jarvey, brad, all towsermouth for that variety
of how's your Auntie-Doris-and-little-Nora-and-the-twins. So we'll
march on markers when this lot's dooby-dooed.'

The physical assumption of Rawcliffe. His body, in clean
pyjamas and wrapped in a Union Jack that Manuel had bought
for a few dirhams in, of all places, the Big Fat White Doggy
Wog, sat next to Easy Walker in what Enderby took to be the co-
pilot's seat. At least a kind of half-eaten steering-wheel or joy-
stick in front of Rawcliffe twitched and turned in sympathy with
Easy Walker's. And also dead Rawcliffe had his share of very
lively dials and meters and emergency instructions, exclamation-
pointed. His arms were pinioned beneath the flag, and he was
corded at neck, waist, thighs, and ankles. No danger of his, its,
flailing around if it-he came back to life.

'You sure he's footed the old garbage-can proper?' Easy
Walker had asked while they had been bundling him in. 'Because there's been cases. There's this case now, brad. Tell you

after. Maybe you minced it all masterman.'

Enderby sat behind Rawcliffe, an empty seat next to him. It was a small but neat aircraft, American-made, though there was a spelling mistake, Enderby noted, in one of the instructions on the instrument-panel: *jetison*. That did not make him doubt the airworthiness of the craft, for it was always a matter of every man to his own trade. This one of piloting seemed as much a trade of Easy Walker's as any of the others he professed. He had cried conversationally above the engine even as, tearing down the runway, he brought the speed up to air-speed:

'A real donk passy too, there'll be there. Left the whole bimbang kadoozer to you then, has he, brad?'

'There's the question of,' Enderby had shouted. 'That one of mine, I mean.'

'Welcome to Bird County,' Easy Walker had yelled as the craft nosed into the old-gold Moroccan air. The late afternoon sky to themselves, except for rare gulls and, far to port, a migrant exaltation of brownish birds that, after a rest on the top of Gibraltar, were crossing the Straits for their African wintering. No Air Maroc flight till very much later. Below on the cabochon-cut Mediterranean very few boats, though what looked like a rich man's yacht gleamed to starboard. It was still the sun's time. The moon, thin last night, was not watching over Rawcliffe's ascension into heaven. Fattened, she would draw at him vainly from the deep, gnawed by fishes, his flag defiled. Over the aircraft wireless strange English crackled from Tangier control tower. Easy Walker ignored it. Aft lay Ceuta.

'There was one,' he yelled without effort, 'Ricker Sugden did for like his booze brad when he kicked. Do too for this jarvey, I reckon.' He recited, drowning the engine:

> 'Dragged from his doings in the roar of youth,
>   Snipped like the stem of a caldicot flower,
>   Snarled time's up ere he'd quaffed his hour,
> Tossed to the tearing of the dour dog's tooth.'

'That's not quite right for Rawcliffe,' Enderby shouted. It wasn't, either. The right one was in all the anthologies, but Enderby's calling of it would never prevail against this of Ricker Sugden's. It was the right one only because it was the only one.

'Bye, my brad, let the bright booze pour
    That is suds of stars in the Milky Way,
    And its door swing open all the joylit day
And the heavenlord landlord cry you time no more.'

'Not one of his best,' called Enderby, but he was not heard. Not obscure enough, too much meaning. Poor Rawcliffe. Traitor Rawcliffe rather, but he had paid. Your suit is granted. What suit? To be granted a cell, smallest unit of life. Enderby feebly tried to give out to sea, sky and Easy Walker that last stanza ('His salts have long drained into alien soil'), and then saw how inappropriate it really was. His soil would drain soon into alien salt. There was nothing for Rawcliffe. But it was something to rest in bones, rags of flag fluttering, at the sea's bottom between two continents. It was a kind of poem. Easy Walker cried:

'Nowsy wowsy. You right for the shove, brad?' Enderby nodded, forgetting that Easy Walker's eyes were ahead and there was no driving mirror. The corpse of Rawcliffe had lolled to rest against the perspex of the starboard door. Enderby roughly pushed it so that it began to topple gracefully against Easy Walker. 'Watch it, watch it, brad.' Leaning over, Enderby turned the door-handle, panting. It was rather stiff. Suddenly it opened and swung, and the huge roaring air without seemed to pull at him, but he dug his nails into Rawcliffe's seat-back. 'Nowsy wowsy powsy.' Easy Walker made the craft list hard to starboard. A torrent of frozen air was rushing in up diagonally now. Enderby clawed at the corpse through its flag-shroud, heaving it out, but, falling to the air, it seemed to be merely buoyed up by it. 'Blast you, Rawcliffe,' went Enderby for the last time. 'Righty right,' Easy Walker sang, and he kicked out at a dead shin. Then he listed further. Enderby pounded and pushed. As it were reluctantly, Rawcliffe's body launched itself into this quite inferior region of the sky, lower, surely, than Parnassus. 'Got him, brad,' meaning space had. The tricolor, crude in this sapphire and turquoise ambience, span slowly down. 'Gone.' Without sound, and with lips parted only as for a cigarette, the sea took him. Here lies one whose name was *not* writ in water, he had once said in his cups.

It was hard to get that door, which had swung open to its

limit, back in place. But Easy Walker lurched violently to port and the door hurtled in and, on a lurch that brought them both lying on their sides as at a Roman supper, it slammed to. Then he righted the craft and, widely circling in the air, its nose sniffed round towards home. Home: what else could you call it? Green Africa ahead, then the geometry of the little airport, then a sudden urgent love for the runway. A three-point landing of the kind called insolently skilled, a taxiing towards Easy Walker's waiting Volkswagen.

'Talking about passports,' Enderby said as they sped through the brown country outside town, 'I'd like that back if you've still got it. I let it go too soon.'

'Not poss, brad. Swallowed up, that, in the great dirty passy-hungry what-does-your-dad-do. Have his, though, your need being greater than. Dead jarveys help the living from their heart of darkness. Still. A pig of a pity.'

'What I mean is,' said Enderby, 'I'm entitled to an official identity of some sort.' But was he? And, if so, why? He might yet be taken somewhere, but he had no intention of making a move of his own. And, anyway, did bearing a name matter? Rawcliffe would be glad to be called anything or nothing if he could be alive again.

'There was the time I got this passy just as the jarvey as todded it seemed like as to take off. But he came to, yes he did, when it was already swapping fumblers. Well, you're all right, I'd say, with this Rawcliffe jarvey. He won't come up, no, not never no more. Different from this jarvey back in Great Dirty Mum.'

When they arrived back at *El Acantilado Verde*, Rawcliffe's other verbal monument, Easy Walker was eager to see what shady treasures there might be to buy cheap and sell dear. The three boys sat, in clean white, at a table by the bar-counter, playing some game which involved the linking of little fingers. They had some difficulty in composing their faces to a funeral look. 'All finished,' Enderby said. '*Finito.*' But there must be a better Spanish word than that. *Consommado?* It sounded soupish. '*Consummatum,*' he said, pushing down to the roots.

'March on markers,' said Easy Walker. He was very deft. The amount of pornography he uncovered was shocking. It was

mostly in the cartridge-box book-shelves, though previously—
because of the austerity of the binding—unsuspected by Enderby. 'Here,' said Easy Walker, 'is some right donk fladge for
such as takes a swizzle to it,' showing Enderby Victorian steel-
engravings of bloody wounds, lovingly detailed, and knobbed
whips and knotted thongs. 'And here's them shoving up the old
kazerzy with it, very painful for my shekels and sherbet. And
here,' Easy Walker said, shock on his unshockable, 'is what I
would not have if it was my own Aunt Ada as did it, brad.
Cause there's limitations to all bozzles, has to be, stands.' In his
hands trembled a leather-bound folio of what, to squinting Enderby, seemed at first to be illustrations to the Bible. But they
were very perverted illustrations, and there was one that made
Enderby feel sick. 'I mean,' Easy Walker said, slamming the
book shut, 'that was bad enough in itself without making it
worse and dirty sexual.' It was the first time Enderby had heard
him use plain language. 'Making a mock of it like that jarvey I
said. When a jarvey snuffs it's not up to him to come back, up-
your-piping and that. All right for him in here,' he bowed his
head, 'because he was what he was and no up-my-tickle. But
this jarvey like I said. And there was like that saucepan-lid,
Lazarus his all-the-same. And crucifixions too in this one, very
dirty. Very clear that came off.'

'What?' said Enderby. 'Who?' Time himself will bring you in
his high-powered car. And supposing the car doesn't go on to
pick someone else up but, instead, goes back to the garage.
Things as they were before, or as near as you could get them.
He would not be surprised, he would not be surprised at anything. 'You mean,' said Enderby, 'Yod Crewsy. You mean he's
not dead after all.'

Easy Walker nodded and nodded. 'Laid out, brad, in some
arsee plum-and-apple in the Smoke. Then all them teens broop-
ing round, going sniff sniff. Turn-the-handles lighted all about
him in his best whistle. And his three brads keeping double-
scotch, two at his toots and one behind his uncle. Then he flicks
open and says "Where am I?" Got it this morning on the talkbox,
in the near-and-far, coming here.'

Enderby nodded and nodded. Bitch. Blasphemous bitch. Very
clever. Easily done, bribed doctors or not even that. Genuine

error. Clinical death and real death. And now sermons about miracles and popsters flocking to give thanks. Our Thammuz, Adonis, Christ for that matter. 'And,' Enderby said, 'I suppose there was one sly pseudo-mourner, come to see, his only chance, his handiwork, lurking in the shadows of the chapel, and, when this body rose from the dead, he screamed. Screamed that the times have been that, when the brains were out, the man would die, and there an end, but now they rise again, this is more strange than such a murder is.'

Easy Walker shook his head, baffled. 'Don't get that at all, brad. Forked me on the cobbles and no rare-with-Worcester. Have to mince the papers when they come out, not out yet, not with that, pennywise.'

Enderby shook his head, not baffled. 'No more papers. Bugger the outside world,' he said violently. 'If not that way, some other. I'll hear about it, only a question of waiting. No resurrection for Rawcliffe, not of any kind. They'll crumple his letter up at Scotland Yard, another crank.'

'I'll ghoul these off now,' Easy Walker said, 'dirt-bibles.' He showed new shock on the realisation that his slang had, for once, slung at the gold and pierced it. Enderby then had an intuition that he was going to throw off what must be a home-stitched patchwork of patois and, strayed sheep or remittance-man, speak a true language that was far more middle-class than his, Enderby's. 'It's all dirt and cheating,' he said, and only on the last word (*cheadn*) did the innominate colonial really sound out. He seemed for an instant as feeble as in a plonk hangover. Enderby nodded. He said kindly:

'Come back tomorrow or the next day for the rest of the stuff. Except for what I want, that is. Any heterosexual pornography I'll keep. I've finished with women.'

'Finish with them.' It was clear and bitter. And then: 'What's all them there sling-your-hooks there, brad?' He headed at a set of cartridge-boxes set aside, special.

'Those,' said Enderby, 'are all the anthologies.'

When Easy Walker had left, Enderby ripped open Rawcliffe's mattress with a tarnished curved dagger. There were bundles of dirty notes, high and low in denomination: about, he reckoned, fifteen thousand dirhams. He would buy a new mattress tomorrow; tonight he would make a dog's bed of rugs and cushions. Then he went thoughtfully to examine Rawcliffe's bath and lavatory, rather well-appointed; for the customers there was only a stark, though regularly sluiced, WC off the dining-conservatory. Then he went to the bar. All three boys looked at him in expectation, a composition, as for an early Picasso, of coffee-mug handlers: Antonio sipped wide-eyed; Tetuani warmed both dark brown hands on the mug's belly; Manuel, finished drinking, swung his gently, handle on little finger. 'No,' Enderby said firmly. 'I sleep alone. *Yo duermo solo.*' They nodded with degrees of vigour: they had merely wanted to know. Manuel said:

'Open up bloody shop?'

'*Mañana.*'

'*Quiere café?*' asked Antonio.

Enderby did not resist his yearning towards a resumption of chronic self-imposed dyspepsia. He had convinced himself that he could be healthy enough if he wanted to be. 'Make,' he said slowly, 'very strong tea. *Muy fuerte.* Not tea-bags but spoonfuls of the real stuff. *Comprendido?* Tinned milk. *Leche condensada.*' And later he would eat—What? Something stepmotherly gross—a corned beef stew with bacon added to make floating flowers of grease, a grumbling huddle of boiled spuds, pickled onions. He nodded with relaxed kindness then went for his first for a hell of a long time leisurely session in the lavatory.

Two

'What I say is,' said the oldest of the men, his skin of broken veins and capillaries like an enlargement of a microscopic picture of motor oil, 'there couldn't have been any conspiracy. They choose crack shots. A political assassination is, in our country at least, a rather serious undertaking.'

'It's altogether possible,' said a dried ancient, goitrous thyroid colloidally distended, eyes popping, voice hoarse, 'that it was the act of a private entrepreneur. More enthusiasm than skill. They should never have got rid of National Service.'

'Well, that's just what I said, isn't it?'

'Implied, if you will. Hardly said.'

'He too,' said a brisk barking small ex-major, the youngest, about seventy-five, 'might have been resurrected. Wouldn't put anything past them. An everlasting premier.'

'Or he was just a liar.' This was a dithering man with twittering toothless mouth. 'Jealousy of the bug for the flea. Shot at him. Failed to kill. Now tries to make himself a political hero. What do you think, Rawcliffe?'

'I really have no opinion on the matter,' said Enderby. He sat in the fireside-type chair, the table in front of him, paper and ballpoint on the table, not a line added to the lines already there:

As loaves were gifts from Ceres when she laughed,
Thyrsis was Jack, but Crousseau on a raft
Sought Johnjack's rational island—

The sun was weakish, what Tangier called winter inching up. The bottles behind the bar caught that meagre light as if to store anew what was already long stored. Manuel measured out whisky for the old men, retired here for the warmth and fancied cheapness. Manuel was cheerful and honest, to be trusted with the till. Honesty was a Tangerine luxury, to be enjoyed. There were bright pin-up calendars, promising, after the mild though windy winter, torrid abandon renewed, golden flesh, the heart-breaking wagging cruppers of the bikinied young over the golden beaches. And there were plaques advertising Byrrh, Rivoli, Royal Anjou, Carlier, a British beer called Golden Fleece. The Coca-Cola ice-box had been freshly polished by Tetuani. Marie Brizard's name was on the water-jugs, Picon's on the ashtrays. Antonio sang, preparing *tapas* in the kitchen. 'Both politicians and pop-singers,' Enderby said, 'are boils on the bottom of the communal body.' The oldest elder went aaaaargh. He liked that. Writer fellow this Rawcliffe. The apt phrase.

Enderby was not pushing on with the sonnet, nor with the letter he still had to write. The question was, he was thinking, how he was to address her. When he wrote. If he wrote. Dear Vesta: never. Dear Mrs—He'd forgotten her new name. (The address was easy: the publisher of this filthy volume.) An abusive salutation, that would be letting himself down. He had written to his own publisher, for he thought he might need him, them, again. Tiny royalties had accrued: they had been keeping them for him (£5. 7. 9.); they were glad, they said, to know where he was at last. As for this business of plagiarism, that was his affair, since he owned copyright. They themselves were not willing to take action, since they were in the bidding for resurrected Yod Crewsy's next book—a brief prose volume, they understood, humorous, inspirational, even religious. And they enclosed a personal letter, still in its envelope, only recently arrived at the office. Enderby had frowned over the handwriting, female. You and your female hadmirers. With a thudding heart he had opened it up.

Dear Piggy or Hoggy or Dirty (for I don't know what else to call you, do I?),

I was sorry about things and still am. And now this is the only way I can get in touch with you. Because I got it out of that silly girl on the plane that it was all really a mistake and you *had* gone to the wrong room without meaning to do what that silly captain of the plane thought (you know what I'm talking about, don't you). They choose too many of these airhostesses for their looks, though hers weren't much to write home about really, and not their intelligence, and that silly captain was a bit too quick to draw conclusions, and I certainly shan't fly with them again, that courier with the stupid woolly cap on was also very rude, I thought. The number of wrongs that seem to have been done you! I was stupid too, wasn't I, thinking you could have anything to do with that shooting, it must have been my inflamed holiday imagination. I've been thinking about you a lot and am sure you must have been thinking very bad thoughts about me. But could you blame me really? I mean, you were a bit mysterious, no luggage and all. What I *had* to do to try and make amends was to get some of your poems from the library—very difficult, the library had to send off for them—and I found some of them rather obscure and others very sad. Very modern, of course. I can't make up my mind yet about whether I really like them—that sounds ungrateful, doesn't it, but I do like to think of myself as an Honest Person, but one of our junior English lecturers—did I tell you about him? Harold Pritchard, he's trying to get a little book of criticism published— was quite gone on them. He said there were curious resemblances to the poems of Yod Crewsy (the more I think of this whole scandalous business the more convinced I am it was a big publicity stunt and in the presence of the Prime Minister as well and that makes me think less of *him*). Then Harold found the same poem in both books, and that gave him an unholy thrill, he loves anything like a literary scandal. There was no doubt, he said, who stole from whom. So he's written a letter to the Times Literary Supplement and thinks the sparks will fly. Where are you, dear Piggy? I wish I could make proper amends. Looking back I see that despite everything that Seville night was really romantic—love and your sudden inspiration and my dear moon and even your mistake when, bless you, you were looking for me. Write to me and accept my love if you will and forgive me.

Your
Miranda

Sitting here on this quiet week-day, the train from royal Rabat just going by on the single-tracked line that separated the Spanish Avenue from the beach cafés, the ink-paint congealing in his ballpoint, the harmless winter approaching, he thought that, despite the luck that had been granted (*said, and died*), the autumn should, for the sake of justice, flame out with a last act of vengeance. But he could not write the letter and, the letter unwritten, the poem would never flood into the estuary of its sestet. What did he really want from her? His money back? No, this place made enough, even in winter. Her humiliation, her smartness wrecked once more but by more devastating waters than the rain of Castel whatever-it-was, the snivelling, the running eye-shadow, the smooth face collapsed into that of a weary crone? No, not that either. Rawcliffe had taught him pity, that maketh the forests to fail.

'It will die down,' said the goitrous old man, 'and new sensations will come up. That new shiftless generation must be fed with fresh novelties.' He took some Wilson's snuff, then hawked, carked and shivered with the dour pleasure of it.

'Not a religious man,' said the snapping ex-major. 'But when I see a central tenet of my father's faith—he held it, poor devil, through all his suffering—when I see that, I say, turned to a trick or gimmick or whatever the fashionable word is, then I wonder. I wonder what new blasphemy they can devise.' He shuddered his whisky down in one.

'No morals,' said the twittering man. 'No loyalty. They will turn on their friends as if they were enemies. It was at a private party that this youth with the gun boasted in his cups. Isn't that so, Rawcliffe?'

'I don't really know,' said Enderby. 'I don't read the papers.'

'Very wise too,' said the senior elder. 'Stay away from that world. Get on with your job, whatever it is.'

'Sam Foot,' said the goitrous old man. 'A ridiculous name. Probably made up.'

'Samuel Foot,' said Enderby, 'was an eighteenth-century actor and playwright. He was also an agent for small beer. *And they all fell to playing the game of catch as catch can, till the gunpowder ran out at the heels of their boots.*'

There was a silence. 'They did, eh?' said the senior. 'Well suppose I'd better be thinking about getting home for lunch. Takes me longer and longer. Walking, that is.'

'He wrote that,' said Enderby. 'It was a test-piece. This other man said that he could recite anything after hearing it once only.'

'On my way too,' said the ex-major. 'Bit of a blow on the prom.'

The door opened and a girl came in, very tanned. She wore, as for high summer, a simple green frock well above her knees, deep-cut at her young bosom, her golden arms totally bare. She carried a beach-bag. She smiled shyly and went up to Manuel at the bar. 'I understand,' she said, 'that I can hire a changing-cubicle or whatever it's called.' Her voice was low in pitch, the accent classless. Susannah among the elders, Enderby thought. The ex-major said quietly:

'Susannah among the elders.' Enderby could see them feeling old, impotent, lust too tired within to rage at so many opportunities lost, the time gone, perhaps death to be their next season. And himself? He got up and said to the girl:

'Well, you *can* actually, but—' She looked at him from green eyes sprinkled, like a *sireh* quid, with gold. They were set wide apart but not too much: enough for beauty, perhaps honesty; not enough for the panic mindless world of the animals. Hair? Enderby at once, to his surprise, thought of the flower called montbretia. 'What I mean is that, surely, it's getting a bit cold now. This time of the year I mean.'

'I don't feel the cold. A cold sea doesn't frighten me.' As in an allegory or *Punch* title-page, the aged trundled off—winter or war, industrial depression or an all-around bad year—from the presence of youth as peace, spring, a change of government. They creaked and groaned, snorted, limped, winced at arterio-sclerotic calf-ache, went. One or two waved tiredly at Enderby from beyond the closed glass door, a safe distance. 'Could I have one then? For a couple of days. Do I pay in advance?'

'No, no, no need—Certainly. *Un llave,* Manuel.'

'*Numero ocho,*' Manuel smiled.

They all—Tetuani clearing the old men's whisky-glasses, Antonio at the kitchen-door, Manuel from the arena with its furled umbrellas, Enderby turned in his chair—watched her prancing seawards over the deserted sand, in scanty crimson, her hair loose. Enderby turned back in rage to his table. He took paper and wrote fiercely: 'You bitch, you know you ruined my life. You also stole my verse to give to that blasphemous false commercial Lazarus of yours. Well, you won't get away with it. One of the stolen poems had already been published in one of my volumes. I'm going to sue, you're all going to suffer.' And then he could see Vesta standing there, cool, smart in spotless dacron, unperturbed, saying that *she* wouldn't suffer, only that mouthing creature of hers, and he was going to be abandoned anyway, past his peak, the time for the chaotopoeic groups coming, or the duo called Lyserge and Diethyl, or Big D and the Cube and the Hawk and the Blue Acid. Or worse. Enderby took another sheet of paper and wrote:

> Smell and fearful and incorrigible knackers
> With the crouched pole under
> And strings of his inner testes strewn
> Over curried pancreas and where the
> Hollowed afternoon vomits
> Semen of ennui and

And and and. Send it round, signed, to the bloody Doggy Wog, showing that I can beat them at their own game if I want to, but the game isn't worth the, in Walkerian locution, turn-the-handle. And, *amigo* with the onion, I know what's in the *carta* you wanted to bring round to my lodgings where my razor and antisolar spectacle clip-on and few dirty handkerchiefs have been long snapped up by those who had not, that night, yet been betrayed to the police by fat Napo. *Khogh.* It was some word of their language, no deformed proper name from another. And the letter surely says that he saw who did it, *hombre*, and told Scotland Yard as much. A curious and perhaps suspicious lack of treachery from treacherous Spain. Enderby felt ungratefully gloomy. All was set for writing and yet he could not write. Draft after unfinished draft. Gloomily he read through his sonnet octave again.

Augustus on a guinea sat in state. This is the eighteenth century, the Augustan age, and that guinea is a reduction of the sun. *The sun no proper study.* Exactly, the real sun being God and that urban life essentially a product of reason, which the sun melts. And no more sun-kings, only Hanoverians. *But each shaft of filtered light a column.* Meaning that you can't really do without the sun, which gives life, so filter it through smoked glass, using its energy to erect neo-classic structures in architecture or literature (well, *The Rambler*, say, or *The Spectator*, and there's a nuance in 'shaft' suggesting wit). *Classic craft abhorred the arc or arch.* Yes, and those ships sailed a known world, unfloodable by a rational God, and the *arc-en-ciel* covenant is rejected. Something like that. *To circulate (blood or ideas) meant pipes, and pipes were straight.* Clear enough. You need the roundness of the guinea only so that it can roll along the straight streets or something of commercial enterprise. The round bores of the pipes are not seen on the surface, the pipes in essence being means of linking points by the shortest or most syllogistical way. And, to return to that guinea, impress on it the straight line of royal descent. And, to return to that pipe business, remember that pipes were smoked in coffee-houses and that news and ideas circulated there. And that craft business ties up with Lloyd's coffee-house. *As loaves were gifts from Ceres when she laughed, Thyrsis was Jack.* A bit fill-in for rhyme's sake, but, rejecting the sun, you reject life and can only accept it in stylised mythological or eclogue forms. But Jack leads us to Jean-Jacques. *Crousseau on a raft sought Johnjack's rational island—* The pivot coming with the volta. Defoe started it off: overcome Nature with reason. But the hearer will just hear *Crusoe.* Jack is dignified to John, glorification of common, or natural, man. Then make Nature reason and you start to topple into reason's antithesis, you become romantic. Why? A very awkward job, the continuation.

'Lovely.' She had come running in, wet. She wrung a hank of hair, wetting the floor. Fat drops broke on her gold limbs. Her high-arched foot left Man Friday spoors. Seeing her round jigging nates, Enderby could have died with regret and rage. 'Like a fool I brought everything except a towel. Could you possibly—' She smiled, her chin dripping as from a crunching of grapes.

'Just a minute.' He puffed to his bedroom and brought out a bath towel, not yet, if ever to be, used by him, and also the gaudy robe, not greatly stained, that Rawcliffe had died in. He put it round her shoulders. Clear gold skin without a blemish and a flue of ridiculous delicacy. She rubbed her hair dry with vigour, smiling her thanks. Manuel hovered, smiling. She smiled back. Enderby tried to smile.

'Could I,' she smiled, 'have a drink? Something a bit astringent. Let me see—' The bottles smiled. No, they bloody well didn't: Enderby was not going to have that. 'A whisky sour.'

'Weeskee—?'

'I'll do it,' said Enderby. 'Fetch some white of egg. *Clara de huevo.*' Manuel ran into the kitchen. She rubbed herself all over in, with, dead Rawcliffe's brilliant robe. 'A difficult art,' blabbed Enderby, 'making a whisky sour.' That sounded like boasting. 'Americans are very fond of them.' An egg cracked loudly off. She rubbed and rubbed. Enderby got behind the bar and looked for the plastic lemon that contained lemon-juice. Manuel, having brought a tea-cup with egg-white in it and some minute embedded triangles of shell, watched her rub instead of his master mix. 'There,' said Enderby, quite soon.

She took it and sipped. 'Hm. Is nobody else drinking?'

'About time,' Enderby said, 'I had my preprandial, if that's the right word.' He seemed to himself to simper, pouring out straight Scotch.

'Do I pay now or do you give me a bill afterwards? And can I get lunch here, talking about preprandials?'

'Oh,' said Enderby, 'have this one on me. It's a kind of custom here, the first drink of a new customer on the house.' And 'Oh, yes. You can have steak and salad or something like that. Or spaghetti with something or other. Anything you like, really. Within reason, that is.' Reason. That brought him back to that bloody poem. To his shock, he saw her bending over his table, looking openly at his papers.

'Hm,' she said, having sipped again. 'You've certainly got it in for this person, bitch rather.'

'That,' went flustered Enderby, coming round from the counter, 'is of no consequence. I'm not sending it. It was just an idea, that's all. Really,' he said, 'you shouldn't, you know. Private.' But it was your privates you were only too ready to expose, wasn't that so, when you— He felt a kind of tepid pleasure promising warmth, not outrage at all. She sat down in his fireside-type chair. She started reading his octave, frowning a little. A curiously tutorial aura seemed to be forming. Enderby went to sit down on one of the stackable chairs near his table.

'Bring it closer,' she said. 'What's all this about?'

'Well,' babbled Enderby, 'it's a sonnet, very strict. It's an attempt, really, to tie up the Age of Reason with the French Revolution. Or, on another level, the rational and the romantic can be regarded as aspects of each other, if you see what I mean.' Sitting, he moved towards her without getting up, as though this were an invalid chair. 'What I have to do is to show that romantic curves are made out of classical straightnesses. Do you see what I mean?' And then, gloomily, to himself: Probably not. She was young. She had perhaps mourned Yod Crewsy's death, gone to some open-air evangelical meeting on his resurrection.

She closed her eyes tight. 'Keep a triplet pattern in your sestet,' she said. 'A breath between your cdc and your dcd. How will the classical pillars become Gothic arches? The sun will melt them, I suppose. And then you ought to have the guillotine. A very rational machine—sorry about the rhyme, but it's rhymes you're after, isn't it?'

'What,' Enderby asked gravely, 'would you like for lunch? There's Antonio, you see, waiting there ready to cook it.' Antonio stood at the kitchen-door, trying to smile while chewing something. She nodded, not smiling but puckered charmingly, thoughtful. Guillotine, machine, seen, scene.

'What are you going to eat?' she asked. 'I'll eat what you eat. Not fish, though. I can't stand fish.'

'Well,' Enderby mumbled, 'I don't normally till— We close for the siesta, you see, and then I usually have—'

'I hate eating on my own. Besides, we've got to work this thing out. Is it something with meat in it?'

'Well,' Enderby said, 'I have a sort of stew going most of the time. Beef and potatoes and turnips and things. I don't know whether you'd like it, really.'

'With pickled onions,' she said. 'And Worcestershire sauce, plenty of it. I like gross things sometimes.' Enderby blushed. 'I like to come down to earth sometimes.'

'Here with your family?' She didn't answer. Monied, probably. 'Where are you staying? The Rif? The El Greco?'

'Oh,' vaguely. 'It's right up the hill. Now, then. Try it.'

'Eh?' And, while Tetuani set places in the conservatory, he tried it.

> Sought Johnjack's rational island, loath to wait
> Till the sun, slighted, took revenge so that
> The pillars nodded, melted, and were seen
> As Gothic shadows where a goddess sat—

'Volta not strong enough. The rhyme-words are far too weak. That *that* is shocking.'

Then, over the thick stew, grossly over-sauced, with pickled onions crunched whole on the side and a bottle of thick red eely alumy local wine, they, he rather, literally sweated over the rest of the sestet.

> For, after all, that rational machine,
>   Imposed on all men by the technocrat,
> Was patented by Dr Guillotine.

'This is terrible,' she said. 'Such bloody clumsiness.' She breathed on him (though a young lady should not eat, because of the known redolence of onions, onions) onions. 'I'd like a bit of cheese now,' she crunched. 'Have you any Black Diamond cheddar? Not too fresh, if that's possible. I like it a bit hard.'

'Would you also like,' asked Enderby humbly, 'some very strong tea? We do a very good line in that.'

'It must be really strong, though. I'm glad there's something you do a very good line in. These lines are a bloody disgrace. And you call yourself a poet.'

'I didn't—I never—' But she smiled when she said it.

Three

Enderby dreamt about her that night. It was a nightmare really. She was playing the piano in her scanty green dress for a gang of near-closing-time pot-swinging male singers. But it was not a pub so much as a long dark gymnasium. On top of the piano lay a yawning black dog, and Enderby, knowing it was evil, tried to warn her against it, but she and the singers only laughed. At last, though, he dragged her out protesting into the winter night (but she did not seem to feel the cold) of a grimy Northern industrial town. They had to get away quickly, by bus or tram or cab, or the dog would be out after her. He rushed her, still protesting, to a main road, and he stopped, with no difficulty, a southbound truck. She began to think the adventure funny and she made jokes to the driver. But she did not see that the driver was the dog. Enderby had to open the truck cabin-door while the vehicle was in motion and get her on to the road again to thumb a new lift. Again it was the dog. And again. And again. The new drivers were always the old dog and, moreover, though they barked they were southbound, they would almost at once turn left and left again, taking their passengers back north. Finally Enderby lost her and found himself in a town very much like Tangier, though in a summer too scorching for North Africa. He had a room but it was at the top of a high stair. Entering, he met with no surprise this girl and her mother, an older Miss Boland. His heart pounded, he was pale, they kindly gave him a glass of water. But then, though there was no wind, the shutters of the window began to vibrate, and he heard a distant rather silly voice that somehow resembled his own. 'I'm coming,' it said. The girl screamed now, saying that it was the dog. But he swam up through leagues of ocean, gasping for air. Then he awoke.

He had foul dyspepsia, and, switching on the bedside lamp,

he took ten Bisodol tablets. But the word *love*, he noticed, was in his mouth in the form of a remotish pickled-onion aftertaste, and he resented that. The moon was dim. Some Moorish drunks quarrelled in the distance and, more distant, real dogs started a chain of barking. He was not having it, it was all over. He drank from a bottle of Vittel, went brarrgh (and she had done that too, just once and with no excuse-me), then padded in his pyjama top to the bathroom. The striplight above the mirror suddenly granted him a grousing image of The Poet. He sat down on the lavatory seat and, a big heterosexual pornographic volume on his knees as writing-board, he tried to get the dream into a poem, see what it was all about. It was a slow job.

> At the end of the dark hall he found his love
> Who, flushed and gay,
> > Pounded with a walking hand and flying fingers
> > The grinning stained teeth for a wassail of singers
> That drooped around, while on the lid above
> The dog unnoticed, waiting, lolling lay.

She had been unwilling to give her name, saying it was not relevant. She had gone off about three o'clock, back in green, swinging her towelless beach-bag, giving no clue where she was going. Manuel, out later to pick up the cigarette order, said he had seen her coming out of the Doggy Wog. Enderby was jealous about that: was she helping those filthy drug-takers with their filthy drugged verses? Who was she, what did she want? Was she an anonymous agent of the British Arts Council, sent out to help with culture in, in Blake's phrase, minute particulars?

> He noticed, cried, dragged her away from laughter.
> Lifts on the frantic road
> > From loaded lorries helpful to seek safe south
> > Slyly sidestreeted north. Each driver's mouth,
> Answering her silly jokes, he gasped at after
> The cabin-door slammed shut: the dogteeth showed.

She had better stop being a dream of boyhood, for it was all too late. He had reached haven, hadn't he? He would not be in

the bar tomorrow morning (this morning really); he would be
out taking a walk.

At last, weary, out of the hot noon's humming,
   Mounting his own stair,
     It was no surprise to find a mother and daughter,
      The daughter she. Hospitable, she gave him water.
Windless, the shutters shook.

This was all messed up. The story wouldn't run to another stanza, and this stanza was going to be too long. And the rhythm
was atrocious.

      A quiet voice said: 'I'm coming.'
   'Oh God God it's the dog,' screamed the daughter,
    But he, up the miles of leaden water,
 Frantically beat for air.

A good discussion about that with somebody, over whisky or
stepmother's tea: that was what was needful. The realisation
suddenly shocked him. Had not the poet to be alone? He con-
verted that into bowel language and noised it grimly in the still
night, clenching the appropriate muscles, but the noise was
hollow.

And so she was there again in the lemony Tangerine sunlight
of near-winter, this time bringing her towel. The old men,
perhaps frightened of the gunpowder running out of the heels of
their boots, had stayed away, but there were other customers.
Two youngish film-men, in Morocco to choose locations that
might serve for Arizona, kept going *ja* at each other and greedily
scoffing Antonio's *tapas*—fat black olives; hot fried liver on
bread; Spanish salad of onion, tomato, vinegar, chopped pep-
pers. An Englishman, in fluent but very English Spanish, ex-
pressed to Manuel his love of baseball, a game he had followed
passionately when he lived three miles outside Havana. A quiet
man, perhaps a Russian, sat at the corner of the counter, steadily
and to no effect downing raw Spanish gin.

'Not worth writing,' she said, 'a poem like that.' She had
changed back into a crimson dress even briefer than the green
one. The baseball *aficionado*, greying vapidly handsome, kept
giving her frank glances, but she did not seem to notice. 'You

yourself may be moved by it,' she said, 'because of the emotional impact of the dream itself. But it's dreary old sex images, isn't it, no more. The dog, I mean. North for tumescence. And you're trying to protect me from yourself, or yourself from me—both silly.' Enderby looked at her bitterly, desirable and businesslike as she was. He said:

'That *love* in the first line. I'm sorry about that. I don't mean it, of course. It was just in the dream.'

'All right, we're scrapping it anyway.' And she crumpled the work of three hours of darkness and threw it on the floor. Tetuani gladly picked it up and bore it off to nest with other garbage. 'I think,' she said, 'we'll go for a walk. There's another sonnet we have to work out, isn't there?'

'Another?'

'One you mentioned yesterday. About the Revolt of the Angels or something.'

'I'm not sure that I—' He frowned. She punched him vigorously on the arm, saying:

'Oh, don't dither so. We haven't much time.' She led him out of the bar, stronger than she looked, and the customers, all of whom were new, assumed that Enderby was an old customer who had had enough.

'Look,' Enderby said, when they stood on the esplanade, 'I don't understand anything about this at all. Who are you? What right have you? Not,' he added, 'that I don't appreciate— But really, when you come to consider it—'

The wind whipped rather coldly, but she felt no cold, arms akimbo in her ridiculously brief dress. 'You do waste time, don't you? Now how does it begin?'

They walked in the direction of the Medina, and he managed to hit some of it out into the wind. It was as though she were telling him to get it all up, better up than down.

> Sick of the sycophantic singing, sick
> Of every afternoon's compulsory games—

Sturdy palms set all along the sea-front, the fronds stirred by that wind. The donkeys with loaded panniers, an odd sneering camel.

'That's the general idea, isn't it? Heaven as a minor public school. Did you go to a minor public school?'

'I went,' said Enderby, 'to a Catholic day-school.'

It was Friday, and the devout were shuffling to mosque. The imam or bilal or whatever he was was gargling over a loudspeaker. Brown men, of Rif or Berber stock, followed the voice, looking at her legs, though, with bright-eyed frank but hopeless desire. 'It's a lot of superstitious nonsense,' she said. 'Don't, whatever the temptation, go back to it. Use it as mythology, pluck it bare of images, but don't ever believe in it again. Take the cash in hand and waive the rest.'

'An indifferent poet, Fitzgerald.' Enderby loved her for saying what she had said.

'Very well, let's have something better.'

> Sick of the little cliques of county names,
> The timebomb in his brain began to tick—

Luncheon in a little restaurant crammed with camp military gear, not too far from the Hotel El Greco. It was run by two men in love with each other, one American, the other English. A handsome Moorish boy who waited on seemed himself in love with the Englishman, who was flaxen, bronzed, petulant and given to shouting at the cook. The Moor was not adept at hiding emotion: his big lower lip trembled and his eyes swam. Enderby and she had a thin dull goulash which she said loudly was bloody terrible. The English lover tossed his head and affricated petulantly against his alveolum, then turned up the music—a sexy cocksure American male voice singing, against a Mahlerian orchestra, thin dull café society songs of the 'thirties. She prepared to shout that the bloody noise must be turned off: it was interfering with their rhythm. Enderby said:

'Don't. Please. I've got to live in this town.'

'Yes,' she said, her green eyes, their gold very much metal, hard on him. 'You lack courage. You've been softened by somebody or something. You're frightened of the young and the experimental and the way-out and the black dog. When Shelley said what he said about poets being the unacknowledged legislators of the world, he wasn't really using fancy language. It's only by the exact use of words that people can begin to understand themselves. Poetry isn't a silly little hobby to be practised in the smallest room of the house.'

He blushed. 'What can I do?'

She sighed. 'Get all these old things out of your system first. Then push on.'

> Beating out number. As arithmetic,
>   As short division not divided aims,
>   Resentment flared. But then, carved out in flames,
> He read: *That flower is not for you to pick.*

'It's time,' she said, 'you started work on a long poem.'

'I tried that once. That bastard stole it and vulgarised it. But,' and he looked downhill, seaward, 'he's paid. Wrapped in a Union Jack, being gently gnawed.'

'You can get something here. This is a junction. Deucalion's flood and Noah's. Africa and Europe. Christianity and Islam. Past and future. The black and the white. Two rocks looking across at each other. The Straits may have a submarine tunnel. But it was Mallarmé who said that poetry is made with words, not ideas.'

'How do you know all this? You're so *young.*'

She spat out breath very nastily. 'There you go again. More interested in the false divisions than the true ones. Come on, let's have that sestet.'

The sestet ended in a drinking-shop not far from the Souk or Socco, over glasses of warmish pastis. Drab long robes, hoods, ponchos, ass-beaters, loud gargling Moghrabi, nose-picking children who used the other hand to beg. Sympathetic, Enderby gave them little coins.

> Therefore he picked it. All things thawed to action,
>   Sound, colour. A shrill electric bell
> Summoned the guard. He gathered up his faction,
>   Poised on the brink, thought and created hell.
> Light shimmered in miraculous refraction
>   As, like a bloody thunderbolt, he fell.

'That *bloody,*' Enderby said. 'It's meant really to express grudging admiration. But that only works if the reader knows I've taken the line from Tennyson's poem about the eagle.'

'To hell with the reader. Good. That needs a lot of going over, of course, but you can do that at leisure. When I'm gone, I mean. Now we'd better take a look at that Horatian Ode thing. Can we have dinner at your place?'

'I'd like to take you *out* to dinner,' Enderby said. And, 'When you're gone, you said. When are you going?'

'I'm flying off tomorrow evening. About six.'

Enderby gulped. 'It's been a short stay. You can get a very good dinner at a place called the *Parade*. I could get a taxi and pick you up about—'

'Still curious, aren't you? Bit of a change for you, isn't it, this curiosity about people? You've never cared much for people, have you? From what you've told me, anyway. Your father let you down by marrying your stepmother, and your mother let you down by dying too young. And these others you've mentioned, men and women.'

'My father was all right,' Enderby said. 'I never had anything against him.' He frowned, though ungrudgingly.

'Many years ago,' she said, 'you published a little volume at your own expense. Inevitably it was very badly printed. You had a poem in it called "Independence Day".'

'I'm damned if I remember.'

'A rather bad poem. It started:

> Anciently the man who showed
> Hate to his father with the sword
> Was bundled up in a coarse sack
> With a frantic ape to tear his back
> And the squawking talk of a parrot to mock
> Time's terror of air-and-light's lack
> Black
> And the creeping torpor of a snake.'

'I can't possibly have written that,' went Enderby, worried now. 'I could never possibly have written anything as bad as that.'

'No?' she said. 'Listen.

> Then he was swirled into the sea.
> But that was all balls and talk.
> Nowadays we have changed all that,

Into a cleaner light to walk
And wipe that mire off on the mat.
So when I knew his end was near
My mind was freer
And snapped its thumb and finger then
At the irrelevance of birth,
And I had a better right to the earth
And knew myself more of a man,
Shedding the last squamour of the old skin.'

'That's somebody else,' said Enderby urgently. 'Honestly, it's not me.'

'And you love your mother because you never knew her. For all you know she might have been like your stepmother.'

'It's different now,' pleaded Enderby. 'I forgive my stepmother, I forgive her everything.'

'That's very generous of you. And who do you love?'

'I was just coming to that,' said Enderby with approaching banners of wretchedness. 'What I wanted to say was—'

'All right, all right. Don't pick me up in a taxi. You can't anyway, because you don't know where I am. I'll pick *you* up about eight. Now go home and work on your bloody Horatian Ode. No, leave me here. I go in a different direction.' She seemed needlessly irritable, and Enderby, having once, though briefly, lived with a woman, wondered if it was possibly— She was old enough, wasn't she, to have—

'Gin and hot water,' he suggested kindly, 'are said to work wonders.' But she didn't seem to hear. She seemed to have switched off Enderby like a television image, looking blankly at him as if he had become a blank screen. A very strange girl altogether. But he thought that, having got the better of the moon, he could perhaps this time live with his fear.

Four

She was smartly dressed for the evening in bronze stockings and a brief, but not too brief, gold dress, a gold stole round her tanned shoulders, her hair up at the back. On her left wrist she had a gold chain from which miniscule figurines depended. It was a restaurant of subdued lights, and Enderby could not see what the figurines were or meant. She was perfumed, and the perfume suggested something baked—a delicate but aphrodisi-acal soufflé seasoned with rare liqueurs. Enderby was wearing one of Rawcliffe's Edwardian suits—it did not fit too badly—and even Rawcliffe's gold watch and chain. One thing Enderby did not like about this place was that the mortician *collage* man from the Doggy Wog was in it and was obviously a respected and regular customer. He sat at a table opposite and was eating with his fingers a brace of roast game-birds. He had greeted this girl with a growl of familiarity but now, picking the meat from a backbone, he kept his eyes sternly on her. He did not apparently remember Enderby. She had returned his greeting with an American air-hostess's 'Hi.'

Tonight she was not going to have greasy stew and pickled onions and stepmother's tea. She read the menu intently, as though it contained a Nabokovian cryptogram, and ordered a young hare of the kind called a capuchin, marinated in *marc*, stuffed with its own and some pig's liver as well as breadcrumbs, truffle, and a little preserved turkey-meat, and served with a sauce full of red wine and double cream. Before it she had a small helping of jellied boar. Enderby, confused, said he would have sheep's tongue *en papillotes*, whatever they were, that was. And, after dry martinis which she sent back as neither dry nor cold enough, they had champagne—Bollinger '53. She said it was not very exciting, but it seemed to be the best they had, so they put, at her demand, another bottle on ice while they were drinking this one. Enderby uneasily saw signs of a deliberate intention to get tight. Soon, clanking down her fork, she said:

'A fancied superiority to women. Despise their brains so pretend to despise their bodies as well. Just because you can't have their bodies.'

'I beg your pardon?'

'Juvenilia. One of your,' she belched gently, 'juvenilia.'

'Juvenilia? But I never published any of my juvenilia.' Several bar-customers were interested in the repeated word: a gland in-jection, a sexual posture, a synthetic holiday resort. She began to recite with mocking intensity:

'They fear and hate
the Donne and Dante in him, this
cold
gift to turn heat to a flame, a kiss
to the gate
of a mons-
ter's labyrinth. They hold
and anchor a thin thread—'

'Not so loud,' went Enderby with quiet force, blushing. The
mortician was looking sardonic over a large dish of blood-
coloured ice cream.

'—the tennis party, the parish dance:
stale pus out of dead
pores.'

Someone at the bar, unseen in the dimness, applauded. 'I
didn't write that,' said Enderby. 'You're getting me mixed up
with somebody else.'

'Am I? Am I? I suppose that's possible. There's so much minor
poetry about.'

'What do you mean—minor?'

She downed a long draught of Bollinger, as though the recita-
tion had made her thirsty, belched with no excuse-me, and said:
'There was that other nasty little thing about meeting a girl at a
dance, wasn't there? Juvenilia, again.' Or a disease perhaps, one
of those gruesomely pleasant-sounding ones like salmonella. She
took more champagne and, with world-weary tone and over-
sharp articulation, recited:

'Semitic violins by the wailing wall
Gnash their threnody
For the buried jungle, the tangle of lianas—'

'I think,' Enderby said sternly, 'that I have some right to
know—'

'Or say that was before, in the first flush,
And say that now
A handful of coins, image and milled edge worn,
Is spilled abroad to determine
Our trade of emotions.'

'I mean, apart from how you know all that, and I don't believe it's mine anyway—'

> 'On this background are imposed
> Urges, whose precise nature it is difficult to define:
> Shells shaped by forgotten surges.'

'I'm not having any more of this,' and Enderby grasped her thin wrist firmly. She shook herself free with little effort and said:

'Too rich for you, is it?' She sniffed at his half-eaten sheep's tongue *en papillotes*. 'A lot of things are too rich for you, aren't they? Never mind, mumsy will ook after him den. Let me finish.' Enderby, very wretched, let her.

> 'One understands so little, having no words
> To body forth thoughts, no axe
> To reach flagged soil, no drills
> To pierce to living wells. It would tax
> My energies overmuch now to garner you
> Out of worn coins, worn shells.'

She took another bumper of fuming wine, belched like an elfin trumpet of triumph, then waved smiling across to the mortician. He said:

'That's telling him.'

'You're being bloody unfair,' said Enderby loudly and, to the mortician, more loudly, 'You keep your nose out of this, sod.' The mortician looked at Enderby with very small interest and went on eating ice cream.

'Big untrue postures,' she delivered. 'Pretence. You can't make major poetry out of pretence.'

'I tell you,' said Enderby, 'it was my stepmother's fault, but that's all over now. Pretence, you say,' he added cunningly, 'but very memorable pretence. Not,' he super-added, 'that I wrote that. I'm sure I didn't.' He was pretty sure, anyway.

'I can remember anything,' she said smugly. 'It's a gift.' Then she went *phew*. 'God, it's warm in here.' And she pulled her stole off roughly, showing her glowing young shoulders.

'It's not really warm, you know,' said Enderby. And, hopefully: 'Perhaps it's all that champagne. Perhaps you're not feeling too well.'

'I feel fine,' she said. 'It's the sun within me. I'm a beaker full of the warm south. Nice tension of opposites there: cooled a long age in the deep-delved earth.' She had drunk most of the first bottle and was now doing very well with the second. 'I won't pretend that you wrote that, because you didn't. Poor boy. But his name was *not* writ in water.' Enderby felt chilled when he heard that. 'Posterity,' she then said. 'The poet addresses posterity. And what is posterity? Schoolmarms with snotty kids trailing round the monuments. The poet's tea-mug with an in-grained ring of tannin-stain. The poet's love-letters. The poet's falling hair, trapped in brush-bristles rarely washed. The poet's little failings—well-hidden, but not for ever. And the kids are bored, and the texts are covered with thumb-marks and dirty little marginalia. They've read the poems, oh yes. They're pos-terity. Do you never think of posterity?'

Enderby looked warily at her. 'Well, like everybody else—'

'Minor poets hope that posterity will turn them into major ones. A great man, my dear, who suffered the critics' sneers and the public's neglect. Halitotic breathing over your corpse. Rev-erent treading through the poet's cottage, fingering the pots and pans.'

Enderby started. 'That's brought back a dream. I think it was a dream. The pots and pans fell, and I woke.'

'Oh, come on, let's finish this champagne and go. I can't eat any more of this muck. Creamed leveret's bones, ugh. Let's go and swim.'

'At this hour? And it's very cold, the sea I mean. And be-sides—'

'You don't swim. I know. You're preparing your body for hon-oured corpsedom. You don't do anything with it. All right, you can watch *me* swim.' She filled both their flutes and downed hers, re-filled and downed again.

'What I meant to say was— It's a bit difficult, I know, but—' He called for the bill. '*Cuenta, por favor.*' Quite the little Tan-gerine, he was thinking. Settling here for corpsedom. No, not that. He had his work, hadn't he? And there was this other mat-ter, and he'd better blurt it out now before the bill came. 'I know,' he said stiffly but urgently, 'there's a great disparity of age. But if you could see your way—I mean, we get on all right together. I would leave it to you to decide on the precise nature of the relationship. I ask nothing.' The bill came: another flame-haired Goth of a Spanish waiter, flashing a gold tunthus. It was a lot of dirhams. Enderby counted out note after note after note, all from Rawcliffe's mattress.

'You only ask *me*,' she said. The champagne was done, and she upturned the bottle to hold it like a thyrsus. 'Come on, I'm burning.'

The mortician growled something about that being okay then. She smiled and nodded. 'What do you do over there?' asked Enderby jealously. 'You go over there. The dog place, I mean. I know you do.'

'I go to a lot of places. I'm a beezy leetle girl. The world's bigger than you could ever imagine."

The doorman whistled a *petit taxi* or *taxi chico*. It was a windy night in a hilly street, no more. But a dirty old Moor shuffled to them to offer a small parcel of marijuana for five dirhams. 'Shit,' she said. 'Dilutions for the tourists. All teased out of fag-ends collected from the gutters.' She gave the old man a brief mouthful of what sounded like fluent Arabic. He seemed shocked. Enderby was past being surprised. In the taxi he said:

'What do you say then? The precise nature of the relationship—'

'You leave to me. Right. I heard you the first time.' They rolled seawards. The driver, a moustached thin Moor with a skullcap, kept turning round to have a look at her. She banged him on the shoulder, saying: 'Keep your fucking eyes on the road.' And to Enderby: 'All I want at the moment is my swim. I don't want avowals and the precise nature of the relationship.' She was silent then, and Enderby thought it prudent also to be silent. They came to near the gate, only the single track to cross, which opened on to the beach steps and the— But *El Acantilado Verde* had been painted out and the new name as yet only lightly stencilled. Manuel had a brother who did that sort of thing.

The bar looked grim and functional under the plain lights. 'Come in here,' Enderby invited, leading her to his own room. There were table-lamps, shaded in warm colours, that all came

on together when he clicked the switch by the door. Many of
Rawcliffe's Moorish curiosa were still around, but there was now
a lot of naked shelf-space to be clothed. But with what? He
didn't read much. Perhaps he ought to read more, keep in touch
with the posterity of which she, all said and done, was very nearly a member. Read about media and the opening up of the
psyche with drugs. All sorts of things. Enderby had bought a
bedspread of camel-hair, its design undistinguished, as well as
new sheets and a new mattress. There was still something raffish,
riffish, Rawcliffesque about the bed on the floor, in the middle of
the floor. Enderby had not yet sufficiently breathed on things.

'Hm,' she said. 'How about calling that cook-boy of yours to
see about some coffee? I'd like some coffee afterwards.'

'Oh, he's not here. They all sleep out. *Yo*,' Enderby said, with
painful roguery, '*duermo solo*.' And then: 'Of course, you can't
swim, can you? You forgot, I forgot. You've nothing to swim in.'
He smiled.

'That's right,' she said. 'Nothing. I shall swim in nothing.'
And, before Enderby could say anything, she darted over to his
book-shelves and picked on a gilt-backed folio.

'That,' said Enderby, 'isn't mine. It was left by him. Don't
look at it, please.' Fool, he should have thought. 'And don't
swim with nothing on. It's too cold, there are laws against it, the
police will come along, this is a Muslim country, very strict
about indecency.'

'Indecency,' she said, looking through the volume. 'Yes. Dear
dear dear. That seems more painful than pleasurable.'

'Please don't.' He meant two things. He felt he wanted to
wring his hands. But she dropped the book on the floor and then
started to take her dress off. 'I'll make coffee myself,' he said,
'and there's some rather good cognac. Please don't.'

'Good, we'll have that afterwards.' And she kicked off her
spiky shoes and began to peel down her stockings, sitting on
Enderby's bedside chair to do it more easily. And then. He
gulped, wondering whether to turn his back, but that somehow,
after that book, might seem hypocritical. Bold Enderby, un-
moved, watching. But:

'Go in as you are, by all means, but—' But going in as she

was now meant going in very nearly as she wanted to go in. And now entirely. Oh God. Enderby saw her totally naked, all gold, with no shocking leprous bands where they might, beach decency being observed, be expected to be. He just stood there, a butler called in by her eccentric ladyship. She looked him hard, though soft, in the eyes. He gnashed his teeth at her ghastly young beauty, all revealed. She said:

'Time enough.' Huskily. Then she lay on the camel-hair, eyes not leaving his, and said: 'Love. You meant to say love. Come on, take me. Darling. I'm yours, all yours. When I give I give. You know that.' He did know it. And she held out gold blades of arms, gold foil gleaming in her oxters. And gold below on the mount. 'You said,' she said, 'I must decide on the precise nature of the relationship. Well, I'm deciding. Darling, darling. Come on.'

'No,' gasped Enderby. 'You know I can't. That isn't what I meant.'

'Just like Mr Prufrock. Darling, darling, you can do anything you like. Come, don't keep me waiting.'

'It won't do,' said Enderby, dying. He saw himself there with her, puffing in his slack whiteness. 'I'm sorry I said what I said.'

She suddenly drew her knees up to her chin, embracing her shins, and laughed, not unkindly. 'Minor poet,' she said. 'We know now where we stand, don't we? Never mind. Be thankful for what you've got. Don't ask too much, that's all.' And she leapt from the bed, brushing his hand with the smoothness of her gold flank, just for a fraction of time, as she ran past him to the door, out of the door, out of the building, out of the arena, towards the sea.

Enderby sat on the bed, blood forming patterns in his eyes. His heart growled as it thumped. Off to the bloody sea, where Rawcliffe was. But no. Rawcliffe was in the Mediterranean, east of here. She was out in the fringes of the Atlantic, a bigger sea. One sometimes forgot that it was the Atlantic here, the Atlantic and Africa and all the big stuff. Minor poet in Africa, facing the Atlantic. There would undoubtedly be phosphorescence all round her as she plunged further into the Atlantic.

Five

She didn't come in the following morning, and he didn't expect her. Yet there had been no good-bye, not yet. She had high-heeled into the kitchen, glowing, clothed, even perfumed (yet smelling somehow, to his fancy, of drowned poets) to see him watching the bubbling coffee as if it were an alchemical experiment. And she hadn't liked the coffee: too weak, too minor-poetic. Well, he had never been good at coffee. Tea, now, was altogether a different matter. Anyway, she had to fly: so much to see to before really flying. And then, lightly and without satire, a kiss on each cheek for him, as at the award of some *prix* for minor poetry. And off.

Tossing in his bed, he had wondered about minor poets. There was T. E. Brown, three legs of Man, who had said: 'O black-bird, what a boy you are, how you do go it,' and given to British gardens pot or plastic godwottery. And Leigh Hunt, whom Jenny had kissed. And the woman who'd seen Faunus in Flush, later married to a poet deemed major. *Minor Poets of the Twentieth Century* (OUP, 84s), with a couple or three of his well separated, because of the alphabetical order, from that one of Rawcliffe. But once they had thought *Aurora Leigh* the greatest thing since Shakespeare, and Hopkins to be just jesuitical hysteria. It all depended on posterity. One kiss, two kisses. And he saw that her name didn't matter.

He sighed, but not hopelessly. He had gone back to the Horatian Ode this morning, in a rather crowded bar.

> So will the flux of time and fire,
> The process and the pain, expire,
> And history can bow
> To one eternal now.

He had to get behind the counter, expert, Hogg of the Sty (When you say gin, Piggy knows you mean Yeoman Warder. False smile flashing over the shaker in some glossy advertisement), to mix a Manhattan for a dour Kansan who believed the drink was named for the university town in his own state. And a

young but archaic what-what haw-haw Englishman, doggy scarf
in his open shirt, had brought in two girls, one of them called
Bunty, and said that nobody in this town knew how to mix a
hangman's blood. But he, Enderby, Hogg, knew, and the man
was discomfited. Three old men had been in, the fourth, the one
with skin like microscope slides, not being too well, confined to
his room. Doubt if he'll see another spring. Won the Bisley shoot
in, let me see, when was it? MC and bar, but never talked about
it much.

What was emerging, Enderby saw, was a long poem based on
the characters in *Hamlet*. The Horatian Ode was for the King,
type of the absolute ruler who would seal a timeless Denmark
off from the flux of history. An epithalamium for him and
Gertrude, the passion of the mature. He'd written a good deal of
that in Gloucester Road, when Vesta went off to work for the
day, bitch.

> The greenstick snaps, the slender goldenrod
> Here cannot probe or enter. Thin spring winds
> Freeze blue lovers in unprotected hollows, but
> Summer chimes heavy bells and flesh is fed
> Where fruit bursts, the ground is crawling with
> berries.

Something like that. It would come back to him in time. A long
soliloquy for Hamlet. Marsyas, was he, he Enderby, risking a
minor poet's flaying? Never mind. On with bloody job is best
way, *hombre*.

She came in when he was ready for his stew, followed by tea
and siesta. She was dressed rather demurely, not unlike Miss
Boland, beige suit, skirt to her knees, stockings of a gunmetal
colour, shoes sensible and well-polished. There were blue rings,
half-rings really, under her eyes. She wore a hat like a Victorian
sailor's. She said:

'I've got a cab waiting outside.' Meaning over the sand, up
the steps, across the railway line and pavement, by the kerb with
a palm strongly clashing above. The wind was high. 'You're not
to worry too much about anything,' she said. 'Do what you can
do. Don't try and tame dogs or enter a world of visions and no
syntax.' This was very sybilline talk.

'I'm doing a long poem based on the characters in *Hamlet*. I don't quite know yet what the overall theme is, but I daresay it'll come out in time. Could I make you a cup of tea? Antonio's got the day off. He's gone to see a man in Rabat.'

'Good. No, thanks. I'll be back to visit you. Next year perhaps. I suppose I should have come before, but I have so much to do.' Enderby was aware now that there was no point in asking further questions: taking your degree in English, are you; doing a thesis on contemporary poetry, is that it? These things didn't apply, no more than curiosity, which he no longer felt, about her identity or origin or age. All things to all poets, but to this poet perhaps less than to some others. No envy. Posterity would sort things out. But, of course, posterity was only those snotnosed schoolkids.

'I'm grateful,' he said, though, out of habit, grudgingly. 'You know I am.'

'You can't be blamed,' she said, 'if you've opted to live without love. Something went wrong early. Your juvenilia days.' Enderby frowned slightly. 'Look,' she said, 'I really must rush now. I only came to say good-bye. But not good-bye really,' grimacing at her watch. Enderby stood up, wincing a bit. A spasm in the right calf, altogether appropriate to middle age. 'So,' she said, and she walked the three paces up to him and gave him one brief kiss on the lips. His share, his quota, what he was worth. Her mouth was very warm. *The final kiss and final—* As if she knew, she gave him the referent, leaving the words to him, very briefly grasping his writing fingers, pressing them. Her gloves were beige, of some kind of soft and expensive skin. *Tight pressure of hands.* That was it then, the poem finished. But the whole thing was a lie (opted to live without love), though it would not be a lie to anybody who could use it, somebody young and in love, saying an enforced good-bye to the beloved. Poets, even minor ones, donated the right words, and the small pride might swallow the large envy.

'Right, then,' she said. They went together to the door, almost with the formality of distinguished customer and bowing *patron*. He watched her climb up to her taxi, feeling a spasm of hopeless rage, briefer than a borborygm, at the last sight of her neatly moving buttocks. But he had no right to that feeling, so the feeling quickly modulated, as a nettle-sting modulates to warmth (the bare-legged legionaries had kept themselves warm in British winters by lashing themselves with nettles: might there not be a poem there?), to something which had, as one of its upper partials, that very pride. She waved before getting in, and then called something that sounded a bit like *all the anthologies, anyway*, but a passing coach, full of sightseers collected from the Rif, roared at it. The gear ground, *for time himself will bring*, but this was only a decrepit Moroccan taxi. The wind blew hard. She was gone; like a hypodermic injection it was all over. He wondered if it might not be a pious duty to find out more about Rawcliffe's slender and thwarted *oeuvre*, edit, reprint at expense of mattress. There might be odd things, juvenilia even, concealed about the place, perhaps even in those tomes of pornography. But no, best keep away. He had enough work of his own to do, the duty of at least being better than T. E. Brown or Henley or Leigh Hunt or Sir George Goodby or Shem Macnamara. Whatever the future was going to be about, things ought to be all right, namely not too good, with enough scope for guilt, creation's true dynamo. It would be polite to reply to Miss Boland's letter, perhaps. If she proposed visiting him he could, if he wished, always put her off. He would go in now to his gross stew and stewed tea, then sleep for a while. The C major of this life. Was Browning minor? He turned to face the Atlantic but, going brrrrrr, was glad to be able to hurry in to escape from it.

Six

This, children, is Morocco. Does it not give you a thrill, seeing what you have all heard or read about so often? Pashas and the Beni-Quarain and camels. Mulai Hafid and Abd-el-Kadir. The light-coloured Sherifians, who claim descent from the Prophet. Palmetto and sandarach and argan and tizra. You say it does *not* give you a thrill, Sandra? Well, child, you were never strong on imagination, were you? And I do not wish to hear any of these silly giggly whispers about what *does* give you a thrill. Some of you girls have very few thoughts in your heads. Yes, I mean you too, Andrea. And, Geoffrey, because that elderly Berber is picking his nose you need not feel impelled to do the same. Lions, Bertrand? Lions are much much further south. Leopards here, bears, hyenas and wild pigs. Bustard, partridge and water-fowl. Dromedaries and dashing Barbary horses.

This is Tangier, which, you may not know this, once actually belonged to the British. Part of the dowry of Catherine of Braganza, Portuguese queen of a merry monarch. A pleasant enough town, no longer very distinguished, with some deplorable specimens of architecture. The beach is deserted. This is not the tourist season and, besides, it is the hour of the siesta. The beach cafés are garish, the paint peeling on many, but some of their names are rather charming. The Winston Churchill, the Sun Trap, the Cuppa, the Well Come. Those Hebrew letters there mean *kosher* (it is three consonants, the Semitic languages not greatly favouring the alphabetisation of vowels. Yes, Donald, Arabic too is a Semitic language and is similarly vowel-shy. Why then do not the Jews and Arabs, aware of a common origin in speech and alphabetic method as well as genes, taboos and mythology, get on better together? There, child, you have the eternal mystery of brotherhood. As Blake might have said, Let me hate him, or let me be his brother. But a good question, Donald, and thank you for asking it) which means, of food, not forbidden by religion. A holiday, you see, condones no relaxations of fundamental covenants. Stop grinning, Andrea. I shall lose my temper in a minute.

That one there is having its name repainted. You can see what it will be, in tasteful ultramarine. *La Belle Mer*. Very pretty. Some Frenchman probably, offering a most delicate cuisine, but now neatly sleeping. Listen, you can hear them sleep. Zrrrzzz. Ghraaaaaakh. Ong. Sleep possesses so many of the better sort, and it is sleep that sustains our visitation, to be fractured and fantasticated on waking, perhaps even totally forgotten.

Why are we here? A fair question, Pamela. What has all this to do with literature? I am very glad you asked that. Well, let me say this. Here you have expatriates of Northern stock, water to the oil of the Moors and Berbers and Spanish. Many of them have fled their native lands to escape the rigour of the law. Yes, alas, crimes. Expropriation of funds, common theft, sexual inversion. I thought you would ask that, Sandra. That term *sexual* effects, in your case, an almost voltaic connection. The term means nothing more than philoprogenitive urges deflected into channels that possess no generative significance. What's all that when it's at home? I expected that remark from you, ignorant girl. I shall ignore it. Ignoration is the only rational response to ignorance. Think that one over, you over-developed little flesh-pot.

And among the exiles from the North are artists, musicians, writers. They have sinned, but they have talent. Desperately they exercise their talent here, dreaming of bitter ale and mea-dowsweet but cut off for ever, yes for ever, from the Piccadilly flyover and the Hyde Park State Museum and the Communal Beerhall on Hammersmith Broadway. Those are the British. The Americans weep too nightly into their highballs for the happy shopping evenings in the Dupermarket, the drive-in colour stere-ovideo, the nuclear throb of the fully automated roadglobe. But they practise their arts. It is writers mostly. Up that hill lives a man who has already produced twenty-five volumes of autobiog-raphy: he tears at each instant of his pre-exilic past as though it were a prawn. Another man, on the Calle Larache, eats into his unconscious heart and mounts the regurgitated fragments on fragments of old newspaper. Another man again writes sneering satire, in sub-Popean couplets, on an England already dead. They are small artists, all. Here there is a *rue* Beethoven, also an *avenida* Leonardo da Vinci, a *plaza* de Sade. But no artist here will have a square or thoroughfare named for him. They are nothing.

And yet think what, on three sides, surrounds them, though the fierce Atlantic will give a right orchestration to the muscu-larity of what, to the sun's own surprise, has sprung out of sun-baked Africa and Iberia. The glory of the Lusiad (George, you will please not yawn) and the stoic bravery and heartbreak of the Cid, and the myth of Juan and the chronicle of the gaunter Don on the gaunt horse. Clash of guitars up there and the drum-roll of hammering heels in the dance, and down there the fever of native timpani. And, east, the tales told to the cruel Sultan Shahriyar, and the delicate verse-traceries of Omar this and Abdul that (all right, Benedict, there is no need to snigger: Islamic poetry is not my subject) and Sayid the other thing.

Yawwwwww. Ogre. Uuuuuugh.

The pain of their awakening, not all of them alone, to the coming of the Tangerine evening. All right, we all know that a tangerine is a small orange, much flattened at the poles. Very funny, Geoffrey. But perhaps now you will consider why it is called what it is called. The calligraphic neons will glow—*fa* and *kaf* and *kaf* and *nun* and *tok*—and the shops resume their oil-lit trades. Ladies in yashmaks and caftans will stroll the *rues* or *calles*, and the boys will jeer and giggle at the few male tourists and point at their younger brothers as if they were carcasses of tender lamb. And the writers will groan at their words of the forenoon and despair.

So away! Our camels sniff the evening and are glad. A quotation, if you *must* know, Benedict. Let us leave them, for men must be left to, each, the dreeing of his own weird. A man must contrive such happiness as he can. So must we all. So must we all, Geoffrey and Benedict and George and Donald and Andrea and Pamela and that horrid Sandra and— Oh, get into line there. We take off, into the Atlantic wind. The moon, sickle of Islam, has risen. The planets Marikh and Zuhrah and Zuhal shine. The stars, in American issue army boots, slide silently to their allotted posts. And the words slide into the slots ordained by syntax and glitter, as with atmospheric dust, with those impurities which we call meaning. Away, children! Leave them to it.

> Until the final glacier grips
> Each island, with its dream of ships

And and and and. Keep on. It will come out right, given time and application. You can, when depressed, pluck your own sweet bay or *laurus nobilis*. It grows here. Nobody will pluck it for you. The aromatic leaves are useful in cookery, and you can cure your sick cat with the berries.

Appendix

Some uncollected early poems by F. X. Enderby.

The poems that follow have not, for some reason, appeared in any of the published volumes of Enderby's verse, and the last poem has not previously been published at all. The poems beginning 'Anciently the man who showed . . .', 'They fear and hate the Donne and Dante in him . . .' and 'Semitic violins, by the wailing wall . . .', allegedly from Enderby's juvenile productions, cannot be traced either in published or manuscript form. It may be of interest to note, however, that the catalogue of the ill-fated Gorgon Press, which specialised in verse printed at the author's own expense, lists a volume by one A. Rawcliffe—*Balls and Talk:* Poems 1936. No copies of this volume have as yet come to light.

A.B.

September, 1938

There arose those winning life between two wars,
Born out of one, doomed food for the other,
Floodroars ever in the ears.

Slothlovers hardly, hardly fighters:
Resentment spent against stone, long beaten out of
Minds resigned to the new:
Useless to queue for respirators.

Besides, what worse chaos to come back to.
Home, limbs heavy with mud and work, to sleep
To sweep out a house days deep in dirt.

Knowing finally man would limbs loin face
Efface utterly, leaving in his place
Engines rusting to world's end, heirs to warfare
Fonctionnant d'une manière automatique.

Summer, 1940

Summer swamps the land, the sun imprisons us,
The pen slithers in the examinee's fingers,
And colliding lips of lovers slide on sweat
When, blind, they inherit their tactile world.

Spectacles mist, handveins show blue, the urge to undress
Breeds passion in unexpected places. Barrage balloons
Soar silver in silver ether. Lying on grass,
We watch them, docile monsters, unwind to the zenith.

Drops of that flood out of France, with mud and work
Stained, loll in the trams, drinking their cigarettes,
Their presence defiling the flannels and summer frocks,
The hunters to hound our safety, spoil the summer.

Spring in Camp, 1941

War becomes time, and long logic
On buried premises; spring supervenes
With the circle as badge which, pun and profundity,
Vast, appears line and logical,
But, small, shows travel returning.
Circle is circle, proves nothing, makes nothing,
Swallows up process and end in no argument,
Brings new picture of old time.

Here in barracks is intake of birds,
The sun holds early his orderly room,
The pale company clerk is uneasy
As spring brings odour of other springs.
The truckdriver sings, free of the road,
The load of winter and war becomes
Embarrassing as a younger self.
Words disintegrate; war is words.

The Excursion

The blue of summer morning begs
The country journey to be made,
The sun that gilds the breakfast eggs
Illuminates the marmalade.

A cheque is smiling on the desk.
Remembered smells upon the lane
Breed hunger for the picaresque
To blood the buried springs again.

Here is the pub and here the church
And there our thirty miles of sun,
The river and the rod and the perch,
The noonday drinking just begun.

Let beer beneath the neighbour trees
Swill all that afternoon away,
And onions, crisp to sullen cheese,
Yield the sharp succulence of today.

Today remembers breaking out
The fire that burned the hayfield black.
An army that was grey with drought
Shows to my stick its fossil track.

Returning evening rose on rose
Or pomegranate rouge and ripe;
The lamp upon the pavement throws
The ectoplasm of my pipe.

Eden

History was not just what you learned that scorching day
Of ink and wood and sweat in the classroom, when mention
Of the Duke of Burgundy lost you in a voluptuous dream
Of thirst and Christmas, but that day was part of history.

There were other times, misunderstood by the family,
When you, at fifteen, on your summer evening bed
Believed there were ancient towns you might anciently visit.
There might be a neglected platform on some terminus

And a ticket bought when the clock was off its guard.
Oh, who can dismember the past? The boy on the friendly bed
Lay on the unpossessed mother, the bosom of history,
And is gathered to her at last. And tears I suppose

Still thirst for that reeking unwashed pillow,
That bed ingrained with all the dirt of the past,
The mess and lice and stupidity of the Golden Age,
But a mother and loving, ultimately Eden.

One looks for Eden in history, best left unvisited,
For the primal sin is always a present sin,
The thin hand held in the river which can never
Clean off the blood, and so remains bloodless.

And this very moment, this very word will be Eden,
As that boy was already, or is already, in Eden,
While the delicate filthy hand dabbles and dabbles
But leaves the river clean, heartbreakingly clean.